Saving Madonna

Saving Madonna

Kate Bristow

NAVY STREET PRESS

© 2023 by Kate Bristow

All rights reserved. Published in the United States by Navy Street Press, Los Angeles
www.navystreetpress.com

Library of Congress Control Number: 2023944720

ISBN: 979-8-9887919-0-4 (Paperback)

ISBN: 979-8-9887919-1-1 (Ebook)

Book cover design and Cast of Characters illustration by L1graphics.

Image of Urbino used under license from Shutterstock.com.

Map illustration by Sylvia Hofflund.

For Tara and Savannah

And for Huw, who always believed

Sassocorvaro

La Rocca

The church
at San Donato

Casa del Lupo

Ca'Boschetto

Urbino

Ducal Palace

At Ca'Boschetto (House of the Copse)

Paolo and **Antonella Rossi**
Luca, working on the farm
Lorenzo, who has joined the partisans
Marco, still in elementary school

Paolo's brother, **Leonardo Rossi**, and his wife **Maria**
The twins, **Tommaso** and **Matteo**
Their daughter **Giovanna**
Gianni, still in elementary school

Nonna, the matriarch, mother of Paolo and Leonardo

At Casa del Lupo (House of the Wolf)

Francesco and **Elisa Marchetti**
Alessandro, who has joined the partisans
Elena, working with **Pasquale Rotondi**
Their younger daughter **Giulia**
Andrea, working on the farm

Prologue

September 1943, Sant'Angelo in Vado, Italy

Instead of being warm in his own bed, Ricardo Minucci was standing under the portico on the edge of the piazza, sheltering from the piercing wind. His hands shook as he attempted to light a cigarette. He could no longer be sure if it was from the cold or fear. A couple walked past on the other side of the road, their dog meandering in and out of the darkened shop doorways, sniffing. He could hear their laughter as they turned down a narrow street. The man called the dog, and they disappeared from Ricardo's sight.

Five more minutes. This was a fool's errand. He'd give them five more minutes, and then he was heading home. He glanced up and down the cobbled street. Nothing in sight. Ricardo strained to look at his watch in the weak light of the streetlamp.

A low purr. A car was moving slowly down the road toward the piazza. No headlights. Ricardo held himself back beneath the portico, waiting.

The car stopped outside the theater, and the engine was turned off. Ricardo looked around one more time and then decided to move. He walked across the piazza and knocked on the driver's window. It opened a couple of inches.

Ricardo gave the agreed-upon signal. "Are you looking for the cathedral?"

"I'm a friend of the prelate," replied the driver. Ricardo nodded. Right answer. The man opened the car door and got out, stretching his limbs. He shook Ricardo's hand. "Glad you're still here. I was forced to take a short detour."

Ricardo noted that the man was wearing an expensive-looking gabardine raincoat and brown leather shoes. *Not a farmer then.* The two men walked to the rear of the car, and the stranger opened the trunk. He pulled a gray blanket to one side, uncovering a large, thick parcel wrapped in some kind of waterproof paper.

"Not ideal, I know, but we didn't have a lot of time."

Ricardo wasn't sure what to make of this information, so he simply nodded again. He cleared his throat, trying to dislodge the phlegm that seemed to be permanently lodged there.

"My car's parked around the corner. I got word to the superintendent that I'd make the delivery to the Rocca at dawn. I wasn't sure when you would turn up, so I didn't want to promise any sooner."

"Like I said, had a spot of trouble. Over to you now. This is the last leg, hopefully."

Ricardo grunted his assent. "Do you know what's in there?" he asked, pointing at the parcel.

"A couple of small Giorgiones, I understand. Two of his lesser works, but still priceless." The man pulled a silver cigarette case from his pocket and opened it, offering a cigarette to Ricardo. The stranger lit both cigarettes and leaned against the car, inhaling deeply. He didn't seem to be in a hurry to leave.

"Why'd you get involved in this, then?" the man asked, pointing at the trunk. He looked at Ricardo with interest, taking in his patched jacket and worn pants. Ricardo knew he looked like somebody who worked in the fields rather than for an art museum.

"I did my fighting last time around. Still wanted to do my part though." Ricardo wasn't sure why he felt compelled to explain himself. The men stood in companionable silence, smoking. Ricardo was less nervous now that there were two of them. They could be two friends enjoying their last smoke together at the end of the night.

"I was wounded at Isonzo in 1915, in one of the first battles," said Ricardo, feeling the need to clarify. "Our leaders had joined the Allies by then." He grunted again, this time with disdain. "Can't trust those in power. Don't trust them this time around either. Definitely wasn't going to put myself on the front lines again."

"So why do this then?" persisted the man.

"My cousin asked me to help. He works at the museum. Makes sense to me. No telling what damage will be done otherwise."

Ricardo lapsed into silence once more. The two men leaned against the wall of the theater, smoking their cigarettes.

After a few minutes, Ricardo said, "I saw too much of that. Damage, I mean. Wanton destruction. Thieving. Soldiers don't care what happens when they're being shot at. Valuable things get stolen or worse when there's chaos."

The man nodded his agreement. Ricardo crushed his cigarette on the cobblestones. Too much small talk for his liking.

"I'm off. Let me take them then." He lifted the parcel carefully from the trunk. "Safe journey back, Signore. I've got it from here."

Without saying another word, Ricardo carried the parcel across the piazza toward the small street where he had left his car. As he turned the corner, he heard an engine starting up again and the stranger's car beginning to move away.

Ricardo gently placed the parcel in the trunk of his own car. Time to go home and get some sleep. In a few hours, the paintings would be safely hidden in the Rocca, far from the front lines, and any inquisitive German. *Best place for them*, thought Ricardo.

Chapter One

Marco was afraid of the biggest pig. Papà always laughed when Marco complained that the pig was intent on knocking him over. Papà said the pig was an animal and had no emotions, and Marco would never be an effective farmer if he was scared of the animals. But Marco sensed the pig looking at him with his mean, small, beady eyes each time he struggled in with the heavy pail. Feeding the pigs was his least favorite job, and a small jolt of fear went through him every time his mother reminded him of it.

"You're just a *bambino*, Marco," scoffed his cousin Gianni. "Watch me—I'm not afraid of him!" Gianni poked the big pig's flank with the small stick he was carrying and got a grunt in return. The pig attempted to shuffle away, but it was hard for the huge creature to move easily in such a confined space. Gianni turned back to his cousin.

"Come on! Hurry up so we can go and help Luca herd the sheep."

Marco spread the feed into the trough, spilling some of it on the ground, and then, with Gianni's help, scattered fresh hay on the floor. All the pigs in the small room, who had been ignoring them up to this point, stood up and approached the trough.

"Let's go!" shouted Gianni.

The two young boys ran out of the pigsty, hollering at each other. Marco, ever cautious, made sure the small wooden gate was locked behind him. He was all too aware of the punishment his father would mete out if any of the pigs managed to escape. Marco tossed the pail away before the two of them began racing up the hill to the field where Luca and the dogs were attempting to corral the sheep into some kind of order.

It was a beautiful October day in the valley, with clear blue skies and a hint of colder weather in the air. The leaves on the trees were turning russet red, and some had already carpeted the hard ground. The black crows, which Marco had to admit he was also afraid of if he was being honest with himself, huddled together on the barest branches of the oak trees lining the field, cawing loudly like sentinels as the boys ran past.

As they approached the top of the hill, Marco slowed down, his breath ragged. He conceded the race to his cousin and stood for a moment, surveying his valley kingdom. The two-story stone house he shared with his family and his cousin's family looked small from this vantage point. Even the giant oak tree that dominated the front yard did not appear as imposing as it did when Marco and Gianni tried to climb it, which they did frequently. He could see his mother and his aunt unpegging white sheets from the clothesline and his father repairing loose tiles on the slate roof. Wisps of smoke rose from the kitchen chimney. Marco smiled at the sight because he suddenly remembered that a relative of his worst enemy was getting slowly roasted on the fire in the kitchen. He licked his lips in anticipation of the dinner. Few meals had been worth anticipating recently.

Marco looked beyond his home to a small wood that stretched out from the rear of the property down to the narrow white road snaking through the valley toward the distant hilltop town of Peglio. His home was called Ca'Boschetto (House of the Copse) because of these trees, and Marco knew it would soon be time for his father and uncle to gather their friends and bloodhounds for the annual truffle hunt. Their small wood was known far and wide as a fruitful location for the illusive and highly sought-after fungi, and the truffle hunt was one of the highlights of the season.

Beyond the wood, a patchwork of fields that had been parched brown after the harvest in the heat of August was beginning to turn into shades of green from recent rain. Marco spotted a couple of deer making the most of the fresh grass. Something else caught his eye as it glinted in the distance. Marco lifted his hands to his brow to deflect the glare of the autumnal sun. Whatever was flashing in the sunlight was moving toward their farm. The ox-drawn carts that often made this journey on the back road couldn't move that quickly. He squinted. Something was not right.

"Luca! Luca! I can see a car coming. Look at the road!"

His older brother turned away from the flock and walked over to where Marco was standing. Luca stared at the distant vehicle for a minute and his face darkened. "Marco, Gianni, run down to the house and tell Papà that there might be Germans coming. Move!"

The two boys, frightened by the edge in Luca's voice, ran back down the hill. Luca urged the dogs to herd the sheep toward the trees lining the field, where they would all be shielded from both the sun and any prying eyes. He felt his heart racing, but he knew it made sense to stay hidden. Better safe than sorry. Young men of fighting age were prime targets for the recent unwelcome arrivals in their neighborhood. It was rare to see a car on these rough country roads, and Luca had a bad feeling about this one. He remembered that his twin cousins, Tommaso and Matteo, were even further away from the house, repairing fences in another field. *Best they stay there.* Luca watched the car painstakingly make its way along the rutted road toward his home. His father would know what to do.

———

Papà started climbing down from the roof once he heard the shouting as the two boys approached the house. He listened to their garbled sentences as they talked over each other. Marco's father grabbed his bag of tools and stashed them in the back of a wooden cart standing in the yard. He then turned his attention to the boys, who were looking at him with scared faces.

"Boys, run into the house and grab the bottles of wine from the kitchen table."

The two families were preparing for a party to celebrate *Nonna*'s eightieth birthday. Marco's mother and aunt had been cooking for days. Meals, such as they were these days, had been noticeably leaner for months as the two cooks had to make sure they could eke out enough food for the guests. Signor Francesco Marchetti from the neighboring farm, Papà's closest friend, had ridden over earlier in the day with four bottles of his prized red wine as a contribution to the upcoming feast.

"Hide the bottles under the straw in the pigsty. Go now!" Papà pushed Marco and Gianni in the direction of the house while his wife and sister-in-law looked at him in bewilderment.

"Whether it's the militia or Germans, they'll want something. We might have to give them some food. We can't hide the roasting pig, but I'm damned if I'll let them take the wine."

Marco could hear the car getting closer. Fear constricted his chest as he and Gianni raced up the stone steps to the family living quarters on the higher floor. Pushing open the thick oak door, they stumbled into the large room. Marco could see the roasting pig turning on the spit in the kitchen fireplace. The mouthwatering smell from the charred flesh almost derailed him for a moment. His cousin grabbed two of the wine bottles from the table and directed Marco to pick up the other two. Their grandmother woke up from her nap in the comfortable chair by the fire.

"What are you two boys up to?" she muttered, confused by the sudden noise.

The boys ignored her, rushing back through the doorway and clattering down the steps again with the bottles. They ran through the door on the ground floor, where the animal pens were situated. The horses, tethered to their hitching rings, snickered at the interruption. Marco stopped short, just as fearful of facing the big pig again as he was of the approaching car.

"Come on, Marco," Gianni said urgently. "Hurry!"

They hustled into the small room that served as a pigsty through the arched entrance from the stable. The big pig raised its head from the trough. It did not seem at all happy to be disturbed while eating. The boys hesitated for a moment. They looked at each other and, with a mutual nod, rushed to the pile of straw and excrement, fell on their knees, and pushed the bottles into the muck.

"Cover them. Cover them," whispered Gianni in a panic.

Marco wasn't sure if Gianni was keeping his voice down to avoid upsetting the pigs or because he was afraid of what was about to happen. Their job completed, they stood up and attempted to wipe the incriminating mess from their knees. Rather than disturbing the horses again, they ran straight out of the back gate. Marco, following his cousin, saw him run right into the arms of a tall, blond soldier.

"Steady, *ragazzo*," said the stranger in halting Italian. He laughed as he grabbed Gianni's arms and held him back. "What's the emergency?"

Marco stared up at the man's gray peaked cap with an eagle insignia on the front and then down at a pair of highly polished black boots. The three soldiers he could see standing by the car in the middle of the farm-yard were not dressed as smartly.

Marco scanned his father's face, trying to decipher his reaction to these unexpected visitors. Papà's face betrayed nothing. The officer was keeping a tight grip on Gianni. For once, Marco was happy that he had been slower than his cousin.

"Signor Rossi, Major Heinrich at your service." The man holding Gianni bowed his head in the direction of Marco's father. "We heard a rumor in town that congratulations might be in order. Where is your mother?"

"She is napping." Papà's voice sounded curt. He was not being as friendly as he usually was when people came to the house. The Germans smirked at each other and waited for their commanding officer to say something else.

"Well, that is a shame. We heard in the market in Sassocorvaro that your wife was trying to procure extra provisions, so you can understand why I wanted to pay you a visit." The tall slim man smiled and looked at each of the family members in turn.

"Since being posted here I have learned that you and your neighbors do not seem to understand the meaning of the word 'rations'. You farmers have it much better than your compatriots in the cities. But my orders are to impose some discipline around here. We wouldn't want any essential foodstuffs diverted to those *partigiani* hiding in the hills would we?"

Marco could not help shivering. This was not a social visit, and he did not know what the Germans would do if they found the wine. The officer might be smiling, but it seemed to Marco that it wasn't a real smile. He forced himself to stay still, wanting to cry.

Marco's mother stepped forward.

"Signore, we do the best with what the Lord provides. And sometimes he overdelivers. I was able to make ravioli this morning, because I found some wild mushrooms in the woods yesterday. So many! I said to my sister-in-law, here's something to celebrate . . ." She stopped and drew a breath. "I'm sure you aren't interested in all that, Major. What I meant to say is, we have enough pasta for the birthday—we would be happy to give you some if you like." Mamma spoke in her usual cheerful voice without a hint of antagonism. Marco held his breath.

"Sounds delightful, Signora Rossi. Shall we?"

The major let go of Gianni and signaled Mamma to walk in front of him to the steps of the house. Papà and Zia Maria started to follow, but the officer put up his hand. "No need to make a fuss. Why don't you stay here with the young ones?"

Without waiting for a reply, the major turned to his men. He barked a few short orders at them in German. He turned back to Marco's father. "Captain Müller will stay here with you. My men are going to search the lower floor."

Two of the soldiers hurried into the animal quarters on the ground floor while Major Heinrich followed Mamma upstairs to their home. Captain Müller stood tall with his hands behind his back, not saying a word. Marco swallowed hard, trying not to throw up, and squeezed his eyes shut as tears formed. The soldiers would find the wine and then Marco and his family would all be shot. He started shaking again.

The next five minutes dragged on. Marco tried to focus his attention on the hill where he knew Luca was standing under the trees with the sheep and his dogs. His older brother was hidden from view but knowing that he was close made Marco feel better. He did not dare look at his father.

Loud noises came from the house. As the officer came down the steps carrying an earthenware pot, his two men emerged from the lower floor, one of them holding a small, squirming pig. The men were laughing at the squeals coming from the terrified creature. The taller man said something to his superior.

Major Heinrich nodded at his men and then turned to Papa. "So it seems as if you have several animals you forgot to mention, including the roasting pig in the kitchen, Signor Rossi. Your wife has cut some generous slices for me and my men. And she has given us some ravioli. I don't know why you farmers are always complaining about food shortages. I was able to say '*Auguri*' to your mother after all—shame we cannot stay for the feast."

Captain Müller opened the trunk of the car and, taking the pot from the major, placed it inside before getting into the back seat. The two younger soldiers sat in the front, the one holding the wriggling piglet in the passenger seat. The major looked around the farmyard one more time, as if committing it to memory. He gave a short bow to Marco's mother and aunt and then turned to Marco's father, the smile gone.

"I control this area now. The rules will be enforced. *Ci vediamo*, Signore. I am sure we will see you—and your family—very soon."

Chapter Two

Luca stood on the hill under the trees, watching the scene unfold below him. As the German officer grabbed his young cousin, Luca took a sharp intake of breath and silently prayed for his father to not lose his temper. Luca knew to stay where he was—he had seen too many young men hassled by the Germans in town since they had arrived in the area a month ago.

As bad as the previous few years of the war had been, the situation had deteriorated since the summer. Once the Allied forces landed in Sicily, setting off the sequence of events that had led to Mussolini's arrest and ultimately the armistice between the Italian government and the Allies, northern Italy had effectively been under German rule. Mussolini might now be heading his puppet government in Salò, but Luca knew who was in charge. He and his friends had heard the rumors of young Italian men being rounded up by the Germans in Campania and deported to Germany as forced labor.

And the Germans weren't their only problem—members of the Fascist militia still loyal to Mussolini were forcing men to join up to fight the Allied forces. Luca's younger brother Lorenzo and many of Luca's friends had vanished into the hills and villages around the town of Sassocorvaro and joined the resistance in the hope of disrupting the

Germans. Luca felt the usual surge of anger mixed with despair as he recalled the heated conversations between them.

"Luca, we can't just sit back and let the Germans take whatever they want," Lorenzo had said as the brothers and a couple of friends spent one early September morning trudging through a nearby forest, on the lookout for wild boar. "I can tell you now that I'm not going to hang around to be conscripted into Mussolini's army. The Italian Social Republic is a losing cause, that's for sure."

Alessandro, Luca's best friend, grunted in agreement. "I'm sick and tired of working on the farm, knowing the war is going on somewhere else—I feel like a child. And I'm not fighting for the Fascists either." Alessandro hoisted his gun onto his shoulder and turned to face Luca. "But I want to fight for something, *amico*. Otherwise, we'll lose whatever honor we still possess, and Italy will never recover from this horrific mess we've been dragged into. I'm not going to wait for the Yanks and the Brits to arrive to do our fighting for us." He spat on the ground for emphasis and waited for Luca's response.

Luca stood still, trying to formulate his thoughts. "I understand what you're all saying. I do. The right thing is to fight them. I know that. I hate the Nazis as much as you do. But what happens to my family's crops and animals? What about yours, Alessandro? My father and uncle can't do everything, and neither can yours."

Luca could see his friend's expression darkening. Before Alessandro could interrupt, Luca plowed on. "We've lost enough farmhands to this war already. Do you want the crops to wilt in the fields? Who's going to slaughter the pigs when they are ready? People rely on us—they still have to eat, goddammit." Luca was stumbling over his words. He knew it sounded like he was trying to find excuses. His heart was telling him to go with his friends, but his head was urging him to stay at home.

Luca's brother and two friends stared at him with something like contempt on their faces. He stared back at them, and they turned away as if they didn't want to look at him anymore. He swallowed hard.

"Well, I'm going," said Alessandro. "I've heard that a group of *partigiani* is holed up near Ca'Mazzasette: now's the time to step up."

He looked at Luca again. "Otherwise we're going to get conscripted —good luck evading the bastards."

Lorenzo, animated, cuffed Alessandro on the arm. "I'm going with you to join the partisans. I'm in line to be called up next year so might as well get out now. Let's get supplies and our rifles and leave as soon as we can."

Lorenzo turned to his older brother.

"I understand what you're saying, Luca. It'd be even tougher on Papa and Zio Leonardo if we both left. I get it—it's a big farm to manage even with you and me and the twins to help. But this is war. If a field isn't plowed, that's tough, but Papa will have to manage. I'm joining the partisans, and that's that."

Two days later, they were gone.

Luca pulled a battered packet of cigarettes from his overalls and lit one. The nicotine felt good in his throat and lungs. He stared out again at the small figures below him. The sound of high-pitched squeals unnerved him for a moment until one of the figures came out of the house, carrying what looked like one of the piglets. Relief swept over him as he watched the four soldiers drive away down the rutted road. It was going to be fine. Whatever they had taken would be a small price to pay if nobody had been hurt. He stubbed out the cigarette on the nearest tree trunk and whistled to the dogs to keep the sheep together as he started walking down the hill. His father watched him approach.

"Those bastards took some food and a pig," he said as Luca drew close. Papa's face was red. Luca saw his mother reach out to touch his arm as if to calm him down.

"Paolo, it's fine. We still have enough for tonight. It was just a small disturbance. I'm glad Luca and the other boys were in the fields and that your brother and Giovanna weren't here. Let's move on with the day and enjoy this evening." She glanced up at Luca, a huge smile on her face.

Aunt Maria, usually content to say little while her sister-in-law commanded the stage, unexpectedly spoke up. "I'm sure Leonardo and Giovanna will return with more food anyway. They always get good deals for our salamis and cheese in Urbino and my girl will have bartered well. She's good at haggling, that kid."

Maria fondled her son's hair. Gianni's face was still buried in his mother's apron as it had been since he had sought refuge there when the officer had released him. "Gianni, *caro*, why don't you two boys go to the top field and tell Tommaso and Matteo that our guests will be here at seven? I want to make sure that they have plenty of time to wash up before everyone else arrives. Nonna will be cross if her grandsons turn up for the party not having tried to look presentable."

As the sun moved lower in the sky, Luca and the twins, Tommaso and Matteo, hauled oak planks from a towering wood pile near the house. Using empty barrels, they constructed makeshift tables and benches. More wood was piled up in various spots to make small bonfires to be lit later when the air grew colder. Tommaso climbed up onto the branches of the giant oak tree in the middle of the yard and hung lanterns for light. Luca's young cousin Giovanna and her mother placed more lanterns and wildflowers in jam jars on the tables to give the party a festive air.

As seven o'clock approached, neighbors and friends started arriving in horse-drawn carts and the occasional car. A few came on horseback. The guests brought whatever small offerings they could spare: honey, ripe cheeses, a basket of figs, a loaf of bread, flasks of homemade liquor. There had been few reasons to celebrate in recent months, and the valley was looking forward to this rare party.

Gianni and Marco strolled among the guests, filling their glasses with red wine and repeatedly telling the story of how they had saved the party by hiding the four bottles in the pigsty. The story became more embellished as the boys circulated. Nonna sat comfortably in her chair under the ancient oak tree, receiving congratulations and good wishes and kissing everyone on the cheeks with fervor. Her two daughters-in-law hovered, watching her carefully. Between fetching rugs and warmer clothing as the night air chilled and gently diverting visitors when they could see Nonna becoming overwhelmed, the two women were kept busy. The twins grabbed their fiddles—they were accomplished musicians and would drop everything to play—and several of the guests were delighted to have the chance to dance. For one evening, music and laughter rang out across the valley as they had not done in weeks.

Luca stood on the edge of the festivities, looking out at the moon as it rose above the distant hill. Someone poked him hard in his side.

"Hello, my dear friend," whispered a voice he knew well. He spun around.

"Elena, you're here at last! I was waiting for you to come and visit. Are we too dull for you now?"

The young woman laughed and kissed him on both cheeks. "I got back almost a week ago. It's been hectic—a year away is a long time. My mother's been dragging me all over Sassocorvaro. I didn't want to come home, if I'm honest, but Papà and Mamma insisted once they learned that Milan had been heavily bombed again. And I was lucky enough to secure a ride home with Superintendent Rotondi."

Elena paused, then reached out to hold Luca's hands. She leaned back as if examining him. "You look well. Very strong. And very tanned. What happened to the pale boy who liked drawing? Working outside suits you." She smiled somewhat wistfully, as if she was sad to have lost that little boy.

Luca grimaced. "Drawing is for kids. I'm a full-time farmer now. If I don't work, who will?" A surge of anger at his missing brother washed over him, immediately followed by regret at his sharp tone. Elena's brother, Alessandro—his best friend—had left to join the partisans as well. In his annoyance, he had forgotten that.

"I'm guessing you're still mad at Lorenzo for leaving, huh?" said Elena. "Mamma's not happy about Alessandro going either, I can tell you. I get that it makes life harder for you on the farm, but I'm sure living rough isn't easy."

Luca scowled. "Their choice. Probably just another adventure for *mio fratellino*—you remember what he's like."

"For sure—any crazy idea and your little brother was all for it." Elena smiled fleetingly, but her eyes looked sad. She tightened her grip on his hands.

"I hate not knowing where my brother is, though, and whether he is alright." She turned and looked at the hills in the distance as if searching for a glimpse of Alessandro. "I wish they were both here tonight." She dropped his hands and hugged him, hard.

"I missed you, Luca," whispered Elena in his ear. "Milan was lively and busy, but I did miss you."

Luca was taken aback by the ferocity of her embrace. He couldn't recall the two of them ever having hugged before. He had to admit to himself that it wasn't unwelcome. Elena pulled back and looked at him with an appraising glance. Luca wondered how she saw him now. She had changed a lot since they had said goodbye to each other. Her chestnut hair, which she had worn in pigtails for as long as he could remember, was now falling down her back in waves. She had grown taller somehow, and the blue dress she was wearing looked like it belonged on the Corso Vittorio Emanuele II, rather than in a farmyard in the countryside. Elena was now a beautiful woman as opposed to the tomboy and childhood confidante she had once been.

"I missed you too, Elena," Luca said. "I'm glad you're back."

Elena started to speak but checked herself. She looked down at her shoes. "You didn't write though," she said quietly.

Luca squirmed. "I-I wasn't sure I had anything interesting to write about."

"But you said you would. Write, I mean. I would've liked reading about whatever you were doing."

It was Luca's turn to look at the ground. Elena's letters had been full of her adventures in the big city. She had moved on to a glittering world that he could only imagine. He hadn't thought his life of hard labor was of any interest to her. Was she teasing him? He couldn't read her face.

"I'm sorry I never wrote, Elena. Your letters were so colorful that I thought mine would be dull in comparison. Nothing ever changes here —you know that."

Elena laughed, which broke the tension. "Okay, I forgive you, farm boy. But a word of advice: next time a friend asks you to write to them, send them a crumb every now and then. Or else she'll think you've forgotten all about her." She poked him in the ribs again.

"Is that Elena Marchetti? Look at you! You're a city girl now." A woman hurried toward them with her arms outstretched. "I was just talking to your mother. I must tell you she's thrilled that you finally came to your senses and returned home." She enveloped Elena in a tight embrace. "Come and say hello to my girls. I know they'll be excited to hear all the news from Milan."

Elena was whisked away, leaving Luca staring at her back. His friend Antonio sidled up to him. "Now there's a sight for sore eyes. Hard to believe we used to tease her for being the teacher's favorite. Looking at her now I wouldn't mind being Elena's favorite, if you know what I mean."

He smirked at Luca, who gave him a half-hearted push. "She's out of reach for you, Antonio. Come on, let's go and grab more of that pork while there's still some left. Nobody can roast a pig like my mother."

Luca linked arms with his friend and the two men started walking over to the table where food was piled up on large platters. The women of the household were serving the older adults and young children as they sat at the long trestle tables, while the young adults were milling around the platters, helping themselves. Despite the wartime deprivations and rations, the spread was impressive: glistening portions of suckling pig, a few rabbits, large platters of wild mushroom ravioli, roasted root vegetables, slices of prosciutto and salami that had been painstakingly cured for months by Luca's uncle in their curing shed, large wheels of *casciotta* cheese made from ewes' milk from their large flock of sheep combined with cows' milk from Francesco Marchetti's herd, grapes, plums, cherries, flaky *cresce* flatbreads. Luca had not seen so much food in one place since before the war. Their neighbors had been generous in sharing what they had. The two friends picked up their plates and began to serve themselves.

Antonio stopped short, a scowl on his broad face. "Why is old man Bruni here? I thought your father had a beef with him."

Luca looked around and spotted his neighbor standing under the ancient oak tree in deep conversation with the parish priest. The old man kept jabbing his finger in the air as he spoke. Don Antonio, the priest, had his head down and was shuffling his feet in the dirt. He looked in need of rescuing.

Luca sighed. "My father wants to keep Bruni sweet. Better to invite him than to hear him complaining for the next three months. It is hard when we share a boundary line."

"Your father's too kind, Luca. I don't trust that man at all.

Remember how many times we got into trouble as kids because of him? Alessandro got that bad beating from his father the one time he was caught stealing Bruni's apples."

Luca grinned at the scowling Antonio. "That was years ago, and Sandro probably deserved it. Come on, or all the best bits of meat will be gone. I've been watching my little brother stuff his face all evening."

The rest of the night was spent eating, drinking, and dancing, and, in between, catching up on everyone's news. Tommaso and Matteo took a break to wolf down some food but were soon reunited with their fiddles. The music was intoxicating. Old ladies who had not been on a dance floor in years were coaxed to try a few steps. Luca's grandmother, her face flushed and her eyes bright, laughed and clapped from her chair, occasionally shouting out words of praise to her two grandsons for their musical talents.

Despite trying to appear relaxed, Luca kept a close eye on Elena's movements. Everyone wanted a piece of her, it seemed. He overheard his grandmother asking Elena whether the risotto in Milan could possibly be better than the one she had been perfecting for decades in her kitchen. Their old schoolteacher Sister Caterina spent an animated half an hour huddled with Elena probing her about the classical concerts she had attended, and whether she had managed to make it to mass at the Duomo itself. His young cousin Giovanna and her friends needed to know everything in fashion that summer in the big city. He could hear snippets of conversations about hemlines and tailoring and sleeves, all alien concepts to him. But he did not feel like joining the loud debates the men were having around him either as they argued about recent wolf sightings and shotgun bores.

Eventually, when Luca had given up hope of having another conversation with her, Elena managed to evade yet another friendly advance and made her way over to where Luca was standing smoking a cigarette. "So, I think we have a year to catch up on! Especially as you never wrote to me."

Luca groaned. "You go first. My life isn't that exciting, I can assure you."

Elena gave him a brief overview of her working life in Milan: the family she lived with, her associates at the Pinacoteca di Brera, the dances and parties she had attended. "There were a few aerial attacks, but mainly targeting the factories on the edge of the city. We felt pretty safe until this summer."

Elena stopped talking and stared out over the dark fields to the hills beyond. The moon had risen and stars freckled the night sky. A wolf could be heard howling in the distance. She stood looking out across the valley for a full minute. Luca wondered what she was thinking about. Elena turned and locked eyes with him.

"It was terrifying, Luca. Like being in hell itself. The planes came on several nights, waves of them. The bombs kept falling for hours. We had fires all around us. I heard that in parts of the city the wind was so strong that it was like being in the middle of a storm, but with flames rather than rain or hail."

Luca did not know how to respond. Without thinking, he took her hand and squeezed it.

"Many buildings and roads were damaged and people killed or injured. They hit the city hall, numerous churches, Sforza Castle, even the Duomo. There was destruction at the Pinacoteca as well. So that's what I had to focus on even though, after that first night, I was afraid to leave the house. But we knew the bombers would only come at night, so during the day, it felt safer."

Elena described the long days at work, trying to log the most valuable art pieces that had been destroyed or damaged, and the nights spent cowering in the basement of the house where she was living. "My bedroom was in the attic, so during those nightly raids, I didn't get much sleep. I had to make do with a blanket on the floor of the basement. But I was just grateful to be alive each morning. Then the letters started arriving. Mamma was terrified, as you can imagine. She was begging me to come back to the safety of the countryside. Then one morning I got to work, and the superintendent was there."

She told Luca that Pasquale Rotondi, the superintendent responsible for art in Le Marche, was paying an official visit to the Pinacoteca and was surprised to meet someone from Sassocorvaro. He was working with the Pinacoteca staff members to move some of their artworks to safety in Le Marche, far away from the Allied bombs. "We talked after lunch one day and I told him about my parents' fears. He immediately offered to help get me home. I resisted at first, but it made sense. During the drive back, which took a long time because of all the bomb craters and checkpoints, he offered me a job. It's all so hard to believe, really."

Elena laughed and her face lit up. Luca realized he was still holding her hand and, feeling embarrassed, let go.

"So, I am working a few days a week for Signor Rotondi now. Not in his office in the palace in Urbino, but in the Rocca at Sassocorvaro." Elena stopped talking and turned to stare at Luca intently. "Do you know what he has been doing? Rotondi, I mean."

"Like you said, moving art to safety." It was an open secret among the people in the valley. Luca's father and some of their neighbors had helped in the effort. Luca had not been very supportive, but his father had brusquely dismissed his mutterings, telling him that it was clear he didn't understand the importance.

At the beginning of the war, the government had been fearful of the potential damage to Italy's cultural heritage. So, over a period of months, several art curators and officials set up networks to move thousands of priceless works of art from all over Italy—paintings, sculptures, manuscripts, music scores—and hide them in locations away from the major Italian cities. Pasquale Rotondi, the young superintendent in the region of Le Marche, offered to take whatever could be delivered to him. He was working in the Galleria Nazionale, an art museum situated in the Renaissance palace at the heart of the city of Urbino. There were vast underground vaults that Rotondi was confident could be used as hiding places. He also identified the Rocca—a fortress hundreds of years old with thick, imposing walls that stood in the center of the nearby small town of Sassocorvaro—as another safe location. Long chains and complicated transfers were arranged, with people transporting the works across the country. Several people in the surrounding areas had helped move the masterpieces the final few miles to Urbino and Sassocorvaro and unload them. By barge or ox-drawn cart, car or truck, whatever means of transport they could use, Italians delivered paintings by

Caravaggio and Tintoretto, silver chalices from Venetian churches, and music scores written by Rossini.

Luca knew it was going on—he had often caught his father on a Saturday evening, setting off on some mysterious journey—but it had exasperated him. He could not see how it was more important to expend so much effort saving pieces of art when people were struggling to survive. He shrugged his shoulders. "Of course I know. We all know. Not sure if it's worth all that effort, though."

Elena's expression gave nothing away. "Luca, you used to love to draw and paint in school—do you remember? You were quite the artist too." She laughed, and the sound made Luca smile. He had missed it.

"And remember how much we enjoyed those visits to the art museum with Sister Caterina and Professor Martini? How lucky we were to be growing up so close to all that beauty. And we all need beauty, especially now."

"Oh, come on, Elena," said Luca. "All that effort to save some paintings? I'd argue Italy has more important things to worry about."

Elena frowned and her face flushed. "But this is who we are, Luca," she said, her voice betraying her agitation. "It's important. If those beautiful paintings and sculptures and tapestries—all that representation of life—are gone, we'll have lost part of our humanity, for God's sake. I saw what can happen in Milan. I don't want this war to destroy what makes Italy so strong. To me, it is as important as food. It matters."

She stopped, aware people were looking at her. Then she laughed that laugh again. "Okay, enough serious talk. I don't want to argue with you when we've just reunited. Tonight, it's about your grandmother and dancing and forgetting the war. Tonight we will simply celebrate your *Nonna*."

Elena grabbed Luca's hand and pulled him toward the music. "And I just remembered that you hate dancing, but tonight, I don't care what you want."

Chapter Three

"I don't want tonight to be over!"

Elena's younger sister, Giulia, was twirling around their bedroom in her linen nightgown, her brown hair loose around her shoulders. Elena, already tucked up in their shared bed, smiled indulgently as she watched her sister dance to some imaginary tune with an imaginary partner.

"It was a real party, wasn't it, Elena? I wish we hadn't left—I wanted to squeeze every last drop out of it." She stopped dancing, her face flushed, and skipped toward the bed, launching herself onto the covers beside Elena. Giulia sat cross-legged and looked at her sister. "It's different for you," she said, pouting a little. "You must have had so many chances to dance in Milan. All those parties and boys! And I was just stuck here, doing nothing fun, ever. When is this stupid war going to be over?"

Elena wanted to laugh at the angry expression on Giulia's face. Instead, she took her sister's hands in hers. "You're sixteen, and there's time, I promise you. When this is all over, I'll take you to Milan myself. You can meet all the boys—or men—you want."

Giulia shifted impatiently. She snatched her hands away and began shuffling herself under the covers next to Elena. "Did you see how handsome Tommaso looked this evening? That mop of light brown hair falling across his eyes—*bello*. And the way he plays the fiddle." Giulia wrapped her arms around herself, and a smile formed on her face. "We got to dance a little—did you see us?" She looked hopefully at her sister.

"I did, and yes, he is handsome, and yes, he can play. There you are —you don't need to go to Milan in that case." Elena dodged the half-hearted blow aimed at her and giggled. She had missed this, gossiping with her little sister.

"What about you? I saw you huddled with Luca. That made a few people jealous!"

"Don't be silly, Giulia. We've been friends forever—you know that. We had a lot to catch up on, that's all."

Giulia looked at her sister intently. The corners of her mouth turned up into a sly smile. "Yes, but you couldn't see him mooning after you like a lovesick heifer every time you talked to somebody else. I don't think he took his eyes off you all night. I, for one, would be thrilled if you two were together—it would make it easier for me to see Tommaso without it seeming strange."

"Well, I'm not going to walk out with Luca Rossi just so you can spend time with his cousin. Come on, it's late. You and I have to milk the cows early, so I'd like to get some sleep."

Giulia grumbled but leaned over to blow out the candle on her side of the bed. She lay down again, wrapped herself in the bedsheets, and was asleep in minutes. Elena lay awake, thinking about what her sister had said. It was tempting to imagine Luca being more than a friend. When he hadn't replied to her letters, she had begun to think that he didn't care to continue their childhood friendship. It had hurt for a long time. Coming back home, Elena had held off visiting him and his family, not wanting to be confronted with his indifference. Despite trying to steel herself, Elena had felt her heart flutter when she had first spotted him that evening. Maybe Luca wasn't lying. Maybe he really hadn't known what to write. Perhaps Giulia was right, and it could be more than a childhood friendship. *We'll see*, thought Elena. *We'll have to see.*

The next day was Sunday with its obligatory outing to church. Elena had become lax in Milan about this particular ritual, but there was no escape from her mother's watchful eye now that she was back home. This morning, though, it did not seem like an obligation, knowing the Rossi families would be there as well. She and Giulia hurried through their morning chores and tried to make themselves look presentable before they left the house. Giulia spent so long trying to decide what color ribbon to use to tie her hair that her father lost his temper.

"The good Lord does not care, Giulia. Get into the cart right now."

Giulia hurried out of the house and clambered up beside her brother Andrea, who was looking as furious as their father. Elena smiled at her younger siblings. They might be a year older than when she had left, but they still knew how to irritate each other. She sighed, wishing that her older brother, Alessandro, was with them. He always knew how to make them all laugh. Elena wondered when she would be able to see him again. She refused to contemplate the more frightening scenario— that he might be injured or killed while fighting for the partisans and that she might never see him again.

There it was again. That little flutter. Elena swallowed hard. She watched Luca helping his grandmother get down from their cart and willed him to turn around and notice her. When he eventually did and broke into a wide smile, Elena felt her cheeks burning. What on earth was wrong with her? She smiled back and started smoothing out the creases in her dress to give her hands something to do.

"How are you all?" called out Antonella, Luca's mother. She was wearing a bright floral dress with a matching hat. Elena stifled a grin. Antonella Rossi was joy personified, and she always dressed accordingly. It was a mystery to Elena how such a perpetually cheerful woman had given birth to such a serious child as Luca. Antonella hurried over to greet them and soon the families were intermingled, with voices rising as they tried to make themselves heard.

"You have to come over to Ca'Boschetto later—I want to chat about the party. What fun we all had! I swear I even saw Signor Bruni smiling at one point. Who'd have believed it?" Antonella kept up a steady stream of conversation with Elena's mother, Elisa, while the others huddled in small groups, laughing and reminiscing about the evening before. Luca and Elena stood silently at the edge of the group.

"Did you—"

"I was hoping—"

The two of them laughed.

"It was such a good party, Luca. Was your grandmother happy?" asked Elena.

"She was! She said it was the best birthday she's had since my grand-father died. I think even she was shocked at how many people bothered to come."

"We wouldn't have missed it for the world," said Elena.

"Well, obviously we knew your family would be there! That goes without saying."

They fell silent again. Luca looked at Elena. "Do come over later. I'll be in the fields—no days off for me—but I would love to hear more about Milan, honestly. I'm sure you have a lot more stories you can share."

"I'd like that very much," said Elena. She locked eyes with Luca, as her confidence came back. "I definitely want to hear all about what you've been doing too. You owe me for all the letters you never wrote. It might take a while."

Chapter Four

As early as elementary school Elena had stood out. All the children of the valley attended the small school in the nearby town of Sassocorvaro run by the nuns of the local convent. Sister Caterina, who taught the older students, had been struck immediately by the quiet intelligence of the girl. Elena would listen to the lesson intently and then ask the most surprising questions. Her essays were thoughtful, and her competence with numbers unrivaled. Sister Caterina was at a loss as to how this farmer's daughter had acquired the intellect to be such an accomplished student.

She began asking Elena to help the younger children with their reading and to assist her with grading their sums. During recess, rather than playing with the other children, Elena would sit next to Sister Caterina and bombard her with questions about her life before entering the convent. Elena was intrigued to discover that the young nun had been brought up in Milan and was the fifth daughter of a wealthy family with interests in music and the arts. Before long Sister Caterina found herself talking about piano pieces she had learned to play, paintings she had seen and all the other subjects that a young girl of means would be expected to study. Elena devoured all of it.

All this talk gave Sister Caterina an idea. She reached out to a renowned art scholar who had worked at the Galleria Nazionale in the Ducal Palace of Urbino but had chosen to retire in sleepy Sassocorvaro, rather than remain in the bustling city several miles away. At the Galleria Nazionale the professor had been one of the people responsible for the safekeeping of the priceless works of art displayed inside, pieces by Piero della Francesco, Giovanni Santi, Timoteo Viti, and the much-loved local son, Raphael, who was born in the city several hundred years ago.

Over coffee at the café in the main piazza in Sassocorvaro one morning Sister Caterina nervously put forward her idea.

"Professor Martini, how would you feel about escorting me and a handful of ten-year-old children to the museum one day?"

The professor looked at the young nun with amusement. "Well, Sister Caterina, I was not expecting you to ask that. You are a very unusual daughter of the Church, I must say."

Sister Caterina smiled but persisted with her request. "I see no reason why the children should not be exposed to high culture particularly as such wonderful examples are right here on our doorstep."

Professor Martini thought about this for a minute but then shook his head. "But they're all going to be farmers and shopkeepers, aren't they? The girls aren't even going to work—they'll no doubt be married off before they turn eighteen. I'm not sure that visiting a museum is going to be of much use to them."

Sister Caterina leaned toward the professor. "Most of the paintings are religious, are they not?" she said firmly. "I see it as an opportunity to show these children the glory of God expressed in so many different ways."

Not being able to find a suitable response to this line of reasoning the professor reluctantly agreed to lead an outing to the museum. So the following Monday Sister Caterina and Professor Martini herded fifteen boys and girls to the bus stop where they caught the bus to Urbino.

Years later Elena could still remember the first time she had laid eyes on the two fairytale towers that adorned the front of the palace high up on the hill. The children had poured excitedly from the bus once it stopped in the market square outside the city walls and had stood in small groups staring up at the vision above them. After climbing up the steep helicoid ramp that led to the upper part of the city and making their way two by two through the narrow streets, the chattering children had finally been led through the giant wooden doors of the palace by their teacher.

Standing inside that awe-inspiring space Elena had at first been overwhelmed but ultimately uplifted by its magnificence. The gracious arches and long stone corridors led to enormous halls lined with tapestries and paintings. Elena had never seen such elegance. She tried to focus on what the professor was saying as he stood in front of certain pieces but it was hard to do so when she was so moved by the paintings themselves. Elena glanced at her schoolmates but only Luca seemed as mesmerized as she was. The two of them sat next to each other on the long bus ride home chatting about the paintings they had liked the most and ignoring the roughhousing of the boys around them.

The professor must have enjoyed his stint as an art guide because the outing was repeated on several occasions much to Elena's delight. She dreaded the end of the school year when she was supposed to graduate and finish her education, unlike the boys who would continue for a few more years. Girls were still obliged to take part in the Opera Nazionale Balilla, the overarching youth organization founded by Mussolini and the Fascist Party with the goal of creating model Fascist citizens. But young Elena was not excited at the thought of learning how to be a good wife and homemaker which was the extent of the curriculum for girls.

Elena's despair at the thought of finishing her formal education was evident to Sister Caterina. The young teacher wrestled with the issue for a few days and then wrote a letter to one of her older sisters, who was now happily married to a count and living on a vast estate outside Ferrara. A few weeks later Sister Caterina received the reply and funds she had hoped for.

"Elena, how would you feel about staying on to help me with the younger ones?" asked Sister Caterina one day during recess. "I've managed to procure a small stipend to pay you a token amount so hopefully your parents will be agreeable. What do you think, young lady?"

Elena was taken aback. She looked up at the nun with wide eyes. "You mean I could stay? I could still come to school every day?" Elena had been praying fervently every night for such a miracle but now that it seemed to have happened, she thought she must be dreaming.

"Yes, every day. And when you're not supervising the little ones, I'm happy for you to sit with the boys in their lessons. Would you like that?"

Elena was so shocked that she couldn't speak. She stared at Sister Caterina with a wide grin on her face.

"I'll take that as a yes then. I'll ask your father for permission. Hopefully your mother won't mind losing your help around the house for a couple more years."

Elena's father was surprised by the nun's request but after discussing it with his friend Paolo Rossi, Signor Marchetti agreed to the unusual arrangement. He was happy to receive some extra income, however meager, although he complained privately to his wife that he hoped this didn't mean that Elena was thinking of joining a convent.

"I'm hoping for some strong grandchildren at some point. To help me on the farm. So I don't want her locked up behind convent walls for the rest of her life." His wife Elisa resisted pointing out that Sister Caterina was hardly locked up but kept quiet.

So Elena managed to remain in school. The younger children did not have much formal education so Elena had plenty of time to join the boys in their lessons. She sat at the back next to Luca and absorbed everything she was told. By this time the art professor had been converted to the concept of art as a civilizing mechanism so he decided to offer the older children a weekly art history lesson. This quickly became Luca's and Elena's favorite class. They sat week after week engrossed in the stories of Michelangelo, Botticelli, Donatello and the other greats of renaissance art. Elena hardly dared breathe, afraid that Professor Martini would one day decide that a girl had no place in the classroom and would demand that she stop attending.

To Elena's relief the opposite occurred. The professor was as impressed as Sister Caterina had been with this young girl's intelligence. He found himself increasingly directing his lessons at Elena and looking forward to reading her essays each week.

As her sixteenth birthday approached Elena knew that her time at the school was running out. The boys in her year had left school and joined the workforce. Elena's older brother Alessandro had been working in the fields with his father for a couple of years. Even Elena's younger sister Giulia had finished school and was doing all the chores that should have fallen on Elena's shoulders. Giulia was constantly complaining to her mother and asking when Elena might be done with this school nonsense. Elena did not think that she would be lucky enough to have a second miracle granted to her. While Giulia slept beside her Elena lay awake staring at the beams in the ceiling trying to formulate a plan. All she knew was that she wanted to be around art. She did not know what that meant or how she would make it happen but she felt she would never be happy remaining at her family farm in the middle of the countryside. Art had no place in the rustic house she called home and she wanted to be immersed in it.

One afternoon after an engrossing hour discussing the painting of the Sistine Chapel, Elena steeled herself and went up to talk to the professor. She explained how her mother was pushing for her to give up being Sister Caterina's assistant and to return to the farm to help with the domestic chores. She told the older man how revelatory his teaching had been and how she hated the thought of giving it all up. Professor Martini looked at her with interest and after a minute's silence said the words that would change the direction of Elena's life once more.

"We'll have to do something about that, young lady."

Before the end of the month Elena found herself explaining to her parents that the professor had procured her an apprenticeship at the Pinacoteca di Brera in Milan together with an attic bedroom in the home of an art historian who had worked in Urbino some years ago. Her parents, fourth-generation farmers who had never traveled further than fifty miles from where they were born, had always wondered where their second child had acquired her academic leaning and, if truth be told, were a little afraid of this outspoken, confident girl.

Her mother was flustered by this brazen request and slightly irritated that her daughter had found a way to delay yet again her assumption of domestic duties.

"But you're just turning sixteen," her mother said. "Who will take care of you in such a huge city?"

"Mamma, I'll be fine. There'll be other young women, I'm sure, and

Professor Martini says the family is very kind and will be supportive. There's a small salary but if I work hard, I'll soon be earning more money. I can send some back to you—I know you could use a little extra."

Elena's father, though old-fashioned in many respects, and more interested in the fate of his two sons than that of his two daughters, nodded and turned to his wife.

"It's up to you, Elisa. Our daughter is perfectly capable of taking care of herself. I'm sure the professor knows what he is proposing and we'll have one less mouth to feed."

His wife was taken aback at how quickly her husband had capitulated and didn't have the strength to keep fighting her headstrong daughter. So Elena had been blessed with her second miracle. She made a point of offering extra prayers when she next attended Mass as well as stitching a small bookmark for her beloved teacher Sister Caterina as a thank you for all her years of support. Elena knew that the nun had more to do with her good fortune than any higher power.

One year later the seventeen-year-old Elena had already made huge strides towards her dream of becoming an art curator. She had loved her time in Milan and had learned much. The curators and historians at the Pinacoteca had been as charmed by this young woman as Sister Caterina and Professor Martini had been and happily took her on as a project, teaching her whatever they could. But once the heavy bombing campaign started in August 1943, Elena knew it was only a matter of time before her parents would demand her return to the safety of the countryside.

The arrival of Signor Rotondi from the art museum in Urbino and his offer of a ride home had made it inevitable. Elena instinctively warmed to this unassuming man, with his gentle eyes and boyish face. He had to be in his mid-thirties but despite sporting a small neat mustache he did not look that much older than she was. As they drove back to Sassocorvaro together, Signor Rotondi described what he was doing in detail. He was managing three different locations where he was hiding art and he thought Elena was exactly the competent person he needed to help him keep track of everything. He would make space for her at the Rocca in Sassocorvaro, which was the location of the three closest to her home, and he knew her presence would give him much-needed support with the overwhelming administrative requirements.

It was a compromise but Elena knew she was lucky. She would work hard on the days she was at the farm to keep her mother happy. And she would do whatever it took to show Pasquale Rotondi that she was an art curator in training. Maybe she wouldn't have to abandon her dreams after all.

Chapter Five

Elena found herself smiling despite the steep hill she was struggling to cycle up. It had been a couple of weeks since the party at Ca'Boschetto, and she had managed to spend time with Luca almost every day. The Rossi and Marchetti families were close friends and neighbors, and their parents visited each other often. Elena's home, Casa del Lupo, sat on a high outcrop on one of the hills surrounding the valley. It was called the House of the Wolf because wolves roamed the wilder parts of the countryside. Elena's father, Francesco, was constantly on edge, especially during calving season. Many a night, Elena had heard unearthly screams coming from the fields as a wolf managed to break in to steal one of the newborn animals. The screams would usually be followed by a volley of shots from Francesco's rifle.

From their farmyard, they could look down into the valley at Ca'Boschetto. As a young boy, Elena's brother Alessandro had set up a communication system with Luca using lanterns, and the two friends had spent many an evening flashing signals to each other from their respective houses. Elena had always felt strangely comforted by the fact that they could see their neighbors down below, even though in reality, it would take them fifteen minutes by road to actually reach each other.

Elena's father, Francesco, and Luca's father, Paolo, were always helping each other out on their farms. Paolo often said he was as close to Francesco as he was to his own brother, Leonardo. Their wives joked that the two men should have married each other given the amount of time they spent together.

Nobody remarked on the fact that, since the birthday party, Luca had started coming with his father to Casa del Lupo more frequently than usual, or that Elena seemed keen to accompany her mother when she made one of her visits to see her friends Antonella and Maria at Ca'Boschetto. Elena would chat to Antonella, Maria, and Luca's grandmother for a while, then casually announce that she was going to walk up the hill to see the sheep or walk in the fields for some fresh air. Her little outings always took her to where Luca was working. Luca would seize the opportunity to take a break and the two friends would sit on the hard ground and talk. They talked about their lives and their dreams for the future after the war. Luca shared his resentment toward his brother for leaving the farm, along with his fears that something terrible would happen to him.

"I was always there to protect him when we were boys. You remember what a troublemaker he was?"

"He's doing what he thinks is right though. You can't fault him for that."

"I can agree with the partisan cause and still be mad at my brother for leaving me with all the work."

"Well, don't forget Alessandro is with him. Hopefully the two of them will keep each other out of trouble."

Elena told him more about her life in Milan and her ambition to become a curator like her employer. "I'm not naive. I know it's going to be harder for me as a woman, but I know I can do it. I'm just as good as any man."

"I'm sure you are," said Luca. "You were always the smartest student at school." Whenever he thought she was not looking, Luca would sneak a glance at her smooth alabaster skin and her thick chestnut hair. She was intelligent and beautiful yet easy to talk to. She was unlike any woman he had ever known.

Elena hardly recognized the young man Luca had become since she had left for Milan. Luca had those dark, brooding looks all the romantic leads seemed to possess in the novels Elena devoured whenever she was able to get her hands on any. She had always thought of him as a quiet, serious boy overshadowed by his loud, boisterous younger brother. All the children in the valley spent a great deal of time together when they weren't helping their parents on their farms. Once released from elementary school they would roam the countryside in a pack, fishing in the stream that wound through the floor of the valley or climbing trees or building camps in the various woods. Sometimes they would stumble across a pack of wild boar and have to run away, screeching and hollering at the top of their lungs.

Despite being younger than some of the others, Lorenzo was always the ringleader, coming up with an endless list of new adventures. Luca was the voice of reason, pointing out what danger lurked in whatever activity on which they were about to embark. Elena felt the injustice when Luca would invariably be blamed by his father for some scrape Lorenzo had gotten them into. But Luca never denounced his brother or tried to evade punishment, and all the children respected him for that.

And now that thin, wiry boy had become a muscular farmer. Elena watched Luca's strong arms as he sledgehammered a few errant fence posts. She spent many a night lying in bed trying to imagine what it would feel like to be enveloped in those arms.

Thoughts of Luca occupied Elena that morning until she arrived, out of breath, in the piazza in Sassocorvaro. Elena rode into the square outside the Rocca and handed her bicycle to a small boy standing in front of the café. The first morning she had arrived for work, Pietro had volunteered to keep her bicycle safe for the day in return for a few small coins. Elena had been sure that her bike would not have come to any harm in sleepy Sassocorvaro, but she admired the boy's gumption and agreed to the arrangement.

"Morning, Pietro, take good care of it, please!"

The boy grinned and doffed his cap as he had seen his father do when a pretty woman walked by the café his parents managed. "Do you want a *caffè d'orzo*? I can make it for you! Mamma has been teaching me."

Elena smiled indulgently at the hopeful face. "Well, I've already had one at breakfast, but I'm sure a second one would help me recover from the ride. I swear that ride gets longer every day."

Elena sat at one of the small tables outside the café, waiting for Pietro to come back from the barn where he stored her bicycle each day. His mother came out of the café, wiping her hands on her floral apron.

"*Buongiorno*, Elena! What can I bring you today?"

"I think your son wants to make me a drink, Anna. Am I mad to have accepted?"

The woman laughed. "As long as he doesn't burn himself like he did last week. He's too impatient sometimes, that kid." Anna motioned to her son, who was hurrying toward them.

"Come on, Pietro—Signorina Marchetti can't wait all day. I'm sure she has very important things to do for the superintendent." She grabbed her son as he got close and wrapped him in a bear hug. "What am I going to do with you, eh?"

Pietro struggled free and ran into the café followed by his mother. Elena sat in peace, her eyes closed, feeling the morning sun on her face. It was getting colder every day and she wanted to grab hold of the intermittent warmth whenever she could.

Pietro's passable *caffè d'orzo* warmed her up and she started walking toward the Rocca, where she would spend the day. The sun had dissipated the early morning gloom and the dark stone walls appeared slightly less imposing than usual. Elena walked through the arch into the ancient fortress and made her way toward the small room that had been converted into an office for her. She was surprised to see Pasquale there, looking flustered, which was not like him at all.

"*Buongiorno*, Signor Rotondi, nice to see you here! How are you today?"

The superintendent looked up and managed a smile. "Elena, I have told you—please call me Pasquale. 'Signor Rotondi' makes me feel like an old man."

Elena smiled and sat at her desk. She watched her boss pulling out fat files from the filing cabinets that lined the walls and making frantic notes in his notebook.

"Is-is everything alright, Signor—sorry, Pasquale?"

Pasquale stopped what he was doing and turned to her. His face looked tired, and he seemed frightened. For a moment, Elena thought he was not going to say anything, but after an interminably long time, he blurted out, "I think we might be in serious trouble."

Chapter Six

Pasquale stood up and took a deep breath as if fortifying himself. Elena waited, sensing that something momentous had happened.

"I was at the palace in Carpegna early this morning and the Germans arrived," Pasquale said. He paused. "They were conducting a search of the premises and found some of our crates."

Elena knew that was bad news. When the Rocca in Sassocorvaro had become too full of artworks stored inside for safekeeping, Pasquale had arranged for the overflow to be stored at the palace in nearby Carpegna. Since the arrival of the Germans in recent weeks, he had been sharing his concerns with her that the art would be discovered and pillaged.

"Luckily for us, I had already removed all the identifying labels from the crates. I was worried this might happen. They did open some of them, however, the ones containing Rossini's music scores. These Germans were just foot soldiers—they had no idea what the papers were, and we were able to persuade them that it was simply old paperwork, inferior music. Luckily, they didn't bother to open any more—the next crates were packed with paintings by Raphael. They've left now, but I'm worried that they will come back and somebody higher up or more alert will realize how important the contents of those crates are."

The two of them exchanged looks—no words were needed. They had both heard the rumors that Hitler was demanding all works of art discovered in Italy to be transported to Germany. The German leader had extravagant plans to build the greatest art museum Europe had ever seen, packed with the finest Renaissance art. The threat to Italy's cultural heritage was no longer indiscriminate bombing by the Allies. Paintings, sculptures, silverware, frescoes—if the rumors were true, they were all being stolen and taken on trains to the fatherland, no doubt destined for the future museum in Hitler's hometown of Linz, Austria.

Pasquale took a deep breath and exhaled audibly. "I have a plan. I will need help, lots of it, and permission from the Vatican, but we need to move everything we have saved to Rome. The Vatican is the only safe place in Italy right now—safe from the Allies and safe from the Germans. They have all agreed not to touch it. If we can somehow transport everything to the Vatican, we can save it all."

Elena burst out laughing. "I'm sorry, but that's madness! There are no trucks and not enough fuel. We will need men, equipment. The roads might be impassable. The Allies are making progress in the south. Surely we should wait for liberation."

Pasquale banged his fist on the desk, in frustration rather than anger. "We'll run out of time! This war could go on for months. And the Germans are here now. They're going to find the art, not just in Carpegna but here as well, and in Urbino, and it'll all be gone before the first British soldier arrives. Trust me—we must move this art to a safer place."

The two of them looked at each other for a few agonizing minutes. Pasquale broke the silence. "I'm worried the Germans might come here to search very soon. They know I come here frequently, as well as to the palace in Urbino. We need to act quickly." He signaled to Elena, who got up from her desk and walked toward him. Pasquale pointed to the paper on the table in front of him. Elena could see that he had drawn up a crude floorplan of the fortress. The two of them leaned over it.

"First, we need to hide the crates stored here in the Rocca," said Pasquale, drawing crosses on the map showing the various locations they had been using. "You know the semicircular corridor on the upper floor? We can block it off. I have called Signor Montagna, the builder. He's coming over this morning and I'm going to ask him to build us some false walls. Together with the curators, let's hide the biggest paintings and, at the same time, remove the labels. We need to keep a master list so we know what is in each crate, but I don't want to make it easy for the Germans if they do decide to call on us."

Elena nodded in agreement—that seemed like a solid plan and more than achievable. She herself had become concerned about the growing piles of crates in the building, and if they were hidden, she would be able to breathe a little easier.

"Next," said Pasquale, "I want to move a few of the smaller paintings immediately to the underground rooms at the Ducal Palace in Urbino. We'll have a lot more space to play with there, despite the number of crates already hidden. There are so many rooms underground that we could block some of them off, and hopefully nobody would be any wiser. I talked it over on the phone with my wife before you arrived—she's nervous that we will be found out, but she thinks at least we'll be doing something proactive."

Elena nodded again. She had met Pasquale's wife, Zea, a couple of times since she had moved back home. She was drawn to her at once, this smart woman who was a well-respected art historian in her own right and who struck Elena as the perfect foil for her husband.

A knock on the door of the office made them both start.

"Signor Rotondi? Are you in?" came a deep, gruff voice from the corridor.

"It's Montagna. Perfect timing. Let's start making lists while he starts on construction."

Signor Montagna listened with amusement while Pasquale explained what he wanted.

"Signor Rotondi, I've had some strange jobs in my time, but this is an odd one for sure."

"As long as you don't make this a story to tell over a glass of wine, Montagna," said Pasquale.

The builder shook his head. "You don't have to worry about me, Signor Rotondi. I am the very soul of discretion. And the last thing I need is the German army breathing down my neck. Or the Blackshirts. Can't stand any of them." He brandished his trowel. "This'll be done in no time. Trust me. Nobody's going to spot anything amiss when I'm done."

———

Over the next few hours, Pasquale, Elena, and the other curators sorted through the crates, Elena making long inventory lists and the men shifting the crates to the upper floor in the Rocca. By late afternoon, they had reduced the number of visible crates significantly. They stood watching as Signor Montagna started sealing up the first wall.

"This will take me a few days, Signore, but everything will be fairly well camouflaged by the time I have finished everything."

Satisfied, Pasquale turned back to Elena and the curators. "Now we wrap up the smaller pieces."

They got to work, using Pasquale's master inventory list to pull out some key pieces. As the paintings appeared, one by one, from their crates, Elena was unexpectedly moved by their beauty. Four of Bellini's Madonna paintings, *The Tempest* by Giorgione, Mantegna's *St George*— all masterpieces, any one of which would be the prized possession of a famous art museum. She felt blessed to be in the presence of such greatness. Pasquale noticed her mood. They stood side by side for a moment.

Pasquale gestured at Bellini's *Madonna with Sleeping Baby* and said emphatically, "This is worth risking everything for. Look at it—its humanity, its luminescence. Without art, we are mere brutes."

Elena nodded, suppressing a lump in her throat. She was afraid of the occupying Germans and what they might do to take the art. She also understood Pasquale's passion. Standing in that room, looking at the beauty in front of her, she did not want this painting stolen—or any of them, for that matter. What kind of art curator would she be if she did not try to do something to keep these works of art hidden?

Elena looked at Pasquale. "I have to be honest. I am afraid, but I do want to help you."

Pasquale looked fondly at his young assistant. "Elena, I do not intend to make this any more dangerous for you than I have to. Hopefully this little subterfuge will help. But—and I mean this sincerely—if at any point you want to stop, let me know. I don't want you to feel that you have to be involved, you understand?"

Elena nodded, not trusting herself to speak.

They loaded whatever they could fit into Pasquale's small car outside the Rocca, taking care to cover the paintings with blankets.

"Maybe the Germans will think one of my daughters is asleep in the back seat," Pasquale joked.

Elena did not think it was a laughing matter. "Be careful, Pasquale —please. We need both you and the art to make it out of this mess intact."

She shook his hand, but the gesture seemed too small given the importance of the moment. Elena watched the small car lurch away from the imposing building. She hoped the plan would work, but she could do nothing more that evening. She just had to pray that Pasquale wasn't stopped by the Germans.

Chapter Seven

Pasquale slowed down as he approached the city. It had been a nerve-wracking journey—something about transporting priceless works of art made every pothole and every curve in the road more terrifying. He had not been sure whether to try to drive at his normal speed to avoid attracting suspicion or to drive extremely slowly to prevent damage to the paintings. Fortunately, Pasquale had been stuck behind a slow-moving truck for most of the journey, which, on any other day, would have irritated him, but today it offered the perfect cover. He started to breathe a little easier as he approached Urbino.

As he drew close to Porta Valbona, he spotted Zea standing by the ancient gateway into the city. She was waving frantically to attract his attention, but, at the same time, was trying not to seem too agitated. He pulled over to the side of the road and she hurried toward him.

"The Germans are at the palace," Zea said as soon as she was in the passenger seat. "You cannot take the paintings there."

"*Porco cane!*" exclaimed Pasquale. Zea rubbed his thigh affectionately. It was very unlike her calm husband to swear.

"What shall we do?" she asked.

They sat in silence for a few minutes, thinking. Pasquale rubbed his mustache in an agitated fashion, trying to work out what the best plan of action might be. Then Zea spoke decisively. "We take them back to Villa Tortorina. We rented it for the holidays, so it is not our real home, and nobody will think to search for them there. Frankly, it'll be safer than taking them back to Sassocorvaro at this time of night."

Pasquale hesitated and then nodded. His wife was right—the Germans would never think to come to the villa, and they would be able to hide the artworks there for a day or two, until they came up with a better plan. He made a U-turn and drove a few miles to the beautiful house where the family was staying. The two of them carried the precious cargo one piece at a time into the house.

Pasquale said, "Let's put the Giorgione under our bed. I think it is the most valuable. And we should hide the others in different places."

The couple worked silently, taking great care not to damage anything. Pasquale felt that he only started breathing again when the last painting was hidden.

They sat at the table with hot drinks in front of them. Zea smiled, then shook her head in disbelief. "I cannot believe this is happening—one day we'll look back at tonight and think that we imagined it. We've done some crazy things together, but this might be the craziest."

Pasquale took her hand and caressed it. "*Carina*, there's nobody I'd rather have by my side right now." He leaned forward and kissed her gently.

Zea's face lit up. "You know what? I have an idea. I'll 'take to my bed' for the next day or so, and you tell the children and everyone else that I am sick. If the Germans do come looking, that might put them off snooping too much. We can hint that it is something contagious."

She laughed out loud. "Hey, at least I will have a much-needed rest!"

The children were a little surprised at their mother's sudden illness when they were informed of it the next morning, but, like all small children, within minutes they had moved on to something else more interesting. It was a stressful day for their father, though. He found himself pacing in the grounds outside the house, unable to settle for very long. He resolved to wait a day or so and then venture to Urbino to find out what the situation was. If the Germans were still at the palace, they would have to come up with another plan.

The next day, Pasquale called Elena in the office at the Rocca. He told her that his wife was sick and that he would be staying at Villa Tortorina for a few days. He was afraid to say much else over the phone, but Elena was smart enough not to ask. It frustrated her that she did not know what had happened to the paintings, but she felt relieved that no Germans had appeared at the Rocca that morning. She was not sure what she would do if they did, with Pasquale absent. Should she just act innocent, saying she merely typed letters? For the first few hours of the day, Elena mirrored her boss by pacing up and down the corridors of the ancient building, but by eleven o'clock, with no sign of any visitors, she decided to carry on as normal. Besides, she had other things to think about.

Luca had come up to Casa del Lupo the previous night to ask Elena if she intended to go to the dance in San Donato on Saturday. He had managed to make it seem like a friend asking a friend, but his agitation gave away his nervousness.

"I'd love to go with you, Luca," she said forcefully. Elena was not one for playing it coy.

Luca had seemed a little startled and blushed. "Oh, that's great. I can pick you up in the cart at seven, seeing that you live closer to San Donato than we do."

Luca hurried away without even coming in to say hello to Elena's parents or to ask for permission, which Elena's father thought was rude until she told him to stop being so old-fashioned. "It is 1943, Papa! Young people go to dances all the time! Besides, I was going out in Milan without you even being aware, and you have known Luca his whole life."

Her father muttered something under his breath about disrespectful daughters, but her mother smiled knowingly. She knew Elena was Francesco's favorite and therefore got away with things none of the other children dared to do.

"I will help you choose a dress, *passerotta*. What fun!"

So Elena had better things to think about than the Germans turning up unexpectedly and the day passed peacefully. At five, she packed up her typewriter, swept her eyes over the office, pleased with how tidy it was, and made her way out of the Rocca. She made sure the gate was locked securely and stepped into the piazza. Her heart dropped—across the square, by the café, she saw a group of Germans surrounding Pietro. The soldiers towered over the child intimidatingly.

Elena took a deep breath and strode across the cobblestones more forcefully than she usually did. The Germans turned to look at her as she approached.

"Ah, Signorina Marchetti, if I am not mistaken," said the tallest soldier, who appeared to be in charge. He made a short bow and held out his hand. "Major Heinrich. A little bird told me that you've returned from Milan recently."

Elena stood still, refusing to take the major's hand.

The man laughed. "I also heard rumors that you are—how should I put it—a little feisty. Where is your boss today? It appears he is missing." He nodded at the frightened Pietro standing next to him. "My young friend here says he has not seen him today."

Elena smiled at Pietro to reassure him and then turned to the major. "Major Heinrich, Superintendent Rotondi has merely taken a few days off to tend to his sick wife and his children. No mystery at all, I can assure you. Now if you'll excuse me . . ."

Elena started to move past the small group, but the German put his hand on her arm. He was still smiling at her, but he gripped her tightly. "Leaving so soon? Why don't you join us for a drink? I haven't been here that long and I'd like to get to know all the civilians I am responsible for."

Elena felt her heart beating strongly. She knew annoying this man was a dangerous move, but she had no intention of staying a minute longer. She calmly removed his hand from her arm and smiled at him. "Major Heinrich, unfortunately my mother gets very concerned if I don't arrive home at the appointed time. She isn't even keen on me having a job outside the home, so you can understand my desire to keep her happy. Pietro, can you fetch my bicycle, please?"

Pietro scuttled away, glad for the excuse to remove himself from the situation. Major Heinrich smiled again, but the smile did not reach his piercing blue eyes. The overall effect was unnerving. "Well, a dutiful daughter must of course listen to her mother. I certainly don't want to be the cause of any anxiety. Please tell your boss when he finally appears that we are looking forward to a visit to the Rocca. We are making sure everything is in order." The major bowed again and, with a wave of his hand, walked away, followed by his subordinates.

Elena was shaking as she walked toward the café. She sat down at one of the outside tables to steady herself.

"Your boss needs to stop sneaking around," said a gruff voice. Elena turned her head and found herself looking at Signor Bruni, Luca's neighbor, nursing a glass of wine at another table. "He'll get all of us in trouble if he's not careful." The old man scowled at her.

"*Buonasera*, Signor Bruni. Are you enjoying your wine?" The last thing Elena wanted to do was engage in a long conversation with the irascible man about the comings and goings at the Rocca.

"I've had better," replied Signor Bruni. "Where has Rotondi been then? The major was asking around."

"It's none of the major's business. Signor Rotondi is an employee of the Italian government. He keeps his own schedule. Besides, his office is in Urbino, not here." Elena was flustered. She would not usually speak so sharply to her elder, but the major's interrogation had scared her.

"We would all be safer if everyone knew which way the wind is blowing. The Germans are here, so you'd better get used to it. They're making the rules now." Signor Bruni picked up a newspaper lying on the table next to him and opened it aggressively. Elena ignored him.

"Signorina, that was scary!" whispered Pietro as he emerged from behind the café with Elena's bicycle. The boy's tanned face had gone very pale.

"Pietro, men like him want you to be scared, you understand?" said Elena, louder than she intended. She could hear Signor Bruni grunt, but she kept talking. "That is how they control us. Don't worry about the Germans—they will be gone soon enough. Just don't do anything stupid, okay?" Elena ruffled the boy's hair and dropped several small coins into his palm.

"Here are a few extra liras for looking after the bike so well today."

She rode away, leaving Pietro gazing after her with a look of adoration and Signor Bruni with a scowl on his ruddy face.

———

The same evening, a few miles away at Villa Tortorina, once the children were in bed, Pasquale and Zea lit the candles in their bedroom. Pasquale could not resist kneeling on the floor and gently removing the Giorgione from under the bed. He laid it on the bedcover and carefully unwrapped it. The two of them stood looking at it reverentially. The candlelight flickered across the moody scene, bathing the young woman and her baby in light.

"*The Tempest* was always one of my favorites," whispered Zea. "It is an enigma. Who is the young shepherd? Who is the woman? A storm is coming—what does it represent? I love that we will never truly know. And tonight, we gaze on this, just the two of us. It is an extraordinary honor."

They smiled at each other. Pasquale reached out and caressed his wife's face. He was at peace, an emotion he rarely felt anymore. Tonight, he knew this painting was safe. Other paintings were safe elsewhere in the house. His wife was by his side, and their two daughters were in the next room, sleeping soundly. Tonight, everything was alright in the world. Tomorrow, they would wake up and face whatever was coming together.

Chapter Eight

W ithin a few days, Pasquale learned that the Germans had left Urbino for the time being so with a huge sense of relief, he moved the paintings from his rental villa to the underground rooms of the Ducal Palace and hid them well with the help of his assistants. Elena was relieved when he returned to the office in Sassocorvaro and told her the good news. But Pasquale brushed her enthusiastic comments aside.

"This is just the first tiny step," Pasquale said. "I have written to the relevant authorities in Rome. Hopefully we will receive their blessing and material support for my plan. We must move all the works as soon as we can: the paintings, the sculptures, the music scores, all of it."

Elena nodded but felt slightly sick. She had no idea how they were supposed to achieve this, and she was terrified of being found out by the Germans. The encounter with Major Heinrich had thrown her off balance—the man seemed to guess that something was going on. But Pasquale appeared to have returned to work with renewed vigor and an inflated sense of what was possible.

"Alright. While we wait for word from Rome, let's organize transport. Elena, call everyone you can think of to find out if they have a truck or even a large car we can borrow for a couple of days. Say it is for official museum business."

Elena did not say a word for a minute or two, not wanting to contradict her boss. She tried to find the most diplomatic thing to say. "Pasquale, this is a very rural community, as you well know. Even the farmers I know don't always have a vehicle. My father still plows his fields with oxen, then takes his produce to the market in a horse-drawn cart. We do own a truck, but we only use it when we absolutely must. It won't be easy to find one vehicle, let alone a few that are available for us to borrow. And as for fuel—" Elena stopped, knowing full well that Pasquale was aware of the fuel shortages.

He smiled at her. "This is why I have given you the task, my dear Elena. If anyone can procure a vehicle, it will be you. And if not, we'll have to come up with another plan."

Elena smiled back, fortified by Pasquale's confidence in her. Moving all the art to Rome seemed like an impossible task—her immediate concern was proving to her boss that she had what it took to be a good art curator like him. If finding transport got her closer to her goal, then that was what she would focus on. Elena was going to try her hardest to make him proud.

Three days later, Elena was not feeling quite so confident. Everyone she had approached in Sassocorvaro had either laughed out loud or stared at her with incredulity. Elena hated the fact that she was ending the week having failed to make any headway, but she was also secretly relieved that Pasquale had not yet heard back from the Vatican. Without permission from the papal authorities, this crazy plan was not going ahead anyway.

Elena gave herself a pep talk that Friday, telling herself sternly that she would start the following week with renewed energy for the task at hand. She might even pluck up the courage to speak to her father, although she was convinced that he was the last person who would agree to help them.

In the meantime, she turned her attention to the immediate task of getting ready for the dance on Saturday evening. Her mother had been unusually helpful when it came to the dress, considering this was something Mamma would normally regard as frivolous and a waste of energy when real work needed to be done. She had procured green fabric from somewhere—Elena did not dare ask where—and had managed to produce a pretty dress made for dancing. Elena felt spoiled, considering she owned a couple of dresses she had purchased while in Milan. But here in the countryside, they looked slightly ridiculous. The dance was being held in a barn at the edge of the village and one of Elena's Milanese dresses would definitely stand out.

Elena and her mother had had a brief argument when Elena had asked for the hem to be shortened by a couple of inches, but looking at her mother's face, she had decided not to pursue the matter. She was just grateful to have something appropriate to wear and for her mother's support for the outing with Luca.

Elena had another surprise when her mother told her younger siblings in no uncertain terms that Elena would have the luxury of a bath on Saturday afternoon and that they would have to wait a day or so to do the same. Her brother Andrea, who was fifteen, was positively giddy at not having to clean up, but the real surprise was Giulia, who always tried to secure the first bath every Saturday and had to be forced out of the water to give the others a turn. Being sixteen years old, Giulia had first tried to argue that she was old enough to go to the dance, but her mother and father were having none of it. Once she saw the futility, Giulia became Elena's strongest supporter and begged to be allowed to do her hair.

"Gosh, I hope Luca asks you to marry him, and then it will be my turn."

Elena giggled. "It's just a dance! We are going as old friends."

"Yes, well, we'll see," said Giulia, with a smirk. "Now hold still—your hair is so knotted."

Chapter Nine

Two hours later, Elena sat next to Luca on the wooden seat in his cart as he guided his horse up the hill to the village of San Donato. Luca seemed tongue-tied, but Elena was not deterred. She kept up a stream of conversation all the way to the village. She told him about her encounter with Major Heinrich, which Luca found a little alarming. She also described her interaction with Signor Bruni, which made Luca grunt.

"He's an annoying old man who needs to learn to mind his own business. My father and uncle are constantly having arguments with him about the most trivial things. You'd think he would have more important things to worry about."

"He's probably very lonely since his wife died. He just wants company, someone to talk to. But, yes, you're right. He needs to adopt a friendlier manner." As the conversation had taken a more serious turn, Elena decided to lighten the mood by talking about the kittens one of their farmhouse cats had just delivered. "Giulia is obsessed, I swear. You'd think she gave birth to them herself. She won't let Papa drown any of them. We are going to be overrun with cats soon. At least we have no problem with mice in our house!"

Luca smiled. "That sounds like Marco. He is far too softhearted to be a farmer. I think my father is beginning to despair."

"No such thing as too softhearted in my book. Your brother's just a kind soul. You men could learn a lot from him," Elena teased. As she spoke, she nonchalantly put her hand on his thigh and squeezed it.

Luca felt as if his whole body was burning. Elena's hand remained there, lightly resting, but it might as well have been an iron grip. Every time he was with her lately he felt his heart beating faster. Everything looked sharper and brighter. He tentatively turned to look at her, but she was facing resolutely forward. She looked even more beautiful than usual this evening. He felt intoxicated just sitting next to her.

Once they arrived at the barn and had tied up the horse by the water trough next to all the other animals, Luca relaxed. He gallantly held out his hand to assist Elena down from her seat and kept hold of it until two of his friends came rushing toward him, hollering.

"You're late as usual, Luca."

Antonio jumped on his friend and started mussing up his long hair. Luca pushed him off but laughed good-naturedly. "At least I washed—you smell like a farmyard."

Antonio scowled. "It's not my fault I work at a tannery." He put his shirt sleeve to his nose and gave it a tentative sniff.

Luca took pity on him. "Forget about it, Antonio. Come on. The music's already started."

The group sauntered into the brightly lit barn, excited to see each other and for an increasingly rare chance to enjoy themselves. It had been a while since the church had put on a dance for the young people in the community, but the priest had decided they deserved an opportunity to escape the current misery of their lives, if only for a few hours. He had witnessed the joy displayed at the Rossi party a few weeks earlier and was hoping to recreate it.

Since the Germans had arrived in the area a few months ago, a pall of fear had settled over the village and the surrounding countryside, and no amount of praying seemed to relieve it. Don Antonio, who had arrived in the parish only a year earlier when the previous priest had died of old age, was not much older than the young people he was trying to reach.

Signora Ricci, who cooked and cleaned for the new priest, and despite being seventy still had a twinkle in her eye, had told him about the dances held before the war, and the idea appealed to him. He spoke to the farmer whose barn had previously hosted the dances, and the man had enthusiastically agreed to the plan. So, for the past few weeks, Don Antonio had been adding a speech to his weekly sermons from the pulpit, extolling the benefits of social activity and community and exhorting the older members of the congregation to let the younger adults in their families attend. Given the number of people, old and young, who had turned up, it seemed to the priest that they had not needed much encouragement.

Soon the makeshift dance floor was full of young men twirling their partners around and their parents on the edge of the barn, casting benevolent eyes on the proceedings. Luca's cousins, Tommaso and Matteo, were playing as vigorously as anyone had ever heard them and their fellow musicians were just as enthusiastic. Their vivacious tunes had everyone on the dance floor. Elena was giddy, refusing to sit still for a minute. When Luca started to fade, she pushed him away from her and grabbed one of her girlfriend's hands instead. "You have no stamina, Rossi!" The two women whirled away.

Luca stood at the edge with Antonio, watching them go. Elena appeared otherworldly tonight, filled with light and spirit. It was as if she was a magnet, drawing everyone toward her and keeping the whole circle bonded. He couldn't take his eyes off her.

"Is it love?" asked Antonio, punching him on the arm. "She's strong-willed, that one! Are you going to be the lucky man who ties her down?"

Luca felt himself blushing and pushed Antonio back. "Elena has always been the life and soul of the party—you know that. Not sure how interested she is in me—she probably had lots of men following her around in Milan."

"Ah, but she isn't in Milan now, is she? And you two—and your families—have been friends forever. Might as well take it one step further."

Luca turned to his friend, about to rebuff him, when he saw some kind of commotion at the barn doors. Heads were turning in that direction. Luca noticed that some young men had entered the barn in a hurry. The music stopped and voices were raised at the back.

"God, it's Lorenzo and Alessandro," shouted Antonio excitedly.

Luca turned and spotted his brother and his best friend, their faces grim, pushing their way through the crowd until they got to where Luca was standing. Elena hurried forward to hug them, but something stopped her. They could have been strangers. Their clothes were torn and dirty and their hair was unkempt. It had only been a year since she had said goodbye to her older brother, but he looked as if he'd aged more than that. Alessandro's face was gaunt, his eyes hollow. He had always been slim, but now his clothes hung from him as if he was a scarecrow. Elena was shocked to see him sporting a ragged beard as well.

The two partisans climbed onto the small wooden stage next to the musicians. Lorenzo nodded at Luca and then turned to face everyone. "We don't have much time," he proclaimed loudly. "One of our sources in Sassocorvaro told us that Mussolini's Fascists are going to round up all the young men they can find this weekend to conscript them into their cause. They've not found many in town, so they are looking further afield."

He hesitated and gazed at the young faces looking at him nervously. "One of our spies on the ground heard them talking about coming here tonight. Someone told them about the dance, and they think they can surprise you. A group of us are staked out on the road, hoping to ambush them, but if we fail—"

He did not need to continue. The young men who had just been laughing and joking with each other knew the seriousness of the moment. Nobody wanted to be caught by the Blackshirts. Luca climbed up next to his brother, gave Lorenzo a stiff hug, and turned to his cousins.

"You two head back home now—you rode here, right?" His cousins nodded. Their pale faces and wide eyes showed how scared they were. They said a hasty farewell to their fellow musicians, gave Lorenzo a hug, and hurried away, clutching their fiddles. Luca looked at Elena.

"You take my cart back to your place. I can't risk being caught on the road, so I'll cut across the fields and hide somewhere. I will try to get to Casa del Lupo later. We all need to lie low for a few days."

Lorenzo nodded. "Our guys will inflict some damage, but that won't stop them. Those thugs don't seem to realize that they are fighting a war they're going to lose. But now that the Germans have arrived to bolster them, things will be very nasty for a while."

Alessandro jumped off the stage and hugged his sister. Elena held on to him, feeling his ribs. One year apart, and this was how they were meeting each other. She held his face in both hands. "Be careful, please. You're brave, for sure, but also foolish. Mamma still cries every night—I can hear her through the walls. Please don't get yourself killed." She hugged him again, then turned to Luca and Antonio.

"Go on, you two. Scram. We've got this. Just don't be caught, okay? The farms need you, or none of us will eat this winter. Let the others do what they need to do, but we don't all need to be fighters. Just leave."

Luca touched his brother's arm in wordless thanks and left the barn with Antonio. Elena turned back to her brother. "Thank you. I know it was a huge risk coming here, and you don't agree with what Luca and the others are doing by staying. But we're all on the same side. Please stay safe. We all have to survive this."

Alessandro nodded. His expression was dark. "We know what we need to do. We're getting a lot of help from most people in the villages and farms. Food, weapons, firewood—they're helping us hide and keeping their mouths shut. But it is not—"

Alessandro was interrupted by a distant explosion. Everyone left in the hall turned toward the doors and started pouring outside. More explosions and gunfire could be heard from further down the hill.

"Sounds like my comrades have engaged with the enemy. Okay, we're out of here. Love you, *sorella mia*—don't do anything foolish." He smiled and touched her cheek. Elena held his hand briefly and then pushed him away. Within seconds, the two young men had disappeared as quickly as they had arrived.

Elena turned to her girlfriends, some of whom were crying. A couple had already untied their pony and climbed onto their cart. Some had bicycles and were hurrying to escape. The older villagers had started walking back to their homes.

"Sounds like the Fascists are a little occupied right now," quipped Elena. A few girls smiled, but their eyes showed their fear. Most of them had a brother, father, uncle, or cousin with the partisans and knew that some of the attackers would not survive the evening. Given the secrecy with which the partisans operated, the families might not know for months, if at all, whether their loved ones were coming home again.

Elena said her goodbyes and climbed onto Luca's cart. She grabbed the flashlight he had left under the seat and turned it on. The light was not strong, but she was grateful for it nonetheless. The horse was a little resistant at first, but she soon turned it around and started trotting down the road toward her home. The sounds of the ambush receded as Elena made her way down the hill on the narrow road. There was no moon tonight, which made the journey harder, but she knew these roads and every curve well. She was more nervous about coming across a pack of wild boar, which would attack if disturbed, and was grateful when she finally saw the gates of Casa del Lupo ahead of her.

Her father was pacing outside the farmhouse, his shotgun over his shoulder. He was listening to the loud noises coming from across the valley. Elena told him what had happened at the barn.

"This is bad. Not good at all. There'll be a price to pay for this, I feel it. I don't want you to go to work on Monday."

"But Papà!"

"Enough. Alessandro roaming around the countryside is bad enough. It's not safe, and you need to stay here until things quiet down again."

Elena knew better than to try to argue with her father when he was like this. She left him outside and went in to talk to her mother. Her mother stood in the kitchen, tears pouring down her cheeks as Elena told her about seeing Alessandro.

"He's alive, Mamma, he's alive. He seemed well," Elena reassured. "He was not part of the ambush, and he left the barn before I did. He's too smart to be caught."

Giulia looked at Elena beseechingly. Elena took a moment to realize what she wanted. "Everyone is safe, okay? Lorenzo and Alessandro made sure of it. Luca got away. The Rossi twins had their horses there. I am sure nobody at the dance tonight was caught." Giulia looked at her sister gratefully. Elena understood her reluctance to ask about Tommaso by name. She had also decided to gloss over Luca's escape as well. No point in giving her mother any ideas.

Elena hugged her mother and her sister tightly. Nobody spoke. It was enough to know that Alessandro's heart was still beating and he was close by, even if Elisa and Giulia had not been lucky enough to embrace him themselves.

Elena was too wide awake to rest. She lay on her bed, listening to Giulia muttering things in her sleep. She heard her mother softly calling to her husband out of a window, and then, after a few minutes, her father stomping into the house and slamming the door. Eventually the noises ceased. Elena knew everyone had retired for the night. She sat up slowly and inched her way out of bed, making sure she did not disturb Giulia. Her slippers were on the floor next to her bed. Quietly, she grabbed a cardigan and a shawl from the chair and went to stand by the window. The two sisters had forgotten to close the shutters, so she was able to look out into the dark farmyard. The firefight appeared to have ended and the night was quiet. She waited, sensing something was about to happen.

After half an hour, Elena had almost given up—her feet were cold and her thin shawl was not keeping her very warm. She was about to go back to bed when she heard the distinct sound of the gate creaking. She put her face to the glass, searching for a movement in the darkness. Luca appeared in the farmyard, quiet as a spirit. He gazed at her window and waved. Elena held out the palm of her hand as if to stop him from coming forward, then turned away. She tiptoed across the room, opened her bedroom door, and inched her way along the corridor. Elena grabbed her coat from the wall hook and exchanged her slippers for a pair of boots. She picked up a large flashlight kept by the front door. The thick door had been bolted, but Elena remembered that her mother had greased the bolt the other day. It slid smoothly as she pulled it. Within a minute, she was in the farmyard. Luca looked at her, his face betraying nothing. She put her finger to her lips and grabbed Luca's hand.

"Come here," she whispered into his ear and pulled him around the single-story house and along the path to the cattle barn. Once inside, they made their way to the ladder and climbed up into the hayloft. With the cows plaintively lowing below them, Elena started piling up straw to make a place to sit and covered it with her coat. She balanced the flashlight on a bale to give them a little light, and the two of them sat facing each other.

"Are you—"

"Did it—"

They both started speaking and stopped. Elena tapped Luca's arm. "You first. Did you see anything or anyone?"

"No, it was fine. We scrambled down the hill and then followed the stream. Antonio went off across the fields toward his house. I made my way here. Nobody saw me and the gunfire did not last long."

Luca hesitated. He looked away into the darkness of the barn, out of reach from the weak glow of the flashlight. He swallowed hard, wondering if he should share what he was thinking. "I-I was terrified, Elena. I thought that—"

Elena pulled him toward her and hugged him. Luca held her with a desperation he rarely felt. His heart was beating so fast, he thought she must be able to feel it through her cardigan and nightdress. He pulled back and studied her face for a reaction.

Elena had never seen Luca look so vulnerable, so defeated. She felt a surge of emotion. *I want to keep this man safe*, she thought. Without thinking, Elena leaned forward to kiss him. Her lips were cold. Luca felt as if he had been touched by an electric charge. He kissed her back, then grabbed the back of her head with both hands. She moaned and held him tighter. Luca felt possessed. He kissed her mouth again and then moved to her neck. Elena arched her back and made little mewing sounds. She pulled at her cardigan, struggling to remove it. Luca gently pushed her backward, and then, still holding her, lowered her to the ground. Elena lay back onto the straw, and Luca lay awkwardly on top of her. She hesitated for a second, then pushed Luca off her. He was alarmed. "God. I'm sorry. I didn't mean to hurt you."

In response, Elena sat up and slowly, languidly, rolled her nightdress up and over her head. She peeked at him with a slight smile, her eyes glistening. The flickering light cast shadows over her pale skin. Luca thought he had never seen anything so beautiful.

"Luca," she whispered. "Luca." She spoke his name as if it was sacred. "I was scared tonight as well. Really scared. But I knew you would come."

She looked at him, boring into his soul. "Because this war—all this —we can't lose each other. I realized this evening. I've only just come back. I don't want to leave you again."

She leaned forward to kiss him again. Luca hesitated, then kissed her back, his tongue forcing its way into her mouth while his hands explored her back, her spine. He gently pushed her down and lowered his mouth to her breasts, kissing first one, then the other. Elena cried out and held the back of his head. It was exquisite—she had never felt such pleasure.

"Don't stop. Please."

Luca felt transported. He moved his hand to caress her right breast while he maneuvered himself lower down to gently lick between her legs. Elena's moans deepened. She fumbled with the buttons of his trousers and moaned again, this time with frustration.

Luca pulled his buttons apart, all caution gone. He wanted her so badly. He did not care if they were caught. He pulled down his trousers and forced his way between Elena's legs. He felt like he would explode. He pushed harder, finding that she was already wet. There was some resistance, only for a few seconds, and then he felt enveloped by her. They cried out in unison, grasping each other as if drowning in a lake. With a shudder, Luca gave a final thrust. As he did, Elena felt the most intense wave come over her, and the two of them crested together, clutching each other's bodies, not wanting to separate.

They lay back on the straw, staring up at the wooden beams, holding hands. Luca finally roused himself and turned to face Elena, propping his body up on his arm. He caressed her face.

"I've wanted you for the longest time," he said in a quiet voice. "I did not even dare to admit that to myself because it was impossible. Even before you left for Milan. You were so unattainable. Look at you— you're smart and worldly, and you—"

Elena put her hand over his mouth. "Hush, Luca. You're an idiot. I wanted this as much as you did." She stroked his cheek. "I know I'm supposed to feel terrible right now. If what my mother and the priests have been saying for years is true, then I'm damned to hell." Even in the dim light, she could see the horror on Luca's face, so she hurried on. "But how can this be wrong? We have been close for as long as I can remember and, since I came back from Milan, I knew it was more. I wanted this as much as you did. I promise you."

Elena snuggled close to him. Luca enveloped her in his arms. They lay still for a few minutes.

"I think everything speeds up in wartime," said Elena. "Girls I knew in Milan would meet a soldier at a dance then three weeks later, they'd be married before he went off again to the front lines. It's as if nobody is prepared to wait in case there is no future." She pulled herself up on her side. "I am not prepared to wait anymore either. I saw the neighbors' house across the road in Milan destroyed by a bomb and everyone inside die in an instant. They had plans and things they wanted to do, I'm sure, and now they're gone. When I came back and saw you that first night, I knew I wanted you. There. I've admitted it now. And tonight proved to me that my instinct was right. I know you feel the same way."

Luca nodded, not daring to speak. She kissed him on the lips and cheeks. "This war will end and we can be together properly. I just need you to stay safe until then, okay?"

Luca pulled her toward him. They lay in the straw, entwined.

"Luca, don't leave just yet."

"I don't ever want to leave you, if I'm being honest."

Luca kissed the top of her head. He felt calm for the first time in months. Elena was right—they needed to stay out of harm's way until this stupid war was over. Lorenzo could do the fighting—Luca was going to stay home, where he was supposed to be.

Chapter Ten

At the same hour, a few miles away, an exhausted group of young men huddled together in another barn. A few lay on the rough ground, straining to breathe. Blood dripped onto the hay from open wounds that others were desperately attempting to patch up. Occasionally, there would be a frantic scramble of activity, followed by guttural noises that faded into silence. The bystanders paused, furiously making the sign of the cross, before they moved on to the next fallen man.

"We lost too many tonight," said Lorenzo in a low voice. He was slumped against the wall of the barn, gripping his aluminum bottle and taking the occasional gulp of water. The grime under his fingernails and the streaks of mud on his arms showed how long it had been since he had taken a bath.

Alessandro nodded. He watched with resignation as one by one the wounded partisans were treated to the best of the group's ability. Five injured men had made it back to the barn a few hours ago, but only two were still alive. Four other men were still unaccounted for. It was unclear how many Fascists had been killed in the ambush, but they all knew that others would soon replace them. The two friends glanced at each other —exhaustion was etched into their young faces.

"Comrades, listen up." Their leader, Erivo Ferri, held up his lantern as if sending a signal to the group. The weary men turned to look at him, anticipating yet another speech from their commanding officer. Lorenzo closed his eyes, not sure if he was ready for a call to arms.

"We lost some good men this evening, true patriots indeed. We inflicted some damage in return, but we also took a hit. I know you mourn their loss, but our liberty depends on us not giving up."

Erivo looked around the barn at the twenty or so men and the few women in front of him.

Some of the men were still in their teens—Erivo sensed they were still tied to their mothers' apron strings. Their faces showed bewilderment and fear, as if wondering how this hell had become their lives. Erivo softened his tone.

"*Ragazzi*, this is hard. Trust me—I know this is hard. This isn't what any of us thought would happen even a short year ago. Here we are in the middle of the country, tending our fields or working in our shops and offices in our small villages and towns. I'm a shoemaker, for God's sake. We never believed the war would come here. Florence, Rome, Milan, Naples—that's where the war was. Well, it's here now.

"Don't go on thinking that somehow Le Marche is safe. Mussolini and his thugs still think they can win and the Germans are not going to go away without a fight. Fuck, there are Nazis now in Sassocorvaro and Urbino! If we want our freedom, then we'll have to fight for it. That means fighting the Germans and, yes, even our fellow Italians if they choose to stick with the *bastardo* Mussolini. We're the true Italians now."

The assembled men and women nodded and grunted in agreement. Erivo hesitated, but then kept talking. "But we need more supplies. We need food, as always, and guns and ammunition. We also need transport. We must be able to move to where we are needed as easily as possible."

The exhausted faces stared at him as if he had asked them to procure gold bullion. Fuel was even harder to come by than precious metals. "Let's rest for a day or so—we know this place is safe for now and we need our two wounded colleagues to heal. We also have to find the men still missing. If they are alive, they'll know to make their way to this barn. So we can't move just yet. We can send out discreet search parties when it gets light."

Erivo paused again, knowing that his fighters were physically and mentally drained. "I realize this is hard to hear, but we must start planning for our next act of resistance. When we've rested, I want you to go back to your families and villages. Like I said, we need more supplies. But only go to those you trust—someone told the militia about the dance this evening, and whoever it was knew that they would not be paying a friendly visit. Traitors are everywhere."

Lorenzo looked at Alessandro as the group started piling up straw to sleep on. The young men did not need to say a word. They both knew that their families were beginning to face shortages. But what was the point of simply surviving if you ended up losing what mattered?

Chapter Eleven

T he sun rose over the hill, casting long shadows over the farmyard. Elena lay in bed, watching the light move, inch by inch, across the terracotta tiles on the floor of her bedroom. She first heard her mother and then her father rise to start their morning tasks, her mother in the kitchen, her father outside on the farm. She did not want to move; she wanted to keep luxuriating in her memories of Luca in the barn, of his touch on her skin, his mouth on hers. Her body ached. She was glad of the physical reminder. She would be with Luca in a couple of hours at church, and the thought made her almost sick with anticipation. She felt different now, as if she had finally become an adult. Her more worldly girlfriends in Milan had whispered to her of their secret trysts with their soldier boyfriends and the forbidden pleasures they had shared. Elena had found the descriptions enticing and terrifying in equal measure. Now she had joined their sisterhood. Would any of her family notice that she was not the same girl she had been the day before?

Breakfast was tense, but not for the reason Elena feared. Francisco shared the terrible news of the evening's incident with Andrea, who had been asleep when Elena had returned the previous night. "But you saw Alessandro?" he asked his sister. "You actually saw him, alive?"

Elena saw the anxiety in his eyes. Andrea always projected inner strength and a careless attitude, as if he was somehow separate from the rest of the family. With a start, she realized that this was simply teenage bravado. He loved and missed his older brother very much.

"He's healthy, Andrea, I promise you. And he wasn't part of the ambush—he went to the dance to warn those who were there. He'll be fine."

"But this is not fine," thundered Elena's father. He slammed his fist down on the kitchen table, making the cups jump. "We are going to church, but that's it for the time being. Nobody is going anywhere else for the next few days, until we find out what happened exactly. The Fascists will want to retaliate, and who knows what the damn Germans will do. I don't want anyone else in this family to behave recklessly, do you understand?"

They all nodded. Elena felt her face burning. She was thinking about the night before in the cattle barn—both of her parents would be scandalized if they knew. She was also thinking about Pasquale's plan to move the art. Elena understood how skeptical her father would be about the idea. He was not someone who understood art or who saw its point. Her father saw art as something only the wealthy cared about. Some people might have money to waste and hours to spend in a museum but working people like her father had too much to do and no time for frivolity. The only reason he had let her go to Milan was because she had been able to send some money back home and because she had been fed by someone else for a year. Francesco Marchetti had always viewed the job itself as meaningless. If his daughter wanted to dabble in art, that was fine, but it was not a real job. If he discovered that her boss had enlisted her to help him move thousands of works of art under the Germans' noses, he would be horrified. No, it was better if that particular plan went unmentioned at home.

It was a somber group that headed to church that morning. The family was greeted by equally dour expressions on the faces of the rest of the congregation as they milled outside the church. Nobody was talking much and whatever conversations were taking place were being had with quiet voices, almost in whispers. Elena scoured the crowd, trying to see Luca. After several minutes, she realized that no young men were present. The village had heeded the words of the partisans the previous evening. Everyone had decided that their sons would not be attending mass.

Within five minutes of Elena's arrival, she saw the Rossi family's largest cart coming up the hill, driven by Signor Rossi himself. Sitting next to him on the narrow bench was his wife and his sister-in-law Maria. Crowded into the rear were Luca's youngest brother, Marco, his uncle, Leonardo, and his younger cousins, Giovanna and Gianni. There was no sign of Luca, or indeed his cousins, Tommaso and Matteo. It made perfect sense to Elena that the young men had stayed home, but she felt a huge disappointment. In that moment, she knew that the next few days, possibly weeks, would be very difficult for all of them.

Elena heard Giulia groan. She looked at her sharply, confused for a few seconds, until she realized that her younger sister was also staring at the cart. Elena was not the only Marchetti who had been hoping to see one of the Rossi men. She grabbed her sister's hand and squeezed it in sympathy.

As the church doors opened to welcome the congregation, a car came hurtling up the narrow road, scattering the stray dogs. Cars were rare on the road, especially on a Sunday. Elena sensed immediately that this did not bode well. Her fears were confirmed a minute later as the car came to a halt in front of the church.

A German soldier sitting in the front passenger seat jumped out as soon as the car stopped and rushed to the rear to open the door. Major Heinrich emerged with a tight smile on his face and stood brushing imaginary specks of dust from the shoulder of his uniform. He walked briskly toward the crowd, who had turned as one to stare at him. The major stopped as he spotted Elena and doffed his cap at her.

"*Buongiorno*, Signorina Marchetti—it is so nice to see you again."

Elena stared straight ahead, trying not to let any emotion show on her face.

Major Heinrich turned to the villagers. "I heard we had a small— how shall I put it—disturbance last night. My counterpart with the local Italian authorities is not a happy man this morning. It appears some criminals stopped his men from carrying out their official duties."

The villagers stood motionless, most stony-faced, some looking terrified. Nobody spoke.

"We know what has been going on in this area—the disruptions by a few traitors. And we also know that they have been getting help. We will find them, and we will kill them. And we will kill anyone who assists them. Is that perfectly clear?"

The major smiled again. The villagers continued to stare back at him. Elena felt terrified—for Alessandro, Lorenzo, and the rest of the partisans, but also for Luca. The man standing in front of them was dangerous. Elena also knew that he would return to the Rocca. Pasquale would be in terrible trouble if his scheme was uncovered. Elena rarely felt afraid of anyone or anything, but she was deeply afraid at that moment, standing in the warm October sunshine outside a small church.

Major Heinrich bowed to Don Antonio, who was still holding the church door, and then turned sharply and marched back to his waiting car. He looked back once more. "We are stronger than you, and we will prevail." The major looked at the villagers with a sneer on his face. "It wasn't my idea to be posted to this godforsaken backwater, I can assure you. But I intend to carry out my duties to the letter. My orders are to keep you all in line. If you think some country villagers can outsmart the Third Reich—" He shook his head as if in disbelief and disappeared into the car's rear seat.

Don Antonio tried to rally the villagers with an upbeat sermon, but it was a losing battle that morning. Even the hymn singing was quieter than usual. Elena and her sister corralled Giovanna, Luca's young cousin, as soon as they left the church an hour later. They had always liked the vivacious girl, despite the fact that she was a little younger than the two of them.

"Gio! What was the atmosphere like at Ca'Boschetto this morning?"

Giulia asked quickly as soon as they were alone. "My father's in a terrible mood and the Nazis' unexpected visit is going to make it much worse."

Giovanna nodded. "Not great. Papa is nervous for the twins, of course. After all, they should have been conscripted already given their age. And Uncle Paolo knows Lorenzo was out with the partisans last night—Luca told him all about it this morning at breakfast."

Elena tried not to flinch at hearing Luca's name. She felt her cheeks going red. Giovanna plowed on without seeming to notice.

"I could tell he was afraid when Lorenzo had first disappeared but now, obviously, things are much worse. I doubt my uncle will let Luca go anywhere for a while. My poor cousin—and my brothers—are going to be trapped on the farm for the foreseeable future."

Elena was torn—she was happy that Luca would hopefully be kept safe by his father and uncle but upset that it would be difficult for the two of them to meet up. She stopped listening as Giulia filled her friend in on what their father had said at breakfast and instead tried to think of how she and Luca were going to be together. Maybe if she invented an errand that would take her to Ca'Boschetto . . . Her reverie was interrupted by her father's raised voice. He was having an animated debate with the other men from the village, and it was getting heated.

"Look. I was not happy when my boy left to join the partisans because I thought it was reckless and I believed that he was too young to have thought through what it might mean. But Alessandro was not wrong. The *partigiani* have the right idea. If we are true Italians, we don't want to be dominated by these damn Germans."

Most of the men around him grunted in agreement. Signor Bruni was not one of them.

"You won't be feeling so gung-ho, Marchetti, when they come back and decide to execute some of us," he said in a dismissive tone. "It happened at Ca'Gallo, remember? The partisans blew up one jeep with a booby trap, and they killed five villagers in retaliation."

Some of the people in the small group started muttering and nodding. Elena's father gave them a scornful glance. "Well, you can do nothing if that's what you prefer, but I'm not going to let my son die. I'm leaving provisions out for him in the barn, and I'm not saying anything if the odd rifle goes missing either. If we're going to die, I'd rather go down fighting. I am too old to be sleeping under hedges like they probably are, but I'll do my part." Francesco turned away resolutely and looked for his family. "Elena, Giulia, Andrea, let's get moving— we're leaving right now."

Elena gave Giovanna a hug and walked quickly to the cart. She did not trust Signor Bruni at all, and her father had just announced publicly that he was helping the partisans. On the other hand, her father's defiant speech had strengthened her resolve, but perhaps not the way in which it was intended. He was right—they were at war whether they liked it or not. She was not ready to take up arms to save her country like her brother, but she wasn't a child. She was tired of being treated as if her life was less important than her brother's. She wanted a career and a family and a life with Luca. For now, she was going to concentrate on helping Pasquale save the paintings and every other precious thing they were guarding. She would show her boss—and her father—that she had what it took to succeed. Finally, she was going to do something that mattered.

Chapter Twelve

T hings were busy in the valley for the next few days. At Ca'Boschetto, Luca was hard at work with his extended family as the olive harvest was upon them. Everybody had a role to play. Their workdays were intense given that they not only had to take care of the pigs and the sheep as usual, but, in addition, the crops were also ready to be brought in. The wheat had been harvested during the long, hot days of August. But now the olives were turning from green to a light purple and needed to be collected before they turned black. It was important that the job was finished before the heavy rain and snow came.

The younger boys were tasked with getting the tarpaulins ready so they could shake down each tree and collect the fruit. It was a task Marco and Gianni always enjoyed as it involved striking the tree with long sticks to dislodge the olives. The group went systematically from tree to tree, collecting as many olives as possible to bring to the communal press in the village to produce precious olive oil.

Then the two families moved on to the fruit trees. The apples were weighing down the branches and would be stored in the cold cellar. Luca's mother and aunt had already canned the excess figs and cherries at the end of the summer. When the crop was bountiful, they could sell or barter the extra jars and fruit at one of the local markets. With the long hours of work, Luca had little time to think about Elena. He saved his reveries for the nights, when he would crawl exhausted into his bed and for a few blissful moments, relive the evening in the barn before sleep overwhelmed him.

After a week of intense work, the two families finally had a moment to rest. Luca's father decided that enough time had passed since the ambush without any signs of retaliatory action by the Italian army or the Germans. Paolo and Leonardo discussed the situation briefly over their morning cups of chicory and decided it would be safe for both families, even the young men, to attend mass later that morning. So, as the sun's rays began warming the autumnal air, two carts set off from Ca'Boschetto toward the village of San Donato.

Luca was fidgeting on the hard wooden bench next to his younger brother. He knew Elena had been at the service the week before because Giovanna had told him all about their conversation and the Germans' unannounced visit. He felt nauseous with anticipation as the carts slowly made their way up the steep hill to the church. As soon as they arrived, Luca spotted Elena's straw hat and bright blue cardigan as she chatted animatedly with some girlfriends. As if Elena sensed his stare, she turned around and her face lit up.

"Luca!" she called before quickly adding, "Giovanna, Tommaso, Matteo, the olive harvest was plentiful?"

Then everyone was chatting at once, desperate to reconnect after their enforced separation during an intense week. Luca said nothing but stood fixated on Elena, as if attempting to capture her image in case of another parting. Elena felt deliriously happy. She turned away from her sister and Giovanna's conversation and touched Luca's arm.

"All good, Luca? You all worked as hard as we did?"

Luca laughed. "It's the same every year—a mad panic at the beginning when my father is convinced that it is going to rain, then the self-congratulations at the end when he tells us all that he timed it perfectly. My uncle's so much easier to deal with. But yes, we got it done. Why were you working hard? Weren't you at your office in Sassocorvaro?"

Elena filled him in with the news that she had not been allowed to go to the Rocca that week. She had ended up working with the family and their farmhands instead. "I think my father was glad of the extra pair of hands, to be honest, although he never said much. But he's decided that I can go back tomorrow. Poor Pasquale would've been quite lost without me this week—I need to find out whether he has heard from the Vatican."

Luca was confused for a moment until he remembered what Elena had told him about the plan to move the art. He assumed that the Pope would agree with him and tell the superintendent in no uncertain terms what he could do with his idea. But he said nothing as Elena was so excited at the thought of returning to the work she loved.

"Do you think you will be able to steal away tonight?" Luca whispered in her ear.

Elena blushed and nodded imperceptibly as Don Antonio started urging the villagers to enter the church. The priest was relaxed about the start time because he knew that being together on Sunday morning meant a lot to the community. These people had such little downtime, and the past few months had been particularly challenging for everyone. Don Antonio thought the good Lord would not mind waiting a few minutes for their prayers.

The service was noticeably more joyful than the previous week's. Elena kept glancing across the aisle at the Rossi family, smiling at young Marco's fidgeting and his mother's hand being firmly planted on his leg to force him to focus. Gianni was not doing any better in the pew behind. His father Leonardo kept glaring at his son in an effort to make Gianni concentrate on the service. Luca smiled at her whenever he saw her looking, and Elena boldly smiled back. She did not care if anyone saw them.

The sunlight shone through the stained-glass windows of the church and lit up the face of the Madonna. The painted wooden statue had stood on one side of the altar for as long as Elena could remember. She had never really examined it before—it was just something that had always been present. It was not a particularly impressive piece, especially when Elena compared it to the artwork she handled every day.

But this morning, her frame of mind and the autumnal sun came together to give the statue an almost celestial beauty. Elena gazed at the calm visage of the Madonna and the innocent expression on the face of her baby son and sighed. In that moment, sitting in the church, she realized she wanted this for herself—a child and a family. It was not something she had ever considered before, even though it was the expected next step for a young woman of her age. The only thing that had excited her mother when her eldest daughter had left for Milan was the thought of the larger pool of potential husbands. But Elena had begun to imagine herself with a career, working in a big city, escaping the rural place where she had grown up. She had chased the dream without trying to figure out where a young man might fit into the picture. In these peaceful moments, Elena accepted the fact that she now wanted Luca, and not only a future with him but also the chance to create a family together. She looked across the church again to see him looking back at her. Her heart leapt at the sight of his dark curls and bronzed skin. This was what she wanted, this man. She lowered her head and started reciting the prayers with the rest of the congregation. Hopefully God would forgive her lapse of concentration.

Chapter Thirteen

Pasquale raised his head as Elena entered her office early the following morning. "You appear very cheerful! What has made you so happy?"

Elena grinned as she sat at her desk. She was in a good mood, but she certainly did not intend to explain the reason to her boss. "I'm just glad to be back! A week away is a long time and seems longer when you're in the fields from dawn to dusk. Look at my hands!" She stood up again and walked over to Pasquale's large table. It was covered with more papers than usual and all the filing cabinets were wide open.

"What's all this? Did something happen?" She picked up the file nearest to her, then saw Pasquale's smiling face.

"Oh my! You look pleased. You heard something?"

"I certainly did," said Pasquale with a certain smugness. "I received a letter saying the Pope has agreed to my plan and he is going to send someone to help us with the transfer."

Pasquale beamed at Elena, who smiled back. He looked so happy that his wild plan might happen. Now that seemed more likely, she felt nothing but trepidation. The bursts of bravado she had felt a few times over the past few days now escaped her. Surely the Germans would not stand idly by while some of the greatest treasures of Western art disappeared on their watch. And what might they do once they found out?

Her fear must have been apparent to Pasquale. He jumped up, his beaming face transformed into a picture of concern for his young assistant. "Elena, dear, please don't trouble yourself. Ours is the righteous cause and I have faith that our quest will prevail." He laughed out loud, leaning back to sit on top of his table, facing Elena.

"Listen to me, sounding like a medieval knight from one of our paintings! I mean, I do believe that this is a worthwhile thing we are undertaking, and I think everything will work out for the best. Come on —let's not worry too much for the moment. We'll have a few weeks to prepare. You can help me draw up a list of the works we would prioritize for this journey and together we will beg, steal, or borrow some transport."

Elena felt reassured. Her boss was right—they had time and a lot of work to do. She could take this one step at a time. She always prided herself on being able to do the best job under any circumstances. She was going to make Pasquale proud of her, whatever the outcome.

Later that evening, Elena lay on the straw in the barn with Luca's arms wrapped around her. They had agreed to meet nightly without any prearranged agreement. If Luca could not make it for some reason, then they would just try again the next night. The events of the past few weeks had persuaded the two of them that they had to live life one day at a time and make the most of any opportunity to be together. Elena filled him in on the events of the day at the office. Luca whistled.

"Well, your boss is something, I have to say. Going straight to the Pope and getting his blessing? That was a bold move. So what happens next?"

Elena hesitated for a few seconds. She knew how Luca would react to what she was about to say. "We need transport. We are hoping the people in Rome can send a convoy, but we need to see what we can provide ourselves. Trucks preferably, but whatever we can find."

Luca sat up and stared at her. He shook his head. "Are you mad? How in God's name are you planning on doing that? Are you going to steal something from the Germans? The Italian army?"

"Well, no. We are hoping someone will let us borrow something." Elena admitted to herself that it sounded rather lame now that she had said it out loud.

Luca laughed sardonically. "Good luck with that. We don't even have enough fuel for ourselves. Nobody is going to give you a truck to drive to Rome. That's a long and dangerous journey at this time, and it would require a lot of fuel. And who says the Germans will let you?"

Elena nodded, feeling miserable. Luca was saying everything she had been thinking. It did seem impossible, yet she had promised Pasquale that she would try. And Elena was not someone who gave up easily.

"There's no need to be so dismissive. I know this seems foolish, but it is important. It matters to me, anyway. I need to prove to Pasquale that I have what it takes to be a curator." She turned away so that Luca would not see the tears in her eyes. Luca reached out his hand and gently turned her face back toward him. He held her head in both hands.

"Elena, *tesoro mio*. I'm sorry. I'm just a farmhand—what do I know about art? But if it matters to you, it matters to me. Let me help you, please. But I have to admit that I'm scared for you. This is going to be so dangerous."

Elena looked at him, at his face etched with both love and fear.

"Luca, thank you. This matters, and not only to me. We can't let the Germans waltz away with our paintings and statues and manuscripts. We just can't. I know it might be dangerous. But even living here is dangerous right now. My brother and yours are in the wild somewhere, and we know they're doing things every day that could get them killed. I cannot do anything like that, but I'm able to do this. We're all saving our country in our own way."

Elena looked at Luca, desperate for him to understand. "I'm fighting for what comes afterward. I want to have a job that I love. I want you. But if I can, I also want to help save the Madonnas and the concertos and the marble statues and holy relics that are part of our country's very soul. Who are we really if we lose all that?"

Elena's eyes burned with fervor. Luca smiled and drew her to him. "Alright, my little fighter. I get it. I give in. I will help you save the Madonnas, if that's what you want."

Chapter Fourteen

Lorenzo and Alessandro huddled together in the woods at the edge of Casa del Lupo. It was coal black with only the faint light from the house being visible. An occasional breeze rustled the leaves above their heads, making the two young men tense up each time, fearful that someone might be approaching their hiding spot. Lorenzo was agitated.

"Come on, Sandro, let's make a move. It's late enough—if we're not careful, your father will be asleep."

Alessandro glanced around one more time. No lights appeared on the distant road and he knew that the likelihood of anyone arriving at this time of night was remote. Still he hesitated. It was not only the fear of being caught by the enemy that was keeping him on edge. He was afraid of the greeting he was going to receive from his father. Alessandro had not seen him for over two months. He had no idea what his father was thinking about his son's sudden departure to join the partisans. He had come back to Casa del Lupo a couple of times in the middle of the night to search for anything useful. He had been grateful for the jars of preserved fruit and the loaves of bread he had found on the bench in the barn. He assumed they were being put there for him. But he did not know who had been leaving them. His mother? One of his siblings? He remained hunched on the ground, blowing air into his hands in an attempt to keep warm.

"Come on," Lorenzo whispered again, more forcefully. "We have to ask him. And if we have no luck, we can visit my father instead."

Lorenzo sounded strong, but he was feeling no braver than his friend. His own father was well known for thinking things through carefully and never acting on impulse. Lorenzo was hoping Signor Marchetti would help them despite his renowned temper, so he would be relieved of the need to go to his own home and start begging.

The two young men scrambled to their feet and gingerly began the trek along the side of the fields toward the farmhouse. The light from the kitchen window grew stronger as they approached the old building. At one point, they were startled as a cat ran out of the shadows and streaked across the yard. They checked their surroundings once more before Alessandro took a tentative step forward and knocked on the wooden door.

"Papa!" he called as loudly as he dared. "It's me, Sandro."

They heard movement inside the building and suddenly the thick door swung open. Alessandro's father stood in the entrance, glaring at them.

"Come inside now," he hissed. "Someone might be watching the house." He pulled his son inside by his arm. Lorenzo quickly followed. A wood fire still burned in the grate and the warm air was a welcome change from the frigid temperature of the woods. Signor Marchetti turned to examine them both, then grabbed his son, pulling him in for a tight embrace. The two men stood still for a minute, saying nothing. Francesco Marchetti's eyes were closed, with his nose buried in his son's shoulder as if trying to take in his scent. He pulled back, still holding Alessandro, and studied his face.

"You've finally grown a beard, eh?"

Alessandro laughed, the tension evaporating. "It is hard to shave when you're in hiding."

His father nodded. "So what's going on? Why the unexpected visit? I thought you would be keeping your heads down. I would go and wake up your mother, but I have a feeling that she might not want to hear this."

The three men made their way to the kitchen table and sat down. Francesco offered them each a mug of hot dandelion tea, which they accepted gratefully. Alessandro took a deep breath.

"Okay, here's the thing. We need help—something big. Although I have been back a couple of times and found a few things in our barn, I wasn't sure—" He looked at his father, who nodded. Relieved, Alessandro pressed on. "Don't get me wrong. We're so grateful for those supplies. And the entire neighborhood is being supportive. Food, water, ammunition—" He stopped, not sure how to continue.

Lorenzo jumped in. "Signor Marchetti, we need to step up our actions. We are getting some intelligence on the movements of the Germans and the Italian militia. We think we can wreak a lot of havoc if we can move fast enough between locations, but that requires reliable transport. We need more vehicles."

A heavy silence fell on the room. Francesco got up from the table and went to stand in front of the waning fire. Lorenzo glanced over at his friend, who raised his eyebrows quizzically.

Without turning back, Francesco spoke quietly. "I understood you were managing to steal jeeps. From the ambushes?"

"A couple, sure. But often they get damaged during the fighting, and we then have to try to make repairs. It's slowing us down."

Francesco turned away from the fire. His face was somber. "Boys, I want to help you. I do. But we only have the one truck. You know that. If I let you take it, I'll have no way to transport my crops or animals to the market in Pesaro. Sure, I can take the cart if I'm only going to Urbino or Sassocorvaro. But any further would be out of the question."

He paused, troubled. "Have you been to Ca'Boschetto, Lorenzo? What does your father say?"

"Not yet, sir. We thought we would come here first."

"I'll tell you what. Why don't I go and talk to Paolo tomorrow? And Leonardo, of course. Maybe the three of us can agree to some kind of sharing arrangement. That way, we all have a means of getting things to the markets further away and we can support the resistance as well."

Lorenzo was shocked. He had not been expecting a positive response. It was a smart plan. His father was more likely to listen to his oldest friend, someone he highly respected. The two men were very different, but Lorenzo knew how much they meant to each other. Lorenzo's father always said that Francesco Marchetti was the best farmer he knew, that he seemed to instinctively know when the weather was going to change and when to plant and harvest crops. His own father did not exactly enjoy farming but did it anyway, just as his father, grandfather, and great-grandfather had before him. Fortunately for his father, Leonardo was a more natural farmer and the two of them made a strong team. In fact, Zio Leonardo had told him many times that he thought it was a waste that his older brother was simply a farmer, as he was as smart as any man around, even the professors at the university in Urbino. Lorenzo always thought that between his father, his uncle, and Signor Marchetti, they would be able to solve any problem life threw at them.

He beamed at Francesco. "Sir, that is a great idea. Thank you. At least my father will listen to you. We can be hopeful that something might be arranged that will benefit us all."

"That's the plan, then. Come back tomorrow night at this time and I'll let you know what has transpired. Don't hold your breath though. It's still a huge commitment to make."

He shook hands with the two young men. "I'll have to tell your mother, Alessandro. She'll be the first person to notice if the truck goes missing. She'll also be angry that I didn't wake her up this evening. So expect to stay for a decent meal tomorrow night, the two of you."

Francesco reached up to one of the racks hanging from the beams and cut down a couple of salamis. "Here. Take these. I'm sure you and your comrades will appreciate them. Now go!"

They smiled and said their goodbyes. Finally, they had some positive news to bring back to the others and a couple of salamis as a bonus. They might not mention the home-cooked meal that awaited them the following evening. No point in making everyone else jealous.

Chapter Fifteen

Her mother's cheerful voice greeted Elena as she arrived home from work the following afternoon. Elena walked into the kitchen to discover a flurry of activity. Her sister was putting a loaf of bread, cheese, and grilled peppers into a large wicker basket on the kitchen table while her mother was stirring something on the stove. The kittens were scuttling underfoot, hoping to catch scraps.

Elena's mother smiled at her. "We are going over to Ca'Boschetto for a while—your father wants to talk to Paolo and Leonardo about something. Afterward, we might have a couple of late-night guests for dinner!" She beckoned Elena over to the stove and whispered in her ear. "Your father says Alessandro and Lorenzo are coming here later to discuss partisan business. But it's a secret—we can't tell anyone, obviously."

Elena smiled. "What amazing news, Mamma! I cannot wait to see them. But why is Papa going to Ca'Boschetto suddenly?"

"Oh, I don't know. Those men are always looking for excuses to talk about something. For me, it's a chance to pay Antonella and Maria a visit. We're all going—we haven't been able to visit each other for a while. Do you want to go with us?"

Elena felt she was blushing. She tried to sound nonchalant. "Why not? Just give me five minutes while I change."

Twenty minutes later, they pulled up outside Ca'Boschetto to be greeted by several dogs and Marco and Gianni running around, chasing the chickens. The rest of the Rossi clan came out of the house to meet them. Luca extended his hand to help Elena's mother down from her wooden seat in the cart. Elena jumped down before he could do the same for her. She smiled at him.

"Welcome!" said Paolo. "Always so nice to see you all." He reached out to shake Francesco's hand. Francesco bent his head to whisper something in his friend's ear. He caught sight of Paolo's brother, Leonardo, coming up behind him and motioned to him to join them. The three old friends, huddled together, started walking away across the yard. Antonella rushed forward and started chattering in her usual machine-gun style.

"These men—honestly. Always something serious to discuss. Come upstairs, Elisa—we can sit and catch up. Nonna is inside—she has been waiting for you. Elena and Giulia, how lovely you both look! Andrea, would you mind helping the boys round up those chickens? I fear they are just playing, not really helping. And when you're done, can the three of you go up to the top of the hill and tell the twins to finish up and join us? Come on, ladies, let's go and eat. I am not waiting for the men."

Without drawing a breath, Antonella took one of Elisa's arms. Her sister-in-law, Maria, grabbed the other and the three women started walking briskly toward the house, already deep in conversation. Elena and Giulia followed, with Giovanna hopping excitedly next to them. Luca stood for a moment, not sure if he should go with the men or the women. His father's conversation had the appearance of being about something very important, but none of the men looked as if they wanted him to join them. And he certainly did not want to join the boys chasing chickens around. He followed the women into the house.

Giovanna and Giulia had disappeared into the bedroom together by the time Luca entered the main room, probably to discuss clothes or shoes or something. Giovanna thought Giulia was the best-dressed girl in the neighborhood and was always trying to emulate her. Nonna was seated in her favorite chair. Elisa sat on the couch closest to her, leaning in while the older woman talked about her recent birthday party. Luca grinned—his grandmother was not going to let the subject go for weeks. Elena was already pouring tiny glasses of the homemade amaro they had brought with them. The other women were fussing about, putting cheese, salami slices, and peppers onto serving plates. Elena passed Luca a glass.

"*Salute!*"

Antonella started exhorting everyone to find a seat. "Come on! Let's sit and eat. I want to hear all the news."

The conversation was still flowing when the men came in half an hour later. Luca saw his father look around the room, then back at his brother and his friend. They nodded as if in silent agreement. Francesco cleared his throat. "Are the boys still outside? We want to tell you something but not if the children are here."

"Yes, it is just us," his wife said. "What is going on?"

"We've decided to help the partisans. Nobody outside our families must know though."

Elena raised her eyebrows at Luca, who shrugged.

"We are going to let Lorenzo and Alessandro take one of our trucks. We have one at Casa del Lupo and the Rossi families have another one. We think it is possible for the three families to share. We don't need to use a truck that often. Anyway, we've hardly any fuel left, so it is probably for the best. The partisans are going to have to work something out on their own on that front."

He paused to gauge the room's reaction. Elena was stunned. She had no clue that this idea was even being discussed. She was also furious with herself for not having asked her father about the truck sooner. She cleared her throat.

"I am guessing Lorenzo or Alessandro made contact last night. How do we know they need a truck?"

Her father scowled at the interruption. He told the assembled group what had transpired the previous evening. Antonella was annoyed that her son had chosen to go to the Marchetti farm, rather than theirs, denying her a chance to see him. Elisa squeezed her friend's hand, trying to suppress her smile, knowing she would see her own son later.

Elena instinctively knew that she should stop talking at this point, but she kept going. "I know this is going to sound insane, but I was going to ask if *I* could borrow a truck."

The entire group stared at her in astonishment. Her father's expression turned from embarrassment to fury, either at the fact that his daughter had spoken at all, interrupting again, or at the very idea of Elena asking for something so audacious. The four women were bemused—what possible use would a young woman have with a vehicle? Luca was startled at first, but then he remembered why Elena was asking. Paolo came to her rescue.

"Dearest Elena, why do you ask? What has happened?"

In halting sentences at first and then with increasing courage, Elena explained what Pasquale was planning. When she finished, the room was silent.

Elena's mother spoke first. "I knew allowing you to go to Milan was a mistake. And now this? What have you got yourself mixed up in? What is that man thinking?" Her voice cracked with emotion. Now it was Antonella's turn to offer comfort. She instinctively put her arm around her friend's shoulder.

"More to the point," Elena's father said, "when did a few paintings become so damned important, eh? Seriously, Elena. Are you out of your mind?"

His face had turned bright red and Elena saw the veins on his forehead pulsing. She stared down at her boots, not daring to glance at Luca, even though she desperately wanted his support.

"Let's not be too hasty, shall we?" said Paolo in a conciliatory manner. He turned and faced the room. "This is unexpected, I know, but I for one wouldn't fault Elena for her request. Signor Rotondi's plan is certainly a wild one, but let's think about it for a while. What he has been doing these past few years is laudatory—at least that is how I view it. Everyone knows what has been going on. It has been an open secret."

He glanced over at his brother and his friend briefly. He was aware that they did not share his view on the secret art convoys. It was one of the rare times that Leonardo had agreed with Signor Bruni, who made his opinion quite plain. But Paolo and several neighbors had volunteered their time—and their animals and vehicles—to help in the final stages of the transport.

"We all know the Germans have been looting since they got here. They have taken our livestock and our crops. It is infuriating. Remember the day of your birthday party, Mother? I was so angry when that arrogant son of a bitch—excuse me, ladies—took one of our small pigs."

Everyone nodded in agreement. This was something they all could get behind.

"We all felt violated, yes? We don't want them here. We don't want Mussolini's thugs here. We want the partisans to help us fight back. All that is true, *vero*? And yes, it does feel like the right thing to do, to help Lorenzo, Alessandro, and the rest in any way we can. But Elena also has a point." Paolo paused—Francesco was squirming a little bit but managing to keep silent.

"I don't want the Germans stealing anything. Not our pigs. Not our wine. Not our boys. And certainly not our heritage. Rotondi has been hiding these masterpieces for months. He has been keeping them safe. These pieces are priceless. They belong to the Italian people—to the whole world, actually. They belong to my children and my children's children. I will grow more wheat. My sow will have another litter. But we will never replace those paintings if they are taken from us. I for one don't want that madman in Berlin to steal what is rightfully ours. Do you?"

Luca gazed at his father in admiration. He had always known that he was an intelligent man who read books and who liked visiting museums on the few occasions he had time for himself. Luca had been eight when his father had first taken him to see the art in the palace in Urbino. He remembered being in awe of the cool rooms and delighted by the trompe l'oeil walls in the duke's study. But the highlights for the young Luca were the paintings. The Madonnas, saints, hunters, landscapes, even a depiction of an ideal city—Luca had never seen anything like them. His rustic home had thick stone walls and very little in the way of furnishings that were not useful.

As they had stood in front of the paintings, one by one, his father had quietly pointed out the brushstrokes, the light, the depiction of the natural world, and how the people were represented. He told Luca about Federico, Duke of Urbino, whose court in the fifteenth century was regarded as the center of the civilized world with its gathering of artists, philosophers, architects, and thinkers, and who had become the patron of some of the most famous Italian painters.

At the time, Luca did not understand everything his father had told him, but once Professor Martini started taking Luca's class to the museum regularly, Luca had grown proud of his city's past and its place in Italy's cultural history. As he listened to his father make his impassioned speech, Luca sensed how much it meant to him. He was momentarily embarrassed that he had been so dismissive of Elena when she had tried to share her belief in Pasquale's mission. He wanted to catch her eye so that he could give her a smile of encouragement, but Elena was transfixed by Paolo.

Francesco cleared his throat. "Great speech, Paolo. You were always the bookish one, that's for sure. I'm just a man of the soil—you know that."

Paolo smiled warmly at his oldest friend. This was a familiar conversation they'd had many times over the past decades.

"And I am not opposed to saving the art, obviously. But I think we have more pressing needs right now. We need to remove the invaders from our lands. I think the truck would be put to better use helping kill Nazis than embarking on a dangerous journey to the Vatican. Rome, for goodness sake! How long does the museum director imagine that is going to take?" Francesco looked around the room, hoping for some support.

"And for the life of me, I don't know why my daughter has to get involved." He looked at Elena, his expression dismissive. "There's plenty to do on the farm; I've told you that before. Still don't know why you insist on pretending that this 'art' business is a real job. The sooner we get you married off the better, in my opinion."

Without waiting to see Elena's reaction, Francesco turned back to Paolo. "The boys are coming to our place late tonight. What do you want me to tell your son, eh? That they can't have a truck because my daughter wants to take some statues and frames to the Pope? It sounds ridiculous even saying it out loud." Francesco stood with his arms crossed, furious. Luca saw his mother biting her bottom lip, which she always did when she was upset. He knew she hated confrontation. He took a tentative step forward and coughed nervously.

"Everybody has valid points to make. Signor Marchetti, you are right, of course. The resistance needs all the help it can get and I want to support my brother in particular." Left unsaid was Luca's guilt at not having gone with him, tempered by his anger at having been left to do more of the farm work.

"And, Papa, you're right as well. Elena and Signor Rotondi are doing valuable work keeping our art secure and safe from the Germans. It is our history and our inheritance, and we gave all that brilliance to the world. I'm proud of that. I don't want to see it all destroyed or stolen." Luca paused and looked at the others. "And we only have two trucks between the three families, so that's a conundrum. Since Lorenzo and Alessandro are returning tonight to hear our answer, I think we should give them the truck."

Elena let out a small cry and put her hand over her mouth.

Luca kept speaking. "I also want to help Elena procure a truck for her paintings. And I want to go with the art to Rome."

Now it was his mother's turn to gasp. "Luca! I already have one son out there breaking my heart. You think I would be pleased to send another one out on some foolhardy mission?"

"Mamma, I don't even know if we can find another truck, but I'm willing to try. I agree with Papa and Elena—it matters to Italy and to what kind of society we are going to be once this war is over, and therefore it matters to me."

Elena looked at him gratefully. Luca saw his father suppress a smile. He felt elated in the moment, but simultaneously afraid of what he might be letting himself in for.

"Wonderful solution, my son," said Paolo. "The diplomat as always! We agreed earlier that Francesco should give Lorenzo and Alessandro their truck, as that's where the boys will go tonight. I am going to donate some precious fuel so they can at least drive it away and hide it somewhere. And tomorrow, Luca, you and I can put our heads together and come up with a plan to help Elena. Now I'm going to go and find some *nocino* that I have hidden away so we can make a toast to peaceful negotiations. I think governments could learn a thing or two from us." He chortled and hurried off in search of a bottle of his homemade walnut liqueur.

The three youngest boys chose that moment to burst through the door, laughing and jostling each other, followed by the twins. It broke the tension in the room and the overlapping conversations started up again. Elena sidled over to Luca. Her hand gently brushed his.

"I love you, Luca Rossi," she whispered.

Chapter Sixteen

The gathering broke up a little later. Elena's mother wanted to hurry home to finish cooking the meal for Alessandro and Lorenzo. Paolo gave Francesco a container of fuel from his barn. The Marchetti family climbed onto their cart for the short journey back. Elena could tell that her father had been slightly mollified by Luca's suggestion, but she also instinctively felt that she had better keep out of his way for a while. She knew her father loved her dearly, but her headstrong ways had been getting her into trouble for years. She was also painfully aware that Luca would probably not make the journey to the barn later that night for fear of accidentally meeting his brother and friend on their secret mission. Elena sighed as the cart bumped its way down the track. Luca's speech had warmed her heart and made her feel even closer to him. How lucky she was to have found this man who understood and supported her. She closed her eyes and thought about touching him and him touching her in return. It took all her strength not to moan out loud. It was going to be a very long evening.

It was dark by the time they got home, and the temperature had dropped. Francesco hurried to the truck with the fuel.

Elisa grabbed her daughter's arm. "Come on, you. He will be

fussing over that vehicle for ages. He'll want to ensure it is roadworthy. By the time he comes in, all will be forgotten."

Elena gave her mother a grateful smile. "Let's cook this dinner, shall we?"

The next few hours, the family chopped vegetables, washed pots and pans, and set the table. Elisa had explained to Giulia and Andrea that their brother was going to come for a late supper with Lorenzo and impressed upon them the need for secrecy. "I don't want you telling your friends, right?"

"We know, Mamma! We aren't little kids anymore." Giulia rolled her eyes at her sister.

Andrea was smiling as he silently followed his mother's instructions to sweep the kitchen floor rather than complain as he sometimes did about being made to do women's work. Elena knew he missed his brother even when he did not talk about it—it was worth going without seeing Luca for a night for a chance for all of them to be together.

By eleven o'clock, Andrea was yawning and Elena's mother was fretting about the overcooked vegetables.

"Mamma, the boys will not have eaten this well in ages," Elena said, giving her a comforting hug. "Trust me."

At that moment, they heard a tentative knock on the door, which made them start despite having been waiting for so long. Francesco opened the door in a hurry and Alessandro and Lorenzo tumbled into the room. After five minutes of hugs and exclamations, Elisa hurried everyone to the table and started serving up dishes of hot stew. Francesco explained to the two young men what had been agreed. Their faces lit up.

"Papà, that is incredible news—thank you for everything," said Alessandro.

Lorenzo was equally enthusiastic. "Signor Marchetti, that's unbelievable. You persuaded my father and uncle—I am so impressed."

"No thanks to this one here." Francesco pointed at Elena. "Her harebrained idea almost derailed everything."

Lorenzo and Alessandro turned to Elena with quizzical expressions. Elena felt her face burning. Yet again her instinct told her not to speak up, but she couldn't help herself. "Well, Signor Rossi and Luca are going to help me, so everything worked out."

Elisa jumped in before her husband could respond. "Let me explain what happened, boys." She summarized the events of the evening: Elena's request, Paolo's speech, and Luca's plan. The two young men were flabbergasted.

"What in God's name were you thinking, *sorella mia*?" said Alessandro. "I know your head is sometimes in the clouds, but this is ridiculous."

Lorenzo said nothing. He was shocked for a different reason. He had always prided himself on being the bold one compared to Luca. He thought his older brother was a hard worker and loyal but very set in his ways. As young boys, Lorenzo had always led the way in their childhood adventures. Invariably, Luca would have to rescue him from some mishap, like when he had fallen in the fast-running stream the day after a winter storm and had nearly been swept away. He found it hard to imagine Luca volunteering to embark on a wild journey at a time when the Germans would be on the lookout for illicit activities. Lorenzo felt a sudden surge of pride.

"Well, it looks like both Rossi boys will be doing their part for Italy. That must be a good thing, right?"

This unexpected comment broke the tension in the room. Elena smiled at Lorenzo and mouthed her thanks.

Her brother put his arm around his mother and kissed her on the cheek. "Mamma, I've been dreaming about your cooking. But tonight you have outdone yourself."

Elisa pushed him away weakly, dismissing the lavish praise, but her face showed how thrilled she was.

Everyone started talking again and the mood became almost festive. Half an hour later, reluctantly, they brought the party to an end.

"Let's get you out of here," said Francesco firmly. "I think it's late enough to drive but take the white roads whenever possible. And if I were you, I wouldn't use headlights. If you drive slowly enough, you should be fine."

Elena saw the sadness in her mother's eyes, so she jumped up and started issuing instructions to her siblings to clear the table. Francesco gave the two young men some last-minute advice on handling the somewhat temperamental vehicle. Hugs were exchanged and Francesco and the two young men moved toward the door.

Lorenzo sidled over to Elena. "I always knew you were different from the rest of us, but my word . . . this scheme of yours is something else. And to persuade Luca to be involved—you really must have sweet-talked him into it."

Elena laughed nervously. Lorenzo smiled back affectionately, then stopped. The expression on his face shifted and his brow furrowed. He stared at Elena in awe. "My God," he whispered. "Now I understand. He's in love with you."

Elena started to deny it, but Lorenzo plowed on. "You were together at the dance, weren't you? Oh, I've been so blind. He's embarking on this crazy quest for you. Who would've guessed?"

Elena leaned in. "Shush, Lorenzo," she implored. "Please don't say anything, especially to my brother. It's early days, and—"

Lorenzo laughed. "Don't you worry about me. Your secret is safe. I'm impressed with my brother though. Elena Marchetti, eh? Punching above his weight, for sure."

"Who's punching who?" asked Andrea from the doorway.

"Nobody, you clown. Come on, Sandro, we need to go." Lorenzo winked at Elena and thanked Elisa for dinner one more time. Within a couple of minutes they were gone.

Chapter Seventeen

Luca was getting frustrated. Two weeks had passed since he had stood up for Elena during the argument about the truck, and he was no closer to procuring her any sort of transport. He had visited all the neighboring farms, except for the one owned by Signor Bruni, to find out if there was any chance of borrowing a vehicle. He had not been surprised to learn that nobody wanted to give up their precious trucks or cars. Even those who had been without fuel for months still clung to the hope that somehow they might be able to find some. It did not help that very few thought that helping the superintendent was a priority given the more immediate issues they were dealing with.

"I have six children to feed, two cows that are ailing, a fence that needs mending, and more besides," complained Signor Conti when Luca had stopped to talk to him that afternoon after coming upon the farmer struggling with barbed wire on the edge of one of his fields. "I can tell you now, moving some paintings around is not at the top of my list. I can't imagine you'll find many takers in these parts, son." Signor Conti looked at him kindly. "I am not saying I want the Germans to take them either. Don't get me wrong." He let off a stream of expletives, as if to emphasize how much he despised the occupiers. "I just think we have to focus on what we can control rather than the things we can't."

Luca nodded and wished him luck. He couldn't blame his neighbors for turning him down. He would have said the same if some fool had come begging to him. He sighed. He was beginning to wish he had not been so keen on making the promise to Elena. He had a horrible feeling that he had simply wanted her to think of him as a hero whereas, in fact, he was only going to let her down.

Luca started wheeling his horse around in the direction of Ca'Boschetto. His father had agreed that they should help Elena, but he was not sure how lenient he was going to be if Luca kept disappearing each afternoon, abandoning work. But the thought of Elena made him desperate to spend time with her. He was so close to Sassocorvaro already, he might as well keep going and surprise her when she finished for the day. If anyone in the town saw him and wondered why he was there and not on the farm, he would say he was going to buy something for his mother. Luca grinned to himself and turned in the direction of the town.

"Well, this is a pleasant surprise," smirked Elena when he walked toward her, reins in hand. "Whatever brings you to Sassocorvaro during the week?"

Luca looked around to see if anybody was watching him. "The thought of you, you beautiful creature. Come and have a drink with me at the café. If anyone asks, I am buying something for Mamma."

Elena laughed. Something seemed to have shifted in Luca over the past few weeks. He was no longer the reticent young man she had reconnected with at his grandmother's birthday party back in October. They had declared their love for each other, and almost every night, they spent hours together in the barn, getting to know each other's bodies intimately. Elena longed for the war to end so they could tell their families and be together officially. It didn't seem right to be so happy when Alessandro and Lorenzo were still in danger.

They walked toward the café, their arms brushing each other but not lingering too long. Elena told Pietro to leave the bicycle where it was for the time being because she and Signor Rossi had met unexpectedly and were going to enjoy an aperitif together before going their separate ways.

Pietro smiled. "I can take the horse, Luca. And I will bring the drinks as well. What would you both like?"

Within minutes, two glasses were on the table together with a small dish of olives and some slivers of casciotta cheese. Luca and Elena sat huddled together in their coats at the small table outside the café, laughing despite the chill in the air. It was already dark, but the two had no intention of going inside the warm café where their conversation might be overheard. Luca shared the dispiriting news about the truck, or the lack of one, but Elena refused to be depressed. She wanted to enjoy these few minutes of normalcy, sitting in a piazza with a glass of wine and the man who loved her. For now, they could pretend the war wasn't happening.

After a while, Luca stood up reluctantly. "I really need to go home. Papà is only going to be lenient with this quest up to a point. And when Mamma starts calling us for dinner—"

Elena got up as well. "My mother always starts panicking if I am half an hour late. I had better grab my bike."

She waved at Pietro, who had been hovering near the door. Luca gave him some money, including what Elena owed him for looking after her bicycle, much to her chagrin.

Luca grinned. "You can buy me a drink another time—I am all in favor of working women, trust me. Come on, Pietro, show me where you've hidden the lady's bicycle and my horse."

The three of them walked around the side of the building to the old stable behind. It was clear that no horses had lived there for years, judging by the crumbling walls and fallen beams. Barrels of wine were stacked along the walls together with piles of discarded jugs, bottles, pieces of metal, and old broken furniture.

"Goodness, this place is a treasure trove, young man," said Luca. "My father would have a field day—" He stopped abruptly, took several steps forward, then feverishly started pulling at a tarpaulin covering something at the back of the stable. Pietro raised his lantern, confused. Luca turned to face them—his expression was triumphant. Behind him in the dim light Elena saw the outline of an old truck covered in cobwebs and dust. The headlights were smashed and the windscreen had a large crack. The tires were deflated. It was obvious the truck had not been used in years.

"Pietro! What is this beauty doing here?" asked Luca. He was grinning at the young boy, who was still looking perplexed.

"I think it was my grandfather's," Pietro said, stuttering. "I really don't know. I have never seen my father drive it. It's been here for as long as I can remember."

Luca let out a jubilant cry and ran forward to hug him, crushing the boy with his strong arms. He turned to Elena and gathered her into the embrace. The three of them were hugging and dancing and laughing uncontrollably. Pietro, unsure what the joke was, was happy to join in.

Fifteen minutes later, Luca and Elena walked away from the café feeling more optimistic than they had in weeks. Pietro's father had been reluctant to assist them at first, assuring Luca that the truck was probably broken beyond repair. But Luca could be very persistent and soon the two men had a deal. Luca was going to bring his tools from the farm that weekend. If he could persuade his father to accompany him, that would be even better. Together they could find out if it was possible to bring the truck back to life. Pietro's father refused to take any money, telling Luca if they did manage to fix the truck it would be a huge blessing.

"Mechanics are not really my thing, Luca, you see," confided Signor Vitali. He wiped his hands on a towel hanging from his ample waistband. "I can make pastries and bread and pour drinks, but give me anything technical to fix, and I am not your man. Have at it and see what you can do. I would be very grateful if you can repair it, to be honest. I had totally forgotten it was in the stable." They had shaken hands. Luca said he would come back on Saturday.

Now Elena was shaking her head, laughing. "You were incredible! I hope you know what you are doing. If you and your father can make this work, Pasquale will be the happiest man in Le Marche. And it will make me look good in front of my boss." She gazed at him in amazement. "To think it was right under our noses all this time. Right across the piazza from the Rocca. It could not be more perfect."

She got on her bicycle and turned to look at him. Luca leaned over and kissed her on the cheek. "Making you happy is all I ever want to do, *carina*," he said in a low voice. "And later tonight I will try to make you even happier." He grinned and mounted his horse.

"Come on, let's stay together on the road as far as your farm. I need you to arrive home safely."

Chapter Eighteen

Pasquale was indeed delighted when Elena arrived at the Rocca the following morning, eager to share the news. Given the luck they had had so far, he hoped the truck wasn't too badly immobilized and that Luca and Paolo Rossi had the skills to fix it.

"If they can do it, then it'll be a great start. I've asked the archbishop of Urbino for assistance as well. He's very keen to move all the religious artifacts such as the altarpieces out of Carpegna and into my hiding places in the palace in Urbino. If we can achieve that, we'll be one step closer to moving it all from Urbino to the Vatican. It looks like we might need a cover story though."

Pasquale had a frown on his face, so Elena pulled up a chair and sat opposite him expectantly.

Pasquale took a letter from the pile in front of him on the desk and waved it at her. "It's frustrating, but my colleagues at the ministry think that in order to obtain all the transport we need and to ensure that the art arrives safely in Rome, we have to tell the Germans something."

Elena was incredulous. "Really? Is that sensible? I mean, surely the whole point is to prevent them from stealing everything."

"*Certo!* But maybe, just maybe, we can find a helpful German. First, a quick history lesson."

Pasquale explained to Elena that during World War I, German troops had destroyed the Louvain library in Belgium, a historic building full of priceless manuscripts. Faced with universal condemnation, including from some of their most influential countrymen, the Germans had set up the *Kunstschutz*, an "art protection" unit, to safeguard cultural treasures during times of war and turmoil. It was ironic, Pasquale added sardonically, that this unit was still operating in another war during which the Germans were responsible for countless acts of destruction and looting of national treasures.

"However," he said with a sigh, "this might work to our advantage. My colleagues in Rome have been communicating with the Kunstschutz unit based in the city, and they believe that they can get them to grant us some kind of official cover for our little expedition. They are trying to obtain trucks and fuel in Rome, which will be very difficult without involving the Germans."

Pasquale laughed at Elena's skeptical expression. "Your face says it all, my dear Elena. I'll admit that I too harbor grave doubts, but if there is a way to obtain official paperwork, it would certainly ease our journey. Don't panic—they aren't going to tell them everything. The paperwork would only talk about returning religious artifacts to the Vatican for safekeeping, rather than everything else. But it would be the cover we need. Nobody would think it strange that we are moving religious objects to the Vatican, given how uncertain the situation is. In the meantime, let's see what Luca and his father achieve with Signor Vitali's truck. I will wait to hear if the archbishop manages to round up any transport. That man has a way of making the faithful believe that, by helping him, they are somehow helping God himself."

Early the following Saturday, as promised, Luca and his father made their way to Signor Vitali's stable, carrying an old toolbox. Elena told her parents that she had to go to the Rocca to finish up some work for her boss, so after an early lunch, she was able to cycle to town to find out how the Rossi men were getting on.

The Saturday market had just drawn to a close and the various stallholders and farmers were packing up their unsold goods. People were milling about, catching up with their neighbors in quiet voices, glancing occasionally at a couple of bored German soldiers who were sitting smoking on the wall on the edge of the piazza. Elena scoured the piazza as she wheeled her bike toward the café. The soldiers did not seem particularly alert and she could not hear any noises from the stable that might attract unwanted attention. Signor Bruni was sitting outside at his usual table, reading the newspaper intently. He did not look up. No other customers were sitting outside. Nobody appeared to notice her as she slipped down the side of the café toward the stable door.

The engine parts were spread out all over the floor, but Paolo assured Elena that things were in pretty good shape. He was sitting on an ancient kitchen chair, eating a panino that Elena guessed had been made by Signor Vitali.

Luca grinned at Elena, tomato juice dribbling down his chin. "Worth doing all this work just to eat this incredible sandwich," he said, waving his own half-eaten one.

He offered Elena a bite, but she waved it away, giggling. "You enjoy it—Mamma's already fed me."

The two men tried to explain to her what they had been doing, but Elena held up her hand. "It all sounds very technical, Signor Rossi, and I'm very impressed. But will it run?"

Paolo smiled at the young woman. "Straight to the point, eh? That is what Antonella is always telling me. Well, I think we can do it. Now that we have stripped everything down, I can see there is no real damage. We have found rust, and we need to change the oil, and we have the windscreen to think about, but—"

They were interrupted by what sounded like orders being barked out and a crowd shouting. The noises grew louder. They looked at each other without speaking. A nosy German would cause them problems.

"Let me go and see what's going on," said Elena quietly. She hurried out of the stable before either man could stop her.

As Elena approached the piazza, she saw a group of German soldiers surrounding a young boy and she heard the watching townspeople calling out in anger. The boy was being held on either side by two soldiers. One of them slapped the boy hard on the cheek. He shrieked.

Elena felt her stomach lurch—it was Pietro, his face blanched white and streaked with tears, his legs filthy and one shoe missing. His father was being held back by two men as he shouted at Major Heinrich, standing on one side.

The major held up his right hand to silence the crowd. "This boy was caught stealing a can of fuel from the military stores several minutes ago. Now why do you imagine he would be doing that?" He looked around the piazza, taking in the anger and fear of the men, women, and children in front of him.

"Let. Him. Go!" shouted Signor Vitali, his face contorted with rage. "He is a child, you bastard."

Major Heinrich smiled. "A child? A child stealing from the German army, that's who he is." He held the boy's chin in one hand, twisting the child's head to stare at him. Pietro was sobbing loudly now and even at a distance, Elena could see a damp patch spreading on the front of his short trousers.

"Who told you to do this, boy? Your father?"

Pietro seemed too paralyzed to speak. He tried to shake his head, but that was impossible in the major's tight grip.

"I don't think a café proprietor who hardly ever leaves town has much need for fuel. I think those so-called partisans hiding in the hills asked you to help them. Is that what happened?"

A hundred feet away, Elena watched Pietro trying hard to think what the right answer might be. He said nothing, his small body jerking with sobs. It appeared he was only standing up because of the two soldiers holding him upright. The major let go of his chin, pushing the boy's head backward.

"Thank goodness somebody saw fit to inform us of the criminal activity taking place. It appears I can count on at least one patriot in this town. After recent events, I was beginning to wonder which side this place is on."

The onlookers started muttering to each other. Someone they knew had betrayed the child. His father pleaded with the major once more.

"Children play silly games all the time. I'm sure it was nothing." His voice was cracking. Elena heard his panic.

"He had to crawl under a barbed wire fence and sneak through a small window in order to break into the building, Signore," said Major Heinrich in a calm voice, staring straight at the café proprietor. "Those are the actions of a criminal, not a child doing something for fun." He turned back to the boy and in one swift movement, drew his pistol from his belt, held it to Pietro's forehead, and pulled the trigger.

Chapter Nineteen

C omplete silence blanketed the piazza for a few seconds, followed by guttural wails from the women watching. Signor Vitali buckled at the knees, only prevented from collapsing onto the hard stone pavement by two men holding him up. As if in some kind of macabre mirror, his dead son was also being held upright by two young German soldiers, whose faces were rigid with shock and who appeared paralyzed by what had transpired. The sides of their faces were splattered with gray and red matter.

Vomit rose up into Elena's mouth and she leaned forward, the contents of her stomach exploding onto the stones. She felt strong arms around her waist and heard Luca's voice whispering urgently in her ear. "I'm here, I'm here, I've got you."

Around them, the townspeople stood in a semicircle, some sobbing loudly, others transfixed. Nobody dared step forward.

The major looked at the crowd impassively. "I warned you what I would do to traitors and thieves and anti-Fascists. He deserved everything he got. Tell your friends hiding in the hills like the cowards they are that they are responsible for this. You are lucky I killed only the boy. Next time, I will execute ten of you."

Elena heard a commotion behind her. Pietro's mother, Anna, ran forward. A few people tried to stop her, but she pushed them aside. She ran to her son, taking him roughly in her arms. The two soldiers let go, shaken by the woman's fury and grief.

"Pietro, Pietro, *mio bambino!*" She sobbed, her shoulders heaving. Awkwardly, struggling with her son's body, she turned to face Major Heinrich, tears pouring down her face. She stared at him, then audibly took a deep breath.

"You . . . you killed him," she said incredulously. "You killed my son." The major stared at the woman emotionlessly. He said nothing.

"We're simple people in a small town who run a café," she said haltingly, her voice cracking but strong. Her voice rang out across the piazza. "Why would you kill my son?" She looked at the townspeople as if searching for answers. "He's a child. A child!" Anna started screaming, an animal cry that rang across the piazza. Elena found it hard to breathe.

Anna's cries grew ragged. Her eyes roamed wildly around the crowd facing her, as if seeking support. Nobody had dared move.

"We didn't want this war!" Anna raised her voice, her face now contorted with rage, and glared at each of the Germans in turn. "You've murdered my child," she said slowly. Her voice grew stronger and louder as she addressed the soldiers. "My only son. The boy who drank milk from my breast and whose head I kissed at night. You've taken him away from me."

Anna turned back to her townspeople, all of whom were staring at the small woman. "If they think," she shouted contemptuously, "that murdering my son will make me a compliant Fascist, then they are stupid as well as inhuman."

One of the soldiers stepped forward as if to take her arm, but she shrugged him off.

"Do not touch me, you bastard. Do. Not. Touch. Me." She spat in his face. The young man blinked but did nothing.

Anna started howling again, raw animal cries, as if her anger and grief had robbed her of human speech. Elena started inching forward, concerned that the woman might collapse. Luca held her tight.

Stumbling, struggling with Pietro's dead weight, Anna walked slowly toward her husband. Released from his neighbors' grip, Signor

Vitali ran forward to meet them. The couple stood in the piazza, their arms around each other, crushing their son between them.

The major looked at them blankly. He signaled to his men, who moved into formation, and then all of them turned and marched away from the square. The townspeople watched them leave, some of them finally finding the courage to shout obscenities at the backs of the soldiers. As Anna and her husband carried their son toward the café, a group of women hurried to join them. Elena spotted Don Antonio walking over from where he had been standing at the edge of the piazza. No doubt he wanted to offer words of comfort to the bereaved couple, but Elena doubted whether anything would alleviate their pain, even prayers.

As Elena watched the priest make his way to the café, she saw Signor Bruni, a look of horror on his face, stand up and walk away quickly. Elena stared at his back. Was he the informant? Surely even Signor Bruni would not do that to a child. Elena shook her head, trying to make sense of it all. She turned to Luca and his father, who was standing next to him.

"Did you see? Did you see what that monster did?" She felt helpless, scared, and angry. The war had truly come to their door and something had shifted within her.

Luca shook his head. "We waited a minute or two when you left, but then we heard the shouting getting louder and more aggressive. I was worried about you, so—" He paused for a moment, his voice catching in his throat. "We heard the shot as we got to the side of the café. For a moment, I thought maybe you—" Again he paused. His face looked stricken. Elena sensed the internal struggle between being grateful she had not been hurt and also devastated that the child they had come to love was the one who had suffered that terrible fate.

"Come back to the stable, my dear child," said Paolo. "You have had a shock and we should find you something to drink."

Elena followed them meekly, still crying, her mind in turmoil. What the hell was she thinking, spending all this time and effort to save some paintings and statues? She was angry. She should have followed her brother and joined the partisans. Women and girls helped with medical aid and cooking. They acted as messengers. A few even had guns and were going on raids with the men. She knew how to shoot—her father had taught all his children at an early age to fend off the wolves and other predators that attacked their animals. Why was she stuck in an office all day, trying to find vehicles to transport Raphael paintings when she could be helping rid the country of these invaders? And now her stupidity had gotten a child killed. She knew why Pietro had stolen the fuel. He would have wanted to impress her and Luca by bringing them something they needed.

Luca wanted to take Elena's pain away. He sat beside her on the floor of the stable, his arm around her, while his father went in search of something to drink, preferably something alcoholic. He pulled out his handkerchief and gave it to her. She blew her nose hard.

"Why is that man so evil? Why did God let it happen? Pietro did not deserve to die." Saying his name out loud made Elena start crying again.

Luca tightened his grip on her. He felt useless.

"I can't do this anymore, Luca. I am going to tell Pasquale I'm done. None of it matters anymore."

Luca stared at her. "What do you mean? You can't stop now. This *does* matter. You said it yourself, remember? If we lose the art, we lose a piece of our humanity."

He was so shocked that, even in her grief, Elena had to smile at him. "So now you are going to try to persuade me? You've changed your tune, Luca."

She caressed his cheek. "But, my darling, shouldn't we do something more important? Maybe our brothers have the right idea after all. Maybe nothing matters if we stay under the yoke of the Fascists. Maybe we need to commit to one righteous cause rather than split our resources like this."

She waved her arm in the direction of the disemboweled truck next to them. "If you can fix this, shouldn't we give it to Alessandro and Lorenzo instead?"

"There are many ways to win a war." Paolo had returned with a dusty bottle and three small glasses. He now stood at the entrance, clearly having overheard the last few sentences.

Luca dropped his arm from Elena's shoulders, but his father shook his head. "No need to pretend anymore, son, at least not in front of me.

It is obvious you care for Elena and she for you. You forget Elena's father is my oldest friend and I have known Elena since birth—your mother and I already think of her as part of the family."

Paolo smiled at the young woman. "Now, young lady, let's discuss what's just happened. Pietro was an innocent victim of an oppressive, cruel regime. The major was looking for someone he could use as a warning to all of us and that poor child happened to be in the wrong place at the wrong time. His parents will never be the same again and we are all diminished by his passing. But—"

Paolo put the bottle and glasses on the small table they had been using as a workbench. He poured three glasses of whatever liquid was in the dusty bottle and passed one to each of them. "Pietro's death will be avenged. I can promise you that. As we speak, the news will be spreading beyond this town and you can be sure that plans will be hatched. Someone in Sassocorvaro won't be sleeping soundly this evening now that they have seen the evil they have unleashed. Informers don't tend to be treated kindly. That doesn't mean we can't also continue with our little project."

Paolo raised his glass. "To Pietro, who was a good son and a sweet soul. May he be at the side of the Lord this very moment."

The three of them raised their glasses and took sips. Elena coughed as the fiery liquid hit the back of her throat.

"I've said it before, and I'll say it again. Don't be distracted. What you and Rotondi are trying to do matters. Art helps us communicate. It helps us remember. It makes us think beyond our small lives. I mean, I am just a farmer living the same life as my ancestors. I wish it was a better life, but there it is." Paolo paused, lost in his thoughts for a minute.

He looked at Luca and Elena. "But whenever I can escape, even for a short time, I look for something bigger than myself. Great art gives me a glimpse of other lives. It allows me to go somewhere else. Without art, we are just like animals, struggling to survive each day. The churches would just be buildings without the altarpieces that reflect the glory of God. We all need to be inspired. And without art, without music, we are destined to be brutes like the monster who carried out this terrible act. I for one believe that we should be better than that."

Paolo's face darkened. Luca was deeply moved by his father's eloquence and fire.

"Elena, Luca, we are going to help Signor Rotondi with his unlikely mission. We're going to get this truck back on the road, and we're going to help transport as many of those pieces to the Vatican as we can. As I said, there are many ways to win a war."

Chapter Twenty

I t was still icy on the piazza in Sassocorvaro as Pasquale arrived midmorning on Monday to check in with Elena. He stopped for a caffè d'orzo at the café. More customers were milling about than usual. A group of women sat surrounding Anna, who was sitting blank-faced at a table in the corner, clutching a worn soft toy. She was oblivious to the noise around her, while her right hand stroked the fake fur of the battered-looking rabbit. Her husband stood behind the bar, his eyes reddened and shoulders slumped, as he busied himself making drinks.

Pasquale quietly offered his condolences for the death of Pietro. Signor Vitali nodded in response. Pasquale downed his drink and left a few extra liras on the counter. He grimaced, thinking of his own children. He could not think of anything helpful to say, so he merely nodded his thanks and left the suffocating room.

Elena looked up from her typewriter as Pasquale entered the office. He noticed her pale face and tear-filled eyes. The child's brutal execution had affected everyone.

Pasquale hesitated for a moment. "How are you doing, Elena? This is a black period for this town for sure."

Elena's devastation showed on her face. "I was in the piazza, Pasquale. I saw it happen."

"Oh you poor child. I had no idea. I heard the news from Signor Montagna yesterday—he came to my house to help me fix a wall in the garden."

Elena told him what had happened on Saturday: the elation of learning that the truck was probably usable, the atrocity that followed minutes later, and the discovery that Pietro had been stealing fuel for them. She started crying again. Pasquale moved closer, putting his arm around her shoulders, and handed her his handkerchief. It went through Elena's head that this was the second time in a few days that a man had given her a handkerchief because of her tears. The thought made her feel weak and useless.

Pasquale cleared his throat. "That must have been a terrible shock. And I know how fond you were of that young lad. Well, we all were. These Germans are savages, pure and simple."

He paused, not sure exactly what to say next. "If you are having second thoughts—"

Elena lifted her head to look at him.

"The shipment, I mean. If you no longer feel safe being involved."

"Quite the opposite, in fact," said Elena decisively. "I mean, don't misunderstand me. I had second thoughts on Saturday. I was so scared and I felt we were responsible for what had happened. I'm still terrified, if I'm being honest. Somebody informed the Germans that Pietro had stolen the fuel. That person could be watching us. But I can't just sit back and do absolutely nothing. They're trying to intimidate us, aren't they? This seems like a small act of disobedience in the great scheme of things, and I want to do my part."

Pasquale could see how tense she was, sitting rigidly in her chair with her face bright red. He bowed his head as if in supplication. "Well, my dear Elena, I'm happy to hear that, for obvious reasons. But I don't want you to think that you have to go through with this madcap scheme because you work for me. Please let me know the minute you have second thoughts. I will totally understand."

Elena nodded and blew her nose using Pasquale's handkerchief. She held it up as if to hand it back to him, then smiled. "I'll keep this for today, if that's okay—I might need it again. Don't worry. I'll make sure it goes in the laundry this weekend."

"No rush." Pasquale smiled fondly at the young woman. "Now, today's agenda. The archbishop has managed to procure a truck from a certain Signor Ceccarelli in Urbino. This gentleman stripped the truck of its parts a couple of months ago and hid them in various places so the Germans couldn't requisition it. But the archbishop persuaded Signor Ceccarelli that helping us out would stand him in good stead in the afterlife. He has even managed to find fuel somewhere. I'm certainly not going to ask any questions. My driver, Signor Pretelli, is bringing it over as we speak. We're heading to Carpegna."

Pasquale planned on removing as much as he could from the palace in Carpegna and bringing everything back to the Rocca. Then he intended to move the entire inventory to Urbino. The crates he had previously hidden in the palace had not taken up much space in the enormous underground vaults, and Pasquale felt that it would be easier to hide everything in one place. If he managed to obtain his reinforcements from Rome and the requisite paperwork, it would be a lot safer if the art was all in a single location.

Elena was happy with this plan for a different reason. Once the art had been moved from the Rocca, she would be in less danger than if it remained ostensibly under her watch in Sassocorvaro.

"Do you still need the truck from the café?" she asked. "Luca says he and his father are going to reassemble it one evening this week."

"Yes indeed. We still need all the transport we can get. I have no idea what will arrive from Rome, or even if they will turn up. I am praying we will have enough."

They were interrupted by a knock on the door. Pasquale opened it to find the ruddy-faced builder, Signor Montagna, standing in the corridor, his cap in his hand.

"Are we ready for some selective demolition, Signor Rotondi?"

The stout man grinned at Elena. It was evident that this clandestine operation had added some spice to his otherwise monotonous work life. It wasn't every day that a small-town builder was asked to participate in hiding priceless works of art from a ruthless invader.

Pasquale smiled. "Is Pretelli outside with the truck yet? And more to the point, did you spot any Germans hovering on your way in?"

"No to both questions," answered Signor Montagna. "But let's start making some holes in the fake walls so when Pretelli gets here, we can move fast."

A few days later, with all the newly-arrived crates from Carpegna temporarily hidden, the next stage of the project began. They knocked down all the false walls created a few weeks earlier, removed the crates hidden inside, and double-checked the master list. When Pretelli arrived once more with the truck from Urbino, Pasquale sent Elena to the café to purchase a few panini for lunch, her real task being to check for any sign of a German patrol. She arrived back twenty minutes later with a bag of food and the positive news that the Germans had apparently disappeared from the town. Pasquale surmised that Major Heinrich believed the horrific public execution on Saturday had subdued the townspeople and that he could afford to utilize his units elsewhere for the time being.

"That is helpful to know. Let's move this stuff out of here as quickly as we can." The small group slowly started carrying the precious cargo down the ramp to the waiting truck. After a couple of trips, a few men who had been smoking in the piazza walked over and, without saying a word, joined in the removal of the crates. Pasquale started to say something in appreciation, but the oldest man, whom he recognized as a porter who worked in the local hospital, shook his head.

"You've been guarding this art for months, Signore. It's an open secret. If you feel it's time to move it, then you must have a good reason. That's all I need to know."

By the time the sixth crate made its way to the truck, twenty men were involved in the chain, and as many women were huddled in small groups watching them. It seemed to Elena that, for the first time since the horrific events of Saturday, the people had something positive to focus on. They might not understand exactly what was happening, but they instinctively wanted to help.

Out of nowhere, a young girl's voice, tentative at first, but soon strengthening, started singing. Startled, Elena turned to look at her. The girl looked familiar to Elena. She was about the same age as her sister Giulia, so they had probably attended school together.

The plaintive aria she was singing was known to Elena. As the notes rose and her breath formed misty clouds in the cold air, the young girl, her eyes closed, seemed to be channeling all the grief Elena had been trying so hard to tamp down. A memory jolted her of sitting in excitement with a girlfriend in Milan listening to her first opera at La Scala. Elena had never seen or heard anything more beautiful: the glittering chandeliers, the velvet seats, the diamonds and furs of the wealthier Milanese in their opera boxes.

It was the music Elena remembered most: Rossini's *Otello* and the opening aria of Act Three that Desdemona sings with such sadness. She remembered proudly telling her new Milanese friend that Rossini had been born not far from Elena's home in the coastal town of Pesaro. Once the evening was over, she had squandered some of her small allowance on a recording of the opera and had played it constantly on the record player in the small living room of the house where she was staying, whenever her landlord's family was out. By some miracle, here was the aria again, sung by a girl in a country town a long way from Milan.

Assisa a' piè d'un salice,
immersa nel dolore,
gemea traffita Isaura
dal più crudele amore.

Seated at the feet of a willow
immersed in grief
Isaura moaned, pierced
by the cruelest love.

Elena stood to one side, making official notes on her clipboard and trying not to let the tears in her eyes fall onto the paper and smudge it. The young girl had somehow found the perfect way to accompany their labors and at the same time relieve their collective grief. Elena was moved by the tacit support of the people of Sassocorvaro. They had witnessed horror yet had not bowed to it. They had been aware of the treasures hiding in their midst and were now determined to help the young superintendent.

Once the truck was full, Pretelli jumped into the driver's seat with Pasquale next to him and started the engine.

Pasquale beckoned to Elena. "We'll be as fast as we can. Try to prepare the rest of the crates. We'll come back for them in a couple of hours. But please keep an eye out. If you notice any signs that those bastards are back, stop at once. Do you understand?"

She nodded and, together with the crowd of townspeople, stood and watched reverentially as the truck made its way carefully out of the piazza toward Urbino. As it disappeared, the group, without a word, turned back to the Rocca and continued the slow task of removing the crates from their hiding places.

By early evening they were finished. The truck had returned empty and then left again, packed with crates. Signor Montagna started fixing the walls inside the Rocca, restoring them to their original state in case the Germans did decide to pay an unexpected visit. It was dark outside and the air had turned bitterly cold. The townspeople had drifted off toward their homes. Elena walked to the stable behind the café to pick up her bicycle. She felt ill thinking of young Pietro. She missed his cheeky face and their little conversations each day. It was hard to imagine the giant hole in the hearts of his parents.

Elena thought about her own father and mother, never expressing their fears out loud but constantly worried about what might happen to Alessandro. The past few days had been surreal, a nightmare she wanted to wake up from. But the events of the afternoon in some small way had loosened the iron bands around her heart a little. She wrapped her scarf tightly around her head and started the cold trip home.

Chapter Twenty-One

A light snow was falling outside when Elena crept out of her bedroom later that evening. She shivered as she tiptoed across the stone floor of the kitchen toward the door of the house, where her coat hung on a hook in the entrance. *Hardly the most romantic of outfits*, she thought as she wound a woolen scarf around her head and put on rubber boots and warm gloves. The barn was going to be even colder. Elena gently pulled back the bolts and opened the door. The ground was already covered with a faint sprinkling of snow, and as she closed the wooden door quietly behind her, she realized her footprints would instantly betray her should either of her parents wake up.

Luca was already up in the hayloft in the barn when she arrived. Her breath formed little clouds as she struggled to remove an outer layer.

"God, it's cold," she whispered.

Luca smiled at her. "At least the animals are keeping the temperature slightly higher inside. Come on, I have stacked up some hay to make a little nest."

Elena was too cold to take off anything other than her coat. She placed it on top of the bed of straw and then lay down, pulling Luca next to her. She gratefully snuggled into Luca's arms. Their two lanterns shone faint light over the scene, illuminating Luca's cheekbones and the dark curls that fell over his forehead. Elena let herself relax.

Luca cleared his throat. "I have some news. I'm not sure how you'll take it."

Elena turned to look at him.

"Lorenzo came to our house earlier tonight. He wanted more ammunition. He told us that they are planning to avenge Pietro's execution."

Elena took a deep breath. This was hardly unexpected, but she was still nervous about what this might mean. "What are they going to do?"

"Lorenzo wouldn't tell us. He said the less information we had, the better. In case, well, you know—"

In case the Germans interrogate us. Elena nodded, sick to her stomach. "Did he say where they were going to attack?"

"No, nothing at all. I can only imagine that they want Germans to suffer, whatever the plan. But if they are smart, they also want to disrupt future activity by the Germans or the Fascists."

Elena nodded again.

"Oh, and they think they know who the informant was. Again, he wouldn't tell us, but I could see he was furious. I would not want to be in that person's shoes. You know what the partisans will likely do to him. Or her."

Elena was shocked. She had not mentioned her hunch to either Luca or Paolo on Saturday. It couldn't be Signor Bruni, could it? He was not a particularly friendly man, but it was hard to believe that he would do something that might hurt a child. She said nothing, hoping she was wrong.

"Well, I have some news too." She told Luca what had happened that afternoon at the Rocca—how the girl's singing had given her some peace. "I'm relieved that we managed to empty the fortress today and no Germans could be seen anywhere. So, if the partisans attack in Sassocorvaro and the Germans search the Rocca, they won't find anything."

Luca was happy that the Rocca was now empty of the works of art —he was desperate to keep Elena as safe as possible. "My father says we can go to the stable on Wednesday evening and finish our work on the truck. I hope the partisans don't do anything for a few days. Does Rotondi still need it?"

Elena told him what Pasquale had said. She was beginning to think that this insane idea might become reality. She was nervous that Luca would still want to take part in the arduous journey to Rome, if only to impress her. "I have a feeling the Vatican is going to come through. They said they will send an official with some kind of papers and transport. This might happen sooner than we think."

Rather than respond, Luca kissed her on the cheek and then more forcefully on her lips. He slipped his hand beneath the layers of clothing to caress her breast. His fingers were cold. Elena arched her back. She felt a flare of heat between her legs.

"*Mio Dio*, I want you, but it's freezing in here," said Luca.

Elena laughed. "I feel the same way. And it's going to become even colder over the next few months. Maybe we will have to find somewhere warmer to meet. I'm not sure I can wait until spring to feel you inside me again."

Elena pushed closer to Luca, their bodies pressing hard against each other. She rubbed her hand on the front of his trousers, then wriggled her fingers inside his clothes. Luca moaned.

The doors of the barn opened and a light appeared at the entrance. In shock, the two of them sat up clumsily, trying to see who was holding the lantern. Elena's heart was beating so hard that she thought it might leave her chest.

"What the hell? Goddammit, you scared me." Elena's brother strode toward them, his fury obvious. He held the lantern up, trying to shed more light on the scene. Elena scrambled to her feet, struggling to put her coat back on.

"Sandro, what are you doing here?" She and Luca made their way down the ladder.

"Well, it's clear to me what you two are doing," said Alessandro.

He scowled at Luca. "Please tell me you're going to marry her, you bastard. That's my sister you are poking."

Elena winced at the crude word. Her cheeks were burning with shame.

"It's not what you think, Sandro," said Luca quickly. "I love her. We want to be together."

Luca tightened his grip around Elena. The two men stood glaring at each other.

Alessandro broke the tension. He sat down abruptly on a bale of hay and grinned at the two of them. "You know what, Luca? If I had to pick anyone for my sister, you would have been high on the list. Okay, I approve." He held out his hand for Luca to shake.

Elena snorted. "I'm right here, you know. I'm not a sow to be mated with. I can make my own mind up, thank you very much."

Her initial terror had been replaced with fury. Goddamn this patriarchal society. Who did her brother think he was? She would marry whom she pleased.

Alessandro smiled at her. "Calm down, Elena. I understand. And I'm not going to tell anyone, okay? Anyway, I came to grab some stuff. Papà always leaves a few supplies for me."

He stood up and went toward the workbench at the back of the barn. Luca and Elena followed him. Luca stood next to Alessandro as he packed a grain sack with the cheeses, cured meats, and box of bullets his father had left out for him.

Luca told him that he had seen Lorenzo earlier on a similar mission to their house. Alessandro was grim as he described the meetings that had been taking place ever since the group had heard about Pietro.

"We're going to retaliate, but I'm not sure how yet. Erivo has information on who told the Germans that Pietro was the thief, so that's been dealt with. That's the easy part. But what we really want is a big target, and we need to inflict pain on those bastards while minimizing the fallout on civilians. It will be tricky, to say the least."

Elena and Luca did not know what to say. They all knew the Germans would respond to any partisan attack and more innocent civilians were bound to die.

"I feel your anger, Sandro. I was in the piazza when that bastard killed Pietro. I'll never forget what I witnessed." Elena shivered, less from the cold than from the memory. "I want to make them bleed too. I want their mothers to weep the way Anna is weeping now."

Alessandro nodded at them both, then lifted the sack onto his right shoulder. "I'd better go. Be careful, you two. You are lucky it was me tonight and not Papà, *sorella mia*."

Elena rushed forward and enveloped him in a hug. "Please try and stay out of harm's way," she whispered in his ear. "I love you. We all love you."

Her brother smiled grimly and turned to leave. He raised his free hand in a fist. "*Fischia il vento!*"

Elena knew the words. It was the first line of a well-known partisan song—*The wind whistles*—but those words had never meant as much to her as they did at that moment. She raised her fist and sang the second line. "*Infuria la bufera*, my dear brother. The storm rages."

Chapter Twenty-Two

Early the next morning, just before dawn, two farmhands arrived at Signor Bruni's farm to find the old man's body hanging from a tree in front of his house. They dropped their bikes onto the ground and ran over to cut him down. A piece of cardboard hung from his neck with words on it. Neither of the farmhands could read, so they removed it once they had cut down the body. One of them found a key hidden under a rock by the front door and let himself into the house to telephone the farmer's daughter and alert the authorities. While one man waited for somebody to arrive who could relieve him of this terrible burden, his friend cycled over to Ca'Boschetto with the sign, hoping to find Paolo and to ask him to read it. He came across Paolo, his brother, and his son in the farmyard, about to start work.

After his initial shock at the news, Paolo took the sign and read it out loud. "'*This man has a child's blood on his hands. All traitors will be punished.*'" He lowered his head. "Bruni was a difficult man, but did he deserve to die? Can we claim to be on the side of righteousness if we condone murder?"

Luca glared at his father. "They did what they had to. I don't condemn them for it. We are all safer now that he's dead." He was thinking about Elena and her mission. The partisans could kill every single informant as far as he was concerned. All he cared about was keeping her safe.

The farmhand took the sign back, thanking Paolo for his help. He couldn't wait to get to town to spread the news. The café would be his first stop.

The weather deteriorated over the next two weeks. Luca and his father managed to get to Sassocorvaro one evening to work on the truck. All anyone could talk about was the execution of Signor Bruni. The consensus was that the old man had deserved it. Pietro was everybody's son, and removing the man who had started the whole terrible chain of events gave people a sense of justice. His daughter had buried him quickly and without ceremony and did not want to dwell on it.

Paolo and Luca spent the evening reinstalling all the cleaned parts in the engine of the truck. They decided the headlights would be left without glass and they had patched up the crack in the windscreen as best they could. The engine had started after several tries, but they had not had an opportunity to test it on the open road yet.

The following day, they found themselves trapped at Ca'Boschetto. Snow fell heavily and obliterated the smaller tracks the farmers used to move from field to field. Elena was no longer able to cycle to Sassocorvaro each day. She managed to send a message to Pasquale, who was staying in his office in the Ducal Palace in Urbino, by handing a letter to one of her father's colleagues who had visited the farm to borrow tools. The letter must have reached its intended recipient, by a circuitous route no doubt, as, five days later, the same man returned to the farm with a reply from Pasquale. The superintendent told Elena not to worry —everything in Sassocorvaro and Carpegna was now under control. He was simply waiting to hear from the Vatican on the next steps.

Elena's mother was happy her daughter was home all day and put her to work milking the cows, canning and baking with her sister. Elena enjoyed spending time with her family, but she felt somewhat removed from them all. She kept thinking about what Alessandro had said about an impending attack. Would they hear anything if it happened? The heavy snow was surely dampening any major activity from either side. Maybe the partisans would wait until the wintery conditions eased up a little.

Elena was also missing the nightly visit from Luca. The snow made it extremely difficult to move around on the country roads, and the temperature in the barn was not conducive to romance. She missed their conversations as much as anything. Luca was becoming the one person she trusted with any secret or wild dream or deeply held fear, without having him judge her. This was what she wanted in her future husband —a best friend who treated her as his equal. She found herself spending time staring out of the window, dreaming about the end of the war and the chance to be with him in public.

Inside the Ducal Palace in Urbino, Pasquale was also spending a lot of time staring out of the window, mainly in frustration at the snowy conditions. He was receiving requests for help from art museums all over northern Italy as curators tried to decide where to hide their most valuable works of art. Since the Germans had invaded, the situation in the north had become more precarious. The one letter he was waiting for had not arrived. It would be Christmas soon, as his young daughters kept reminding him, and he was growing increasingly concerned that he was not going to get the green light from the authorities.

His wandering mind was interrupted by a knock on the door.

"Look what has arrived!" His colleague Signor Renon entered the small room, waving a piece of paper. "A telegram from Rome!" He smiled as he handed it to Pasquale and stood waiting while he opened and read the contents.

"Yes! *Finalmente!*" said Pasquale. He walked over and hugged his colleague. Renon grinned—it was very unlike his friend to be this demonstrative.

"Come on, tell me! Do we have permission?"

"We do indeed, my dear friend, we do indeed."

Pasquale held up the telegram to read it. "There is not much information. '*Expect Signor Emilio Lavagnino, the central inspector of the*

Directorate of Antiquities and Fine Art.'" He looked at Renon. "I know Lavagnino—he is a good man. From what they told me previously, I think he will have some means of transport and the official papers, which will declare that the goods are religious artifacts being returned to the Vatican for safekeeping. That should keep the Germans at bay if they become suspicious. My goodness, it is going to happen, Renon. This audacious plan might work."

The two men smiled at each other. Pasquale felt some of the tension of the past few months dissipate. Somebody important thought this insane idea might succeed. He was impatient to go home to tell Zea the good news. And he had to get word to Elena as well. He needed the master list from Sassocorvaro and, hopefully, the addition of the truck the Rossi men had been working on. Everything suddenly seemed a lot more hopeful. Now all they needed was for the snow to ease up.

Overnight, their luck changed. The following morning, the city woke to blue skies and sunshine. The snow had stopped and the temperature was several degrees higher than it had been for some time. Out in the countryside, the farmers cleared as much snow as they could from their tracks and the white roads leading out of the valleys and hills to the main tarmac road. In Urbino and the surrounding towns, the street cleaners were doing the same. Housewives hurried out of their homes with their ration badges to obtain the essentials that had been running low during the forced wait.

A day later, Elena was surprised to hear a car coming up the recently cleared track to Casa del Lupo. Her father and brother were out in the fields, but her mother and younger sister stood next to her in the yard as they tried to work out who the unexpected visitor might be. Nobody spoke, but Elena suspected, like her, they were hoping it wasn't German soldiers.

Elena breathed a sigh of relief when she recognized Pasquale's car. The superintendent introduced himself to her mother and sister.

"It has been too long, Signora Marchetti. Your daughter has been an excellent assistant, and I want to thank you for letting her work with me. I don't know how I would have managed without her."

Elena's mother brushed the praise aside, but her expression betrayed how pleased she was.

Pasquale turned to Elena. "Signorina Marchetti."

Elena tried not to grin at the formal tone but realized that Pasquale was trying to be polite in front of her mother.

"We have received the instructions we were waiting for, you will be pleased to hear. I was wondering if you might be ready to come to the office in Urbino to help me with the next step. I will obviously give you a lift and bring you back this evening in time for dinner."

Elena nodded. "By the way, I have the list you might need. I was bringing it home each night from the office to ensure it was in safe hands."

Pasquale wanted to kiss her but managed to restrain himself. "Good thinking, Signorina Marchetti. We would not want prying eyes interfering with state business, would we? If you need a couple of minutes—"

Five minutes later, the two of them were on the road.

"So, tell me everything, Pasquale! I cannot believe this is going to happen."

Pasquale quickly explained what had transpired. He turned to look at her. "Did Luca and his father manage to finish repairing the truck?"

"Well, it turned over. They have not been able to drive it outside yet. Shall we make a quick detour and go and ask them?"

Elena felt extremely important as they drove into the yard at Ca'Boschetto. Antonella insisted on making them sit down for pastries while she sent young Marco up the hill to fetch Luca and his father. Elena had butterflies in her stomach while they waited for the men to return.

Pasquale was hesitant to say anything with Antonella and her sister-in-law in the room, but Paolo spoke up. "It's alright, Rotondi. They know the plan. Young Elena told everyone here a few weeks ago when she wanted to take our truck." He laughed, as did the rest of the family.

Elena smiled weakly at Pasquale. "It is a long story—"

Paolo interrupted her. "Never mind that now. Yes, we have the truck ready for you. I can go tomorrow with Luca and then one of us can drive the truck to Urbino and leave it for you at the palace. I am sure it will be fine. Signor Vitali said—"

He paused, his face somber. Everyone looked stricken thinking about the bereaved father.

Paolo cleared his throat. "Signor Vitali is giving us the fuel he had hidden away. He says he never understood much about art, but he will do anything to frustrate the Germans."

A heavy silence fell on the group once more.

"That sounds like a good plan, Signor Rossi," said Pasquale eventually. "Elena and I will be making all the preparations over the next day or two, and hopefully Lavagnino—the emissary from the Vatican—will arrive by then. It would be my best Christmas gift, knowing we got some of these paintings to safety."

Chapter Twenty-Three

The next day, Elena and Pasquale were holed up in the office in the Ducal Palace going over the master list and deciding which pieces to prioritize should there be insufficient transport available. Pasquale wanted to make sure some of the larger altarpieces were moved first, for a couple of reasons. He was sure the Vatican would want the young superintendent to pay special attention to pieces that belonged to the church, as opposed to the Raphael and Titian paintings he personally valued more. But Pasquale was also afraid of the transport being stopped by the Germans. Having a couple of large altarpieces in each truck would make the official cover story more believable.

They were in the middle of working out how many crates an average-sized truck might carry when Renon walked in with the good news that Luca had arrived. Pasquale noticed the blush on Elena's cheeks and once again felt sure that these two young people meant more to each other than being just good friends. The two of them hurried out with Renon to look at the truck.

"What an uplifting sight, Luca," said Pasquale as he walked around the vehicle. "I can assume since you are here that the engine is working fine."

"Oh, yes. She sounds like new. My father was very excited when the engine started first time this morning, but of course he acted as if he had known it would all along."

The two men grinned at each other.

"Well, you and your father deserve all the thanks in the world. This will be very helpful to us." Pasquale went to the back of the truck to check out its capacity.

Luca stood, shuffling his feet. "I was hoping—I thought it might be helpful—"

Elena looked at him nervously.

"Signor Rotondi, I want to drive to Rome," said Luca hurriedly. "I think I can be of enormous help to you."

Pasquale and Renon stared at the young man. They looked lost for words.

"That is very generous of you, Luca," said Pasquale finally. "I am not sure it is the best idea though. What if the convoy is stopped by the Germans? Or Mussolini's men? You will be hard-pressed to explain what you are doing on a mission for the Vatican."

Luca did not know how to respond. He wanted Elena to think highly of him for volunteering, but he had not thought it through. He stood looking at his feet.

"We don't have to make any final decisions now," said Pasquale hurriedly. "Thank you for the offer, Luca. The truck alone is more than enough, seriously. But let's see who and what turns up from Rome. Hopefully we will have enough manpower and transport to make your kind offer moot."

In order to conceal the truck from prying eyes, they decided to drive it inside the palace gates and hide it in the courtyard. It wasn't the safest place, but none of them wanted to leave it outside in the piazza. Once the truck was safe inside, Luca awkwardly asked Pasquale if he might stay for the rest of the day and hitch a ride home with Elena.

Pasquale laughed. "Of course! I didn't expect you to walk home. That would take hours."

Luca found himself having one of the best afternoons he had had since the war began. He followed Pasquale, Renon, and Elena down into the underground areas of the palace and squeezed into the secret rooms they had built to hide the crates. As they opened one crate after another and discussed how they were going to make this plan work, Luca stood to one side, in awe of the beauty in front of him. He was reminded of how art had always moved him when he was a child and how magical those visits to the Ducal Palace had been. At one point, Elena took his hand in the dark and squeezed it hard.

"Isn't this something?" she whispered in his ear. "It is like a dream to me. All this beauty. All this glorious beauty!"

Luca nodded and squeezed her hand back. He felt tears pricking his eyes and was surprised at how emotional he felt. If he had ever felt conflicted about what Elena was trying to do, at that moment any uncertainty vanished. This was worth it—all of it. His brother might think he was crazy, but suddenly everything made perfect sense. He needed all this art to be saved. Italy needed all this art to be saved. Hell, the whole world needed it to be saved. He was just happy he had made a small contribution to making sure it was.

Chapter Twenty-Four

Lorenzo rubbed his chapped hands together in a vain attempt to warm them up. He was relieved that it had finally stopped snowing, but the blue skies and sunshine did not seem to be making any perceivable difference to the frigid temperature inside the drafty barn they had been sleeping in. He leaned on the shovel and took a crumpled cigarette packet out of his pocket. Alessandro stretched his arm out across the pit they were attempting to dig and held out a lighter.

The two men stood in silence, smoking their cigarettes and taking advantage of the lull to think back over the past few weeks. It had been brutal, for sure. One of their comrades who had been badly wounded in the ambush on the Blackshirts had died a couple of nights earlier. His tortured cries had grown weaker during the early hours. It felt as if the whole unit had been awake, listening as his breaths grew more and more labored until they had mercifully ceased. The body had lain on the straw for a day, as the snow made it impossible for them to move it.

Earlier in the morning, their commander, Erivo, had asked two of the late soldier's friends to take his body on horseback to his parents' home so he could be given a decent burial. It was dangerous, but Erivo felt the enemy would have other, more pressing concerns given the foul weather. Whenever humanly possible, they should try to honor the dead. Alessandro and Lorenzo had watched as the two friends silently bundled the man up in his blanket and laid him across one of the horse's backs. It looked medieval, but there did not appear to be a better way to accomplish the gruesome task.

They were almost grateful when Erivo told them it was their turn to dig a new latrine trench. Neither of them relished the task, but it was good to be outside in the sunshine, stretching their limbs and breathing fresh air rather than the fetid air inside the barn, which reeked of blood and death.

A few hours later, they had dug a decent-sized pit, and they gratefully carried their shovels back to the barn. The sky was turning dark. They were looking forward to whatever soup was being prepared for supper. As the two friends entered the barn, they saw the others sitting in a circle, murmuring to each other.

"Rossi, Marchetti. Come and join us. We have some news." Erivo motioned to them to sit down. The commander waited a couple of minutes for everyone to settle, then cleared his throat. He nodded at the two men who had taken their fallen friend home.

"First, we are grateful that you managed to return Comrade D'Angelo to his family. I am sure that was not an easy undertaking, but his parents deserved to have their son back. He died for his homeland and for a righteous cause, and we will always remember him."

The group bowed their heads as if they were in church. There was silence for a minute.

"While they were in the city, our comrades made a point of catching up with our contacts. It looks as if we have some interesting chatter at the German headquarters." The men looked at each other, some with apprehension, some with excitement.

"One of our contacts, a woman who delivers food to the commanding officers, overheard talk of an imminent arrival from Rome. She was born in South Tyrol so she speaks German, which is proving very helpful. A telegram had just been delivered and some officials were on their way to Urbino. She was not in the room long enough to learn more, but she shared with our colleagues that it seemed out of the ordinary. The major was barking orders at his subordinates and preparations seemed to be underway."

Erivo looked at the assembled company, with his brows furrowed. "Obviously, this is not a lot of information to go on, but we must always be alert to anything unusual. We need to find out more. Who is coming? Why are they coming? Is it a new offensive? Are they going to be rounding up civilians? Has something happened further south? Are the Allies making progress? As you know, we want to strike back after the horrific event in Sassocorvaro—this might be the opportunity we have been waiting for."

"Finally!" shouted a voice from the back of the barn. "Those bastards need payback."

"And we will give it to them," said Erivo forcefully. "But we can't go off half-cocked. We need to use our limited resources wisely and effectively. I have sent Esposito and Romano to Urbino this evening to hang out around the bars. All we need is a couple of drunk Nazis with loose lips—Esposito knows enough German to get their drift. Once we have a clearer picture, we can move. It sounded like whoever these visitors are, they will be here in the next day or so, so we will need to act quickly. Until then, let's start organizing, try to sleep, and be prepared to move out tomorrow if necessary."

Alessandro turned to Lorenzo, his face alight. "This is it. We're going to see some action at last. Thank God—I was getting bored of doing chores."

Lorenzo smiled weakly at his friend. "Yeah, about time we did some fighting."

Around them, the atmosphere had turned almost festive as the group chattered about what might be about to take place.

Lorenzo was not feeling quite so brave. Watching young men die slow and agonizing deaths over the past few weeks had weakened his desire for combat. He still believed in the cause, and he had never met anyone as charismatic as Erivo Ferri. He hated the Germans with every cell in his body. Pietro's death had struck him particularly hard. He kept thinking about his little brother Marco, who had been in the same year as Pietro at school. Lorenzo did not want to think about what it would feel like to lose someone you love that much to an invader's bullet.

But living rough for a couple of months had been harder than he had thought. They never had enough to eat and Lorenzo felt the cold in his bones. He had been sleeping on hard floors in various barns for far too long. All he could think about was the bed he shared with Luca and the conversations they used to have late into the night. Maybe he should have stayed a farmer rather than pretending that he was a soldier.

He watched his comrades huddle in small groups, some of them using worn strips of cloth to clean their rifles. He felt removed from them—he wanted to strike a blow against the invaders spreading terror in his neighborhood, yet he was beginning to doubt whether he would have the courage he would need when the time came. Erivo interrupted Lorenzo's reverie.

"Rossi," Erivo said in a low voice, "I noticed you and Marchetti have been managing to deliver a lot of needed goods. Especially that truck. Do you think the two of you might run another errand for us?" He motioned to Alessandro, who hurried over to join them.

"Let's hear what Esposito hears this evening in Urbino. If I think we have something to go on, I will need you to go back to your farms tomorrow night to obtain fuel and more ammunition, if possible. I have a few other men I am going to send out as well, but your families have been particularly helpful. I hope you thank them on our behalf."

Lorenzo and Alessandro nodded.

"Okay, good. Let's wait it out tonight and see what we learn. The next few days will be interesting, to say the least." Erivo patted the two young men on the shoulders and walked off toward another small group.

Alessandro looked at Lorenzo gleefully. "You see, my friend? We are important. We are making a difference. Those German bastards are not going to know what hit them." He linked arms with his friend and pulled him over to the fire, where a large pan of soup was simmering. "Even this slop is going to taste good tonight."

As Alessandro ladled some of the thin soup into his tin cup, Lorenzo followed his friend's lead with an uneasy feeling in his stomach. He prayed silently to a God he hardly believed in anymore that the two of them would still be alive when this nightmare came to an end.

Chapter Twenty-Five

The wind blew fallen leaves in flurries across the piazza as Pasquale hurried from the café to the doors of the Ducal Palace. He shivered in his heavy winter coat. The leaden sky above him spoke of more snow to come after the reprieve of the day before, and Pasquale was worried. He briefly nodded to the guard at the entrance and hurried across the courtyard to his office. He had barely been seated five minutes when Renon rushed in with a paper in his hand.

"They are coming! My God, they are coming. Just got another telegram. They stopped in Perugia to make arrangements for the art being held in that city, but it was a while ago."

Pasquale grabbed the paper and read the short message. Lavagnino was finally on his way. The telegram was noticeably terse and did not say anything about resources, so they would just have to wait to discover what the situation was. But the day was finally here when he would find out whether his audacious plan might work.

It was hard to concentrate on the mundane administrative tasks of a lowly bureaucrat for the next couple of hours. Pasquale found himself taking frequent breaks to wander the halls of the palace, visiting some of his favorite spots. He stood for a while in the duke's tiny study, contemplating its stunningly detailed trompe l'oeil wooden panels. Duke Federico would surely have agreed with his plan to save some of the greatest pieces of Renaissance art the world had ever seen. The man had been a visionary, a humanist, and a patron to some of those very painters. Pasquale read the inscribed Latin quote on the wall, rumored to be Federico's motto—*"virtutibus itur ad astra." With virtue man will reach the stars,* mused Pasquale. He was sure Duke Federico would think his plan virtuous. He wandered out to the small loggia and stood staring out of the window at the hills and snowcapped mountains beyond. Pockets of mist still floated in the valley. The sun had not been able to break through the thick cloud—not great weather for embarking on a perilous journey.

Pasquale's thoughts were interrupted by distant shouting—he recognized the voice of his curator. The visitors must have finally arrived. Pasquale straightened his tie and left the room. Hurrying down the stone stairs, he met Renon on the way up to find him. The two of them did not need to say anything. They had been preparing for this moment for weeks.

Standing in the courtyard was a group of men staring up at the inscriptions engraved in stone on top of the arches on all four sides. As Pasquale approached, he realized that one of them was wearing a German uniform. The group turned and watched the young superintendent as he made his way to the center. The German stood tall and gave a small salute. Another man hurried forward and shook Pasquale's hand.

"Signor Rotondi, I presume. Let me introduce myself. Italo Vannutelli, from the ministry."

Pasquale looked around. "Is Lavagnino here?"

"No. We decided to split up south of the city. Lavagnino has gone on to Carpegna with the trucks, where I believe he will find some crates to collect. We headed straight here. I have all the paperwork from the Vatican, so this should not take too long."

Vannutelli lowered his voice a little. "The gentleman who accompanied us is Lieutenant Scheibert from the Kunstschutz. He is our protection, you might say." His eyes blinked rapidly.

Pasquale hesitated for a couple of moments, not sure how much to say. "Welcome to Urbino, Vannutelli. I am sorry to say Lavagnino has made a wasted journey. Everything is already here in the palace. We thought we would make things easier for you."

Vannutelli stared at him, surprised. Renon and Pasquale exchanged quick glances, then the curator spoke up.

"Signor Vannutelli, I am Signor Renon, one of the curators here. I can drive you to Carpegna to meet Lavagnino and the transport and then bring everyone back here to the palace. How does that sound?"

"We were hoping to turn this around quickly," said Vannutelli. "It looks as if we will need to stay at least tonight."

"No problem at all," replied Pasquale quickly. "I will find rooms for everyone at the *albergo* nearby. As you can imagine, we don't have too many visitors these days. I'm sure they will be glad to have paying guests. Also, I will arrange dinner for everyone this evening. Let's at least try to make this a festive occasion."

Pasquale smiled awkwardly. He was trying to keep his face as passive as possible, but his mind was in turmoil. *A German officer, for God's sake.* This was an unexpected and unpleasant surprise that would make the whole enterprise much riskier. Surely this official would be paying close attention to what was being loaded onto the trucks. He had the beginnings of a crazy idea in his head, but he needed to talk to a couple of confidants first.

Pasquale's thoughts were interrupted by the German, who was walking toward the three men. The man bowed. "Lieutenant Scheibert from the Kunstschutz. It is a pleasure." His Italian was good, Pasquale noted.

"Welcome, Lieutenant. As I said to Vannutelli, there seems to have been some miscommunication. The crates for the Vatican are already here. My colleague Renon is going to take Signor Vannutelli to Carpegna to rendezvous with Lavagnino and explain everything to him. In the meantime, can I get you anything?"

The lieutenant looked at some papers he was holding. "I am supposed to meet a Major Heinrich. He has been sent word of my arrival and apparently he should be in Urbino today."

It took every ounce of mental strength Pasquale possessed not to react visibly. This situation was quickly going from bad to worse. He thought fast. "No problem at all, Lieutenant. I will direct you to the German headquarters. They have taken over one of the municipal buildings." His voice held no judgment—he was trying hard to sound as neutral as possible.

The officer made a small, stiff bow. "That all sounds good, Signore. Let us proceed."

Ten minutes later, Renon and Vannutelli were on their way to Carpegna. The German had been dispatched to meet the major.

Pasquale hurried back to his office and quickly telephoned his home. "Zea, I need guidance and your assistance."

His wife listened patiently while Pasquale explained what had transpired. She whistled softly. "Alright, that is a bit of a curveball. I think we can handle Scheibert. At least his presence makes this official. I'm more concerned with the major being part of this. We all know what he is capable of."

"Yes, you're right," replied Pasquale, gloomily. "But listen—I have an idea. Yes, before you say it, another crazy idea. I have suggested dinner tonight. If you're comfortable attending and I can persuade Elena to come as well, we might be able to distract this officer. He's in the Kunstschutz. If his job is to protect art, he must know something about it. Between you, me, and Elena, that is one subject we can talk about for hours. To keep him—how shall I put it—focused, we can dig up some bottles of the *rosso conero* we've been saving and make it a party. At the same time I can ask Renon and some other men to start loading the trucks. I will argue that it is to save time so they can leave early tomorrow morning. With any luck, the German will be having such a good time that he will be less attentive."

He was met with silence on the other end of the line. Pasquale thought they had been cut off for a moment. Then he heard his wife laughing.

"Pasquale, you never cease to amaze me. Yes, it's crazy, but I'm happy to be your bait. I would be careful how you explain this ruse to Elena's family, though: I'm not sure whether her father will think of it as such a good plan."

Relieved that Zea was willing to participate, Pasquale agreed to pick her up in the car once he had driven over to Elena's home and hopefully managed to convince her to join them. He quickly organized for someone to sort out rooms at the *albergo* and to ask the proprietor to think about what might be provided for a dinner at such short notice.

"Tell them the museum will cover all the costs," he said recklessly. He would worry about the money once this saga was over.

An hour later, Elena's parents had indeed been persuaded that Pasquale and his wife would be taking care of their daughter at this impromptu work dinner and had agreed that she could attend. Elena had quickly changed into a suitable outfit and set off with her boss to collect Zea. As soon as they drove away from the farm, Pasquale told her the real plan.

"Do you think you need Luca to help tonight?" she asked. She was proud that Pasquale wanted to include her in the scheme, but also a little scared that Major Heinrich would be attending the dinner. The thought of Luca being in the vicinity gave her some courage.

"That's a great idea. We need all the help we can get to load the trucks quickly. Let's swing by the Rossi place and talk to him."

For the second time in two days, Elena and Pasquale drove into the yard at Ca'Boschetto. The sky was already beginning to darken and the air was growing colder. Elena was glad she had remembered to grab her warm winter coat. Paolo, Leonardo, Luca and the twins were making their way down from the hills. The working day was much shorter in the winter given the hours of daylight. The five men greeted the new arrivals, with Luca trying not to stare too much at Elena. Her cheeks were flushed with the cold and her brown eyes sparkled. He felt the little surge of joy that happened every time he laid eyes on her.

Pasquale explained for the third time what he was planning to do that evening, this time being more direct than he had been at Elena's home. He trusted that Paolo would immediately grasp that this was the only way to keep the plan on track.

"You go, Luca," said his father immediately. "I'll square it with your mother. We have come this far; we might as well try and finish the job. Good luck, all of you. Just remember to keep that bastard's glass full, Pasquale, not your own."

Pasquale laughed. "Yes, none of us can afford to be drunk. We need our wits about us. Thank you, Paolo. It looks like I owe you once more, my friend."

The two men shook hands. Luca jumped into the back of Pasquale's car. He was happy to grasp any opportunity to be with Elena, but he was nervous. News that the major might be involved in some way was disconcerting. The man had shown what cruel and arbitrary behavior he was capable of. Luca hoped the German would not decide to hang around the palace for too long this evening—the hours ahead were worrying enough to think about without wondering whether Major Heinrich would discover their subterfuge.

Chapter Twenty-Six

As they drove into the piazza outside the Ducal Palace, the occupants of the car found six trucks already parked, guarded by a couple of German soldiers. Pasquale swore under his breath when he saw the men. His wife leaned across and patted his hand.

"Deep breaths, *mio caro*. We've got this."

The four of them exited the car and walked into the palace. More men were now standing in the courtyard talking to each other, with Major Heinrich and Lieutenant Scheibert huddled by themselves some distance away, speaking in low voices. Renon spotted the new arrivals and waved with a smile of relief on his face. A man Elena and Luca did not recognize walked toward them.

"Signor Rotondi, we meet again. Well, this undertaking is certainly becoming more interesting by the hour." He removed his hat and made a short bow to Zea and Elena. "Signor Lavagnino at your service. And who might you lovely ladies be?"

Pasquale shook his hand and quickly introduced everyone. He was careful to say that Luca was one of his assistants—he knew the young man would need to keep a low profile. Before they managed to say anything else, Major Heinrich joined them. He let his gaze fall for several seconds on Elena before he spoke.

"Signorina Marchetti, we must stop meeting like this. You are everywhere, it seems. So, Rotondi, I have read over the paperwork. Everything looks to be in order. If the Pope wants his belongings, who am I to stop him, eh?"

The major smiled at the group. "Where are the pieces currently stored? What's the plan?"

Lavagnino spoke up. "I trust the good superintendent has it all under control. It is certainly easier now that we know everything is here at the Ducal Palace."

An awkward silence ensued, broken by Zea. "I'm sure Lieutenant Scheibert would like to know where he is sleeping this evening, am I right?"

She flashed her dazzling smile at the lieutenant, who looked flustered. "Why don't I take you over to the *albergo* so you have a chance to rest before dinner? Elena and I will make the final arrangements for the meal—I'm sure you would enjoy some decent food after all those hours on the road."

She turned to the major. "Would you like to join us for dinner, Major? I've no idea what we've managed to procure at such short notice, but I brought a few bottles of local red wine with me that we were saving for a special occasion. This might as well be it. They're in our car outside—shall we?"

Disarmed, the major nodded in agreement.

"Well, that's sorted then. Let's head over to the *albergo* now and leave these academics to go through the fine print of the paperwork."

Zea linked her arm through Elena's and started walking toward the doors of the palace. As if hypnotized, the major and the lieutenant followed them.

Lavagnino watched them leave, then let out a low whistle. "Good lord, Rotondi, your wife's something, isn't she? That was the smartest move she could have made. Come on, show me what you've really got hidden here and we can decide how the hell to pull this off."

The men started walking toward the archway on one side of the courtyard that led to a steep slope down into the underground section of the palace. Luca followed them, alarmed at what had transpired. He hated watching Elena go off with that monster. Now it looked as if they would be spending several hours in each other's company. Elena must be feeling unnerved. Suddenly his role looked easy by comparison.

The group proceeded down the steep slope to the lower floor. Lavagnino stared at the enormous arched ceilings and cavernous rooms. "I have heard this palace is an architectural wonder, but my word, this really is magnificent."

Pasquale explained that the duke had made sure that his palace design incorporated every possible modern convenience available. "Well, what was regarded as state of the art in 1445!" Pasquale went on to explain that in the cavernous space below ground, the duke's architects had designed huge stables for the horses, laundry rooms, places to store ice in the winter, storage spaces, large kitchens for the preparation of food, a sewage system, and even a water heating system that allowed the duke and his duchess to enjoy hot baths.

Lavagnino whistled. "The man was a genius. What an amazing place to come to work every day, Rotondi."

Pasquale nodded. "I count my blessings daily. And of course this vast subterranean space meant that we had plenty of places to hide our crates. The Italian army has been hiding armaments in the underground water system since the war started. They figured even if the Allies bombed the palace—which they agreed not to do, by the way, given how historically important it is—the arms would be safe. So we simply avoided the water system and looked elsewhere."

He took the minister to one of the rooms where he and Signor Montagna had constructed the fake walls. He had asked the builder to come the day before and remove some of the plasterwork so they would be able to access the crates.

Lavagnino inspected the handiwork and grinned at Pasquale. "And you, my friend, are also a genius. This is incredible. How many pieces are we talking about?"

"Almost ten thousand in total, I think," said Pasquale modestly.

"Good grief. Okay, we'd better start. How are we going to manage this feat?"

Pasquale laid out his plan. Lavagnino agreed that the dinner was a good subterfuge and should keep the Germans tied up for most of the evening. Pasquale explained that they were planning to drive the trucks into the courtyard. That would mean they would not have too far to go to load the trucks, they could work much faster, and they would be hidden from anyone lurking outside.

After some calculations and scribbling on pieces of paper, they worked out that they would probably be able to take just over a hundred cases on the first trip. Pasquale was concerned for a moment, but Lavagnino assured him that he would return early in the new year. "If we make it this time, the Vatican will be eager to receive the rest. We will have no trouble the second time around."

Pasquale saw the wisdom in that, but it made him nervous. He hated the idea of having to keep the rest of the treasures safeguarded for a few more weeks. Who knew what would happen in the meantime?

Lavagnino noticed his discomfort and put a reassuring hand on his shoulder. "We can do this, trust me. You and your team have done the impossible already. Nobody in Rome believed it when they first heard what you were talking about. You are going to pull this off right under the noses of both the Germans and the Fascists. Tonight will be stressful, I know. The next few days will be stressful too. But I have all the faith in the world that I will get these artworks and music scores to Rome and that we will be celebrating very soon."

Pasquale stood listening. The man was extremely confident that they would succeed. He then turned to Luca. "Lavagnino, this fine young man helped us procure an additional truck. He's offered to drive with your convoy to Rome if you need the extra help."

Lavagnino looked at Luca, his eyes boring into him as if trying to work him out. "That's a rather foolhardy offer, if I may say so. The journey to Rome will be rough, with the potholes, the terrible weather, and the constant risk of an Allied bombardment or a checkpoint search. But then you would have to return alone to Urbino. That might be even more dangerous for you—a young man of military age alone in central Italy. I would imagine Mussolini's lot would love to force you to fight for their lost cause."

Luca looked down at the stone floor, trying to marshal his thoughts. He needed this important man from Rome to understand him. "I just believe there are different ways to win this war, sir. My father and—"

He hesitated, then rushed on, his words tripping over each other. "My father and the woman I love have both argued that these works of art need to be saved, and they're the two wisest people I know. I'm not an academic, Signor Lavagnino, and I don't understand much about art. But I know that hearing a wood pigeon singing to its mate in the early morning fills me with joy. And watching the sun turn the clouds red and orange as it dips below the hills of our valley in the evening makes me forget my aching shoulders for a few minutes as I contemplate its beauty. As a child, I saw paintings on the walls of this palace that moved me in a similar way. I want to be able to bring my own son here one day in the future and show him those same paintings."

The assembled men looked at him with renewed interest. Pasquale thought he had never heard Luca say so much at one time.

Lavagnino held out his hand. "Young man, that is the best reason I have heard so far for this mission. I would be honored to have you on my team."

Surprised, Luca shook the official's hand. "Thank you, sir. I will try to be helpful." He felt a jumble of emotions: fear at the journey he was about to undertake, embarrassment at having bared his soul to a stranger, and pride that this important man had found his words compelling. He could not wait to share all this with Elena.

"Well, what are we waiting for?" asked Pasquale. "Let's drive the trucks inside and start loading. We have an hour before dinner, Lavagnino, so we can at least get things moving. I will leave Renon here in charge while we are at dinner. He knows this list as well as I do." For the first time in a few months, Pasquale was feeling hopeful. If they survived this evening without the Germans finding out that they were packing so many additional items, then they stood a good chance of being successful. Once the convoy was on the road, its fate was in the lap of the gods.

Chapter Twenty-Seven

Erivo looked up as Esposito and Romano hurried into the barn. He had been trying to keep busy all morning while he waited, not always patiently, for them to return from Urbino. Knowing how thorough the two young men usually were when they were sent on a mission, he expected them to come back only when they felt they had mined every possible information source, but it was difficult not knowing what was happening in the city for so many hours. He was nervous that someone might have given them away to the authorities, or that one of them had made an error of judgment that had landed them in trouble. Now Erivo looked at their excited faces as they stood in front of him, desperate to share their news. Aware of the men and women around them, who had all turned their heads to look at their returning comrades expectantly, Erivo motioned to the two men to follow him outside.

They stood several feet away from the barn's entrance. The day was cold, with an overcast sky that threatened snow.

"You look close to bursting, comrades. Come on, share what you've uncovered."

Esposito looked at his friend for reassurance before speaking. "We learned a lot. Just like you said, a few beers in a bar and anyone will open their mouths if they think nobody important is listening."

He quickly confirmed that the Germans had been expecting the arrival of important visitors. The major had arrived at the headquarters the day before. None of the revelers in the bar seemed to have any idea as to exactly who had been expected, though, or why they were coming to Urbino.

"So we decided to stay overnight with my cousin," said Romano, continuing the story. "We thought if we were still in the city this morning, we might be able to find out more. So we went to a couple of our old haunts—the café in Piazza della Repubblica, the butcher's shop my uncle owns—but nobody knew anything. Then Carlo here had the bright idea of paying a visit to one of his old sweethearts." Romano nudged his friend, who started blushing, in the ribs.

"She works as a maid at the *albergo*. Well, as we arrived at the rear entrance, we heard a flurry of activity inside. We hung around at the back in the courtyard, smoking, and once we couldn't hear anything anymore, we slipped inside. Turns out that someone from the museum was asking for rooms for the night for a party that had just arrived from Rome. And he had German soldiers with him."

The two men looked at Erivo, looking for a response to this bombshell. Their leader's face remained impassive, so Romano hurriedly continued. "Carlo's friend said the owner of the *albergo* had asked where their vehicles were and was told that they had trucks which were now parked at the Ducal Palace."

"And that is not all," said Esposito. "They're having dinner tonight at the *albergo*. Major Heinrich is one of the guests—not sure who else. Anyway, my friend says whoever is here is in a hurry. They're supposed to leave again tomorrow morning. The two maids were all complaining because the rooms would have to be cleaned again and the bed linen washed after only one night."

Erivo was impressed. This was all good information. They still did not know exactly what the objective of this journey was, but it had to be big if the major was involving himself. He stood contemplating the news for a few minutes. This might be the chance they had been waiting for. Whatever was going on involved Germans—that was a fact. If his group caused a disruption, that would frustrate whatever plot was brewing.

Erivo patted the shoulders of the two young men. "Well done, you two. Smart thinking to wait until this morning—that gives us a lot more useful information. Seems like we should be planning a little surprise for our visitors. Okay, give me time to think. Don't say anything to the others yet. Go inside and grab something to eat—although I'm assuming your 'friend' probably gave you a pastry or two."

The men laughed, and Romano punched his friend in the ribs again. They headed back to the barn, leaving Erivo to work out his next move.

———

Thirty minutes later, Erivo walked back inside and called the group to order. He stood on an upturned crate, looking at the expectant faces. He had grown very fond of this mismatched crew: young naive men hardly out of childhood; older, cynical communists who had been preaching against the Fascist state for years, finally feeling vindicated; hardened women with strong bodies wanting to play their part alongside the men rather than sitting passively at home. They were all exhausted, dirty, and malnourished, but still determined. Whenever the group lost a comrade, as they had done a few times in the past two weeks, it hit him hard—he felt responsible for each life, knowing his decisions were sending them into harm's way. And he was about to do it again.

"Alright, listen up. A lot to share. Last night, Esposito and Romano learned that the Germans were expecting important guests. They heard talk of arrivals from Rome and that Major Heinrich was in the city to meet with them. And this morning it was confirmed that this unknown group indeed turned up and are staying the night in the city. But—and this is important—they will be leaving again tomorrow morning."

Erivo paused and looked around the barn. He wanted to make sure the audience was still with him.

"So why has this mysterious group arrived? We can hazard a guess.

They arrived in trucks, not cars—that is significant. We know armaments have been stored in the ancient underground water system—our own forces used those tunnels before the Germans got here and since then, the invaders have continued to stockpile weapons and ammunition. It makes sense—those tunnels have stood for hundreds of years and they are far below ground. No aerial bombs can reach them."

All eyes were on him now. They were transfixed. Erivo raised his voice slightly. "I'm convinced that this convoy has come to shift some of these weapons south. Maybe they're running short at the front lines. The Allies have been moving quickly up the peninsula, so it makes sense. Who knows? But whatever they're doing here, this convoy will make a prime target if we decide to hit it. And we would need to do it quickly if they're out of here tomorrow. There's only one main road south from Urbino, as you all know, and it has many sharp curves. We have several good options for mounting an ambush. But only for the first few miles. After that, it's a straight open road until just before Fossombrone, where they either turn right to go through the mountains toward Rome or left to head toward the coast and the port of Ancona. And we have no idea which route they will take. We need to strike them right outside the city."

The room was energized. Erivo sensed the subtle shift in the atmosphere. They had been staying put for too long. This plan offered some action. There were low murmurs as people started whispering to each other.

Erivo held up his hand for silence. "As I said, if they're leaving tomorrow, we have to move quickly. I'm going to break you up into small groups. A few people will head to Urbino immediately and try to find out more precise information on how many people and vehicles we are dealing with. I will lead a small reconnaissance group to the outskirts to work out where on the road we should attack them. Looking at the maps, I want to check out the stretch of road before the station. I think there are a couple of likely spots. Once we've chosen the place, we will head back to one of our safe houses on the edge of the city. I've already spoken to a couple of you about getting more ammunition—we will need extra supplies as soon as possible, so you'll need to head out tonight as well. Bring whatever you can procure to the agreed safe house after midnight, and then we will regroup. We need to leave from here in the early hours and be in place before the sun comes up."

He hesitated for a moment. He knew he was asking a lot from his people and time was short. It would be a miracle if they managed to pull this off. Erivo was also aware that he needed to choose key team members wisely. The ones doing the ambush needed to be seasoned soldiers. He could not afford to take any novices or those who might lose their nerve at a critical moment. He was also facing the depressing reality that they did not have enough weapons, grenades, or incendiary devices for more than a small crew to handle. This would have to be a precise attack.

"Right. Give me ten minutes to draw up lists and then we can head out. Anyone who doesn't want to go, let me know. This is going to be dangerous. I only want those with stiff spines. It's already dark, so we need to move fast."

The room was galvanized. The young men stood up immediately and hovered around Erivo, hoping to be chosen. The older men, confident that their leader would pick seasoned fighters, started picking up rifles and talking in soft voices to each other.

Suddenly, a lone female voice started singing the plaintive words of one of their best-known anthems. One by one, voices joined in until the whole group was singing in unison.

E se io muoio da partigiano,
o bella, ciao!
bella, ciao! bella, ciao, ciao, ciao!
E se io muoio da partigiano,
tu mi devi seppellir.

And if I die as a partisan
Oh, goodbye beautiful,
goodbye beautiful,
goodbye beautiful! Bye! Bye!
And if I die as a partisan
Then you must bury me.

The haunting words filled the barn. Erivo felt his soul stir. He surreptitiously wiped a tear from his eye. He prayed he would not have to bury many men when this was over.

Chapter Twenty-Eight

Elena stood in front of the large fireplace, staring at the flames. She kept looking at the door, hoping Pasquale would turn up before the German officers.

"I need help, Elena," said Zea from the other side of the room. "I'm not sure where to seat everyone."

Elena turned around reluctantly and made her way to the table. The small dining room at the *albergo* had been transformed. Lit candles cast shadows on the ceiling's faded frescoes and whitewashed walls and lent the room a sense of occasion. The silverware on the white linen table-cloth gleamed, and it looked as if the owner of the *albergo* had set out her best crystal glasses for the dinner. Zea was scribbling on a piece of paper.

"I hate doing this to you, but would you mind if I put you next to the lieutenant? I'm sure he will be interested in talking to you about your time at the Pinacoteca di Brera in Milan. He must be some kind of expert to be in that art preservation unit, surely."

Elena swallowed hard and nodded. She was extremely nervous about the upcoming dinner but knew that distracting the Germans was critical to allow the cases to be loaded into the trucks unimpeded.

She looked at Zea. "Where are you going to seat the major?" Elena felt nauseous even thinking about him.

"I'm going to sacrifice myself for that particular task," Zea replied, grimacing. "Don't worry. I've had to sit next to many a pompous art historian or museum head in my career, all thinking they were smarter than me. An arrogant German officer doesn't faze me. Even one who has proved himself to be inhuman."

Elena smiled weakly. She admired Pasquale's wife so much. Zea was a strong, confident woman who was brilliant at her work and who appeared to have the best kind of relationship with her equally talented husband. Elena aspired to have a marriage like theirs.

As if on cue, the door opened and in walked Pasquale and Lavagnino, their faces red from the cold outside and flurries of snow still evident on their coats.

"*Mio Dio*, it's wintery outside." said Pasquale. "Just our luck it has started snowing again. If it keeps going like this, it'll be a tough journey tomorrow."

Lavagnino nodded, removing his overcoat and shaking it. "But we've done well so far, my friend. I'm impressed with your organization and thorough lists. If we can keep this dinner going for a couple of hours, I think the men will be able to finish loading before we return to the Ducal Palace."

Pasquale kissed his wife on the cheek and smiled at Elena. "Are we ready, ladies?"

"All done. We just need our guests to arrive now. I have worked out a strategic seating plan, by the way." Zea winked at the two men.

Lavagnino laughed. "Beautiful and brainy—what a lethal combination. We will put ourselves in your capable hands, Signora Rotondi."

The four Italians looked up as they heard loud German voices approaching the room.

"We can do this," Zea said, and stepped forward with a wide smile to open the door.

An hour later, the room was filled with cigarette smoke and the sounds of knives and forks scraping china. Elena felt a headache coming on and was trying to sip her wine extremely slowly. Her companion, however, was pouring wine for himself freely and the volume of his voice increased with every glass he drank.

"I must say, Signorina Marchetti," the lieutenant said, putting his left hand on top of hers as she rested it on the table. "I was not expecting such pleasant company this evening when I agreed to come on this trip."

He leered at the young woman, who was trying not to stare at the spots of red wine on the soldier's jacket. Elena suppressed a shudder and removed her hand by picking up her knife, ostensibly to cut another piece of roasted pork.

"Your work in the Kunstschutz is certainly fascinating, Lieutenant. Tell me, who's your personal favorite of the Renaissance artists whose work you've been trying to protect during this difficult period?"

It was surreal to be having this conversation with a citizen of the nation directly responsible for the dangers facing the art in the first place, but Elena kept talking. "I'm a big fan of Raphael, of course, but you won't meet anyone from Urbino who professes otherwise. He was born here, so we're going to own him and his genius."

The lieutenant nodded in agreement. "I don't disagree with you about that. The man had talent, of course. But I'm very partial to Caravaggio myself. I love a little brutality in my art. Raphael is a little too soft for my liking."

He smiled at Elena, stabbing a piece of meat with his fork as he did so, as if to emphasize his point. Elena felt queasy thinking about Luca and the others loading the crates into the trucks. She looked around the table, trying to gauge how the other conversations were going.

Zea was managing to look fascinated by the major's long anecdotes about his time in the German army. He had been giving her a blow-by-blow account of the battle for Sicily earlier that year, which, to Elena's ears, sounded like a litany of complaints about the incompetence of Italian leadership during the campaign.

"Just arrogant fools, the lot of them," said the major, his derision obvious. "Absolutely zero strategic sense. Far too many mistakes were made." He took another sip of wine, as if to rinse a bad taste from his mouth. "We would not have lost the island if we had been in charge."

Zea nodded, her face blank. The major took this as his cue to continue his diatribe.

"My unit was forced to retreat under heavy fire. We were fortunate in losing only a dozen or so men. Not how I intended to end my time in combat, I can assure you."

"I'm sure it wasn't," said Zea in an agreeable tone. "Urbino is a long way from Sicily. How did you end up here?" She leaned forward, her expression open.

"Not my idea, I can assure you, my dear woman," said Major Heinrich. He frowned and glared at the other diners. "I did not intend to end up in this backwater, keeping peasants in line." Elena wondered whether he was including the Italians around the table in this description.

"But I go where I'm needed. We have to hold the north, whatever happens. So I'm determined to keep my patch under control. I'm not going to allow any insurrections around here. Any sign of trouble, and I'm going to stamp it out."

I guess that includes nine-year-old boys, thought Elena bitterly. It took every ounce of strength she possessed not to glare at the major. She did not know how Zea was managing to keep a neutral expression.

"A couple more months proving my worth and I'm going to ask to go back to the front lines in the south. They need more men like me making the big decisions—not those flaky Italians."

Elena recognized the aggrieved tone. She had encountered internal politics at the Pinacoteca, where ambitious young men maneuvered to get the juiciest positions and stewed when they were overlooked or, worse, demoted. The major believed he was destined for greatness and was resentful that his brilliance had been overlooked. Men like him could be viewed as minor annoyances in the art world; it was a different matter when they had the power to summarily execute people. Elena shivered, thinking about the men in the underground rooms at the palace.

As if he had read her mind, the major suddenly spoke up from the other side of the table. "As delightful as this meal is, at some point we must go back to check on the trucks. I need to make sure all the pieces on the Vatican's list are accounted for."

Pasquale tried not to look at Lavagnino. "My head curator, Renon, is supervising. He has a copy of the list and he's always very thorough."

"That may be, Rotondi, but I have my orders. I would hate for the Pope to start complaining to my superiors if his favorite altarpiece does not make it to Rome."

Major Heinrich looked around the table with a grin on his face, but Elena heard the sharp edge to his voice.

"Well, I think I'm the one with the most to lose, Major," said Lieutenant Scheibert. "After all, I'm the one who approved this journey and I'm the one responsible for the convoy until we make it back."

The major glared at the younger man. "I think you'll find while you are in this city, I am the commanding officer. And I happen to oversee actual soldiers as opposed to the pack of art historians you allegedly command."

The temperature in the room seemed to have dropped a few degrees. Zea picked up a bottle of wine and refilled the major's glass. "Gentlemen, I happen to have it on good authority that the chef here has a small wheel of aged *parmigiano*. And I spotted a dusty bottle of *vin santo* outside, which I think would go with it rather splendidly."

The major raised his glass and bowed his head in her direction. "That sounds exquisite, Signora Rotondi. And if the *vin santo* is as excellent as this *rosso conero*, then it will be a splendid end to the meal. I'm willing to wait a little longer in that case."

Elena felt her face would crack with all the smiling. This was the longest meal of her life. Zea had worked her magic again to calm the room, but she hoped the evening would continue to go smoothly. She did not dare contemplate what would transpire if the major discovered what was going on at the palace.

Several miles away on a country road, Alessandro and Lorenzo sat in the truck that Alessandro's father had lent to the partisan cause many weeks earlier. They had switched off the headlights to avoid attracting attention, but every few minutes, Lorenzo had to turn on the windshield wipers to clear the glass of snow. The two friends were debating their next move.

"Look," said Alessandro. "I think my father will have left some ammunition in the barn. He tries to leave me something useful every week. If we head to Casa del Lupo, we won't even have to wake anyone up."

He didn't say anything else, but he was anxious to complete this task as quickly as possible. He wanted a piece of the real action and he was now annoyed that the two of them had been sent back to their farms for supplies, rather than heading to the city to carry out reconnaissance work. Alessandro was hoping to be included in the ambush team. The longer they hung out in the country, the less likely that would happen.

"But here's the thing," countered Lorenzo. "We have plenty of stuff at Ca'Boschetto that will be useful. Apart from ammunition, there's an old stock of dynamite. We had to clear some rocks to widen the stream a few years ago, so my uncle blew them up. If I explain the situation to my father and uncle, I'm sure we can take some. It'll be a better use of our time."

"Well, why not do both? It's not so far between our houses. Let's go to Casa del Lupo first, see what's in the barn, and then head to yours. We can talk to your father and hopefully he will give us some useful stuff. That way we'll have covered our bases."

Alessandro was cold and he wanted to move. Lorenzo was usually impetuous. Now he was acting like his father Paolo, carefully considering all the options. It was infuriating at times like this. His own father might not be as smart as Signor Rossi, but he was definitely a man of action.

"Come on, let's move. My feet are freezing."

Lorenzo started the engine and the truck slowly inched forward. Alessandro was nervous about the state of the road. The snow was coming down quite quickly now and the tires on the truck were not in the best condition.

After an agonizingly slow journey, they pulled into the Marchetti farmyard. They followed the track to the rear of the main house and pulled in next to the barn. Hurrying into the barn with a lantern,

Alessandro walked to the rear, where his father usually hid supplies. He was glad not to find his sister and Luca in a compromising position again. Maybe his previous interruption had scared them off their regular late-night rendezvous. Alessandro chuckled to himself as he quickly filled his sack with the root vegetables, a jar of cherries, and a box of bullets that had been left in the usual place. The bullets would not go far, but he was grateful for them as well as the food.

Returning to the truck, Alessandro nodded to Lorenzo, holding up the sack. He then climbed up into the passenger seat. "Let's go. Not much to help us with the ambush, but at least we have a few potatoes and carrots. Oh, and a jar of cherries. And fortunately, nobody woke up."

They drove slowly back down the track. Neither of them noticed the light that appeared at one of the bedroom windows. Francesco watched his truck as it disappeared, then turned to face his wife, who was looking at him expectantly from their bed.

"It was the boys, not Elena. They picked up the supplies in the barn. This work dinner is taking far too long. I hope Rotondi gets her back here soon. This weather isn't safe to drive in, especially in that small car of his."

He was annoyed but trying not to show it. Respectable young women should not be gallivanting this late at night in the city. *Whatever was Rotondi thinking?*

Elisa motioned to him to return to the warmth of the bed. "Stop worrying, Francesco. She'll be back soon. Just be happy that the boys collected the food. I'm sure they're all starving."

Her husband reluctantly got back into bed and blew out the candle. He did not mention the box of ammunition. Hopefully the partisans would put it to good use.

Chapter Twenty-Nine

It was almost midnight when the dinner finally wrapped up. Lieutenant Scheibert was decidedly the worse for wear. He kept slurring his words and attempting to wrap his arm around Elena's shoulders. The major, who, Elena noted, looked as sober as when he had arrived despite the copious glasses of wine, was glaring at his countryman.

As the guests rose from the table, Pasquale and Lavagnino exchanged glances. They were both keen to return to the palace, but they were hoping that the Germans would decide to call it a night given the late hour. They stood by the door with their coats on.

"Thank you for joining us," Zea said diplomatically to the major. "I hope you enjoyed the meal. They managed to produce quite a feast, despite the deprivations, didn't they?"

The major nodded in agreement. "It was delightful. Thank you for organizing everything. Now, if you will excuse us—"

Before Major Heinrich finished the sentence, he was interrupted by a large crash. Lieutenant Scheibert had stumbled backward trying to get out of his chair. He fell onto the floor, snapping one of the wooden legs underneath him.

Before anyone else moved, the major hurried to his side and pulled him unceremoniously to his feet. "For God's sake, man, pull yourself together."

Pasquale carried over the lieutenant's heavy coat. He and Major Heinrich managed to put it on the officer. The major gripped the man's elbow tightly. "I will make sure this man gets to his room. Thank you again for your hospitality."

He turned to Lavagnino and Pasquale. "My inspection can wait. I will see you gentlemen at eight o'clock tomorrow morning in the palace courtyard. I want to check the manifest before the convoy leaves." He bowed to the group and left the room, dragging the lieutenant with him. Elena felt almost sorry for the young man—she imagined Major Heinrich would have plenty to say to him once they were out of earshot.

"Thank the Lord for strong liquor," said Lavagnino. "That was a relief. Let's go and check out what's been done then we need to head to our beds too. I'm sure you would appreciate a few hours of sleep before we meet again."

Pasquale nodded. He had just heard the bells from the church of San Domenico striking midnight. He was worried about how Elena's parents would react to the late return of their daughter. It was going to be at least one o'clock by the time they managed to get to Casa del Lupo, and even later before he and his wife would be able to get to bed.

"Quickly, before the major changes his mind. I want to make sure the men managed to pack everything."

The group left the *albergo* after thanking the proprietor and her staff for the meal. Zea told Pasquale that she would stay to help tidy up —the chef had offered her leftovers for her children, and she wanted to compensate her friend, the owner, for the broken chair. Pasquale smiled —he knew Zea also wanted a chance to catch up on the latest gossip in the city. He told her that they would come and collect her as soon as they were finished at the palace.

The snow was already an inch thick on the cobblestones outside. Elena shivered as the wind blew across the piazza, but she was relieved that they had managed to avoid an inquisition that evening. Entering the palace through the large oak doors she could see that the courtyard was a hive of activity. All the trucks were loaded up with tarpaulin-covered crates, containing masterpieces of Western art, as Elena was well aware. Being inside the courtyard without the howling wind meant that the air did not feel as bitterly cold as it had in the large piazza. But the snow was still falling, and the temperature dropped as they descended into the underground rooms at the palace. The men were carrying the last of the crates up the ramp when the party arrived. They were relieved to see no Germans with them.

"Perfect timing," said Vannutelli, flourishing the list. "Everything is packed up and ready to go. We loaded a large altarpiece in the back of each truck, so if anyone decides to open a crate, that'll be the first thing he will find."

Pasquale, Lavagnino, Renon, and Vannutelli huddled together, conferring on the list. The other men took the opportunity to step away for a cigarette. Luca and Elena moved to one side and Luca surreptitiously took her hand.

"How was it, *carissima*? I am guessing the plan worked since the Germans are not here."

Elena gave him a chaste peck on the cheek. "We had a couple of dicey moments, but my God, Zea is brilliant. I don't think she is afraid of anything or anyone." She filled him in on the details of the evening.

"Well, at least you got to feast. We were not so lucky," said Luca ruefully. He saw Elena's face fall and hurriedly continued. "Don't worry. Giorgio says he has some pasta at his house that we can eat."

Luca pointed at a short, stout young man leaning against one of the thick stone walls smoking. "You remember him from school? He works here in the palace now, which is why he was drafted in to help load the trucks. I think I'm going to stay with him tonight. There'll hardly be enough time for your boss to drive both you and me home, and if I do drive with them to Rome tomorrow, I'd rather be here early."

Elena was crestfallen, but the plan made sense. As it was, she would be terribly late getting home. She hoped her parents were already fast asleep and that she could slip into the house without them noticing what time it was. She was a little resentful that as someone who had lived away for a year she was still treated as a child at home, but, unfortunately, she could not see that changing until she got married and had a home of her own. The sooner the better in her opinion.

"The major said he would be back at eight o'clock, so I'm guessing we will be back by then too. Lavagnino mentioned earlier that he wants to be out of here by nine at the latest. Are you still sure you want to do this, Luca? The roads are going to be treacherous if it keeps snowing."

Luca nodded resolutely. "If anything, the weather makes my decision easier. I know how to navigate these roads in this type of weather and where all the potholes are—these Romans won't have a clue. I'm going to suggest I take the lead in the convoy tomorrow, at least for the initial stretch. That way, they can all follow me and hopefully we'll make it without mishap."

Elena looked around the dimly lit room to see if anyone was watching, then hugged Luca tightly. "Just don't try to be a hero, okay?" she whispered in his ear. "I want you back here before Christmas in one piece."

As Elena and Luca prepared to say goodbye to each other for the evening, out in the countryside, Alessandro and Lorenzo were about to arrive at Ca'Boschetto. No lights were visible at the house, which was to be expected given the lateness of the hour. Lorenzo was trying to decide the best way to wake up his father without rousing the entire household. He had remembered his father and uncle having a conversation a couple of months ago about hiding the dynamite in case anyone came to search the farm, but he had no idea where they had ended up moving it. For all he knew, the cache was buried in one of the fields. This suddenly seemed like a foolish idea.

They sat in the truck for a minute or two, wondering whether they should abort the mission. Erivo might not be impressed with the paltry box of bullets, which was all they had to show for their evening so far, but Lorenzo was now second-guessing his previous enthusiasm for a late-night conversation with his father. If the dynamite was indeed buried, it would be almost impossible to dig it up at this hour, with snow already on the hard ground.

Alessandro was annoyed at his friend's hesitation. He was anxious to drive to Urbino, but he did not want to turn up empty-handed either. "Come on, we're here now. Your father might be angry initially, but he always comes around. He'll understand why this is important."

"But it's pitch black out here, freezing cold, and still snowing. If this dynamite isn't in a convenient place, we'll never be able to get to it at this hour."

Alessandro was getting increasingly aggravated. An hour ago, his friend was suggesting they avoid going to Alessandro's farm at all because of the potentially bigger haul here, and now he was hesitating outside his own home. Lorenzo was usually the first to make a move, however ill advised. This was proving to be a wasted evening.

"Let's think logically. Give me a list of the easiest hiding places first. We can start with those without waking anyone up. If we find nothing in the next thirty minutes, then we can decide what to do next."

Lorenzo thought for a moment. The pigsty was his father's favorite place to stash things because most people were averse to the stench. The wooden shed where his father and uncle cured the meat was another good bet—plenty of potential hiding places in there. Mulling it over, he decided it made sense to start in the shed, as it was certainly the cleaner option and his father would be unlikely to hide the dynamite on the ground floor of the house itself.

The two friends reluctantly left the relative warmth of the truck's cabin and slowly made their way around the house to the curing shed. The smell that assailed them as they entered made them realize how hungry they were. Lorenzo's uncle was famous in the neighborhood for the quality of his salami—Alessandro's mouth watered at the thought of it. Would one salami be missed? Pushing the haunches of meat aside, they began searching for a likely hiding place. Lorenzo began tapping some of the barrels used for brining.

"Got it," he said after a few minutes. "This one sounds different."

He prized open the lid. As he raised the lantern, Alessandro caught sight of the sticks of dynamite inside nestled in straw.

"Thank God we didn't have to go looking in the pigsty," said Lorenzo. "Let's take the whole barrel. I'll deal with their wrath the next time I come home."

Struggling a little, they managed to carry the barrel across the farmyard, taking care not to slip on the icy patches that were forming.

Gently, they wedged it in the rear of the truck wrapped in the threadbare blankets they had bought with them in case the truck broke down and they were stranded in the subzero temperatures.

"Let's get out of here. And be careful driving on these roads. Dynamite can be very unstable once it has been stored for a long time. The nitroglycerin tends to leak out. I don't like the idea of crashing into a tree with a potential bomb on board," said Alessandro.

They set off on the road to Urbino, elated that they now had something substantial to bring to the mission. Alessandro was convinced that they had done enough to secure spots on the ambush team and started chatting excitedly about finally taking part in the fighting.

The journey to the city was uneventful, except for the moment when they saw headlights on the road ahead, slowly coming toward them. Alessandro quickly ducked down in the passenger seat and Lorenzo pulled his cap down, hiding his face. As the headlights grew bigger, he was relieved to find that it was a small car. It was impossible to see the occupants, blinded as he was by the lights, but the vehicle kept coming. Within seconds of passing them, its taillights had disappeared into the darkness. *Someone local, and someone not looking for trouble,* thought Lorenzo.

In the car, Pasquale was having almost identical thoughts.

Chapter Thirty

T he abandoned vestry next to the monastery had not seen so much action in years. Over the past hour or so, people had been slinking into the large space, hurrying over to their leader to give him their reports. Guns had been cleaned and ammunition gathered in small piles. A large map was spread out on a table, covered with mysterious markings and notes. Everywhere Lorenzo looked, men were engaged in the tasks needed if this attack was going to be successful.

When Lorenzo and Alessandro had finally arrived, Erivo had been excited by the addition of the dynamite, but, as usual, had maintained his calm demeanor. He had motioned to his second in command, a slim, dour man called Giuseppe Luzzatto known to have been an explosives expert in Mussolini's army before the collapse of the Fascist regime. Giuseppe never spoke much, but it was rumored that his family was of Jewish descent, despite having been ostensibly Catholic for as long as anyone could remember. His grandmother still lived in what had been the Jewish ghetto, in a small house next to the synagogue in Urbino.

Giuseppe never discussed the war or the stories that had started circulating about Jews disappearing from cities all over Italy, but he was known to have deserted from the army even before the armistice had been signed with the Allies. His old friend Erivo had sought him out when the partisan unit was formed. If anybody could work out how best to use the dynamite, it was Giuseppe.

It was now three o'clock in the morning. A few men were slumped against the walls, trying to grab some moments of sleep before the night ended. Lorenzo longed to join them, but he was afraid of being asleep when Erivo made his final decisions on the plan.

As if his leader was reading his mind, Erivo suddenly cleared his throat and asked everyone to gather around the table. Lorenzo nudged Alessandro. "This is it. Finally."

Looking at the expectant faces in front of him, Erivo felt unusually nervous. He prided himself on being a rational man who made logical decisions. Tonight, he felt like he was behaving totally against form. Had they had enough time to plan this properly? Despite additional snippets of information that had come in over the past couple of hours, it did not feel like they knew enough. The one glaring missing piece of the puzzle was the objective of the convoy.

Collecting armaments from the palace tunnels seemed like the obvious goal, but something was bothering him. Why had these trucks come all the way from Rome? Surely other places much closer to the Eternal City were housing German armaments. The fact that German soldiers had been spotted and Major Heinrich was involved certainly lent credence to the theory that this was all in aid of the German war effort. But what if his assumption was wrong? He looked at his unit, this bedraggled collection of proud Italians. He did not want to lose any of them to a mistake.

"So here's the plan, such as it is. A few of us drove out to the station earlier. We scouted the road and found a good location. It's a small, wooded copse on a bend, below the hill where the duke's mausoleum is situated. A good hiding spot, and, more importantly, away from any houses. I don't want any civilians inadvertently dragged into this."

Lorenzo straightened up at the word "civilians." He liked the idea that he was a soldier, albeit a very different kind of soldier.

"Now I want to keep this small, as you know. You've all done sterling work in the past twenty-four hours, but to avoid detection, I think it's best if we keep the core team tight. I am going to only take just over a dozen men with me."

The room groaned. The thirty-five people in the vestry all harbored dreams of being chosen.

Erivo held up his hand to silence them. "You're all capable of doing this, I know. But some will simply be more useful than others given their prior training, or their skill set, or their personality. I'll call out the names. Once you know who is going with me, I want the rest of you to head back to the barn. No ifs or buts, okay? It will be dangerous to be found anywhere near Urbino if we pull this off."

Left unsaid was the risk to the chosen crew. If they all survived the ambush, and if nobody was wounded, it would be difficult enough to disappear in the carnage and escape. If anyone was killed or wounded, it would be a different story. Carrying even one injured man would add to the dangers facing them. Erivo did not want anyone who did not have an essential role in the ambush hanging around the city.

Erivo started to read the names from the piece of paper in his hand. Luzzatto, the explosives expert, was the first name, to nobody's surprise. Erivo stopped the list after eight names.

"This is the main attacking force. Giuseppe and I will plant the explosives. We are going to use a downed tree in the copse that we spotted earlier. We will drag it to the side of the road and hide the explosives inside. The two of us will manage the detonation. Everyone else will have rifles and grenades. We learned earlier that there are seven trucks in this convoy, so we will have one man with a line of sight on each truck."

The men he had selected nodded—everything Erivo had outlined made sense.

He cleared his throat and continued. "In addition, we will take five extra men, all armed. I want to leave one of our trucks one mile up the road closer to the city. I want a driver to wait with the truck—it'll give us a chance to get anyone wounded away from the scene. The rest of the ambush group will make their way back by foot. The other four men will act as front and rear guards, two men further down the road from where the ambush is taking place and the other two just before it. Their role will be to pick off anyone who escapes the main ambush. Bear in mind this will be in daylight. One of the German guards was spouting off in a bar earlier this evening, saying that they were leaving by nine o'clock in the morning. So we have little room for error and we don't want any witnesses to survive."

The last sentence hung in the air like a storm cloud. Lorenzo glanced sideways at Alessandro, whose face was white. Neither of them had ever killed a man. Would this be the day that would change?

"Leonardo Ferrari. Marco Romano. Bella Mazzi." There was a low grumbling in the room. All eyes turned to look at a young woman dressed in army fatigues and standing in the shadows.

"You all know Mazzi is a better shot than almost anyone," said Erivo sharply. "She's going." The young woman stared defiantly at the group, her face grim.

"Lorenzo Rossi. Alessandro Marchetti." Lorenzo nudged Alessandro with his elbow. He felt elated and terrified simultaneously. They were in.

Five minutes later, the plan was finalized. Alessandro was less than pleased to discover that he was the designated driver for the getaway truck, but at least he was part of the team. Lorenzo was given the job of covering the road with Bella Mazzi in case any of the Germans tried to escape back to Urbino. Two more men were told to head south of the ambush location.

"Right. One more task. Esposito, you rode here, yes? I want you to position yourself somewhere near the palace and check out the convoy from afar. You'll need a cover story in case someone gets suspicious. Maybe visit your 'friend' again at the *albergo*."

The men laughed. Carlo's face was bright red.

"When you determine that the convoy is ready to head out, ride to the ambush site as fast as you can to warn us all. One man on a horse will be much faster than a truck convoy, particularly on these snowy roads. That should give us at least twenty minutes' warning. Then you can take one of the small country tracks back, avoiding the main road."

Erivo looked at the assembled group. "Anyone whose name I have not called out can head back to the barn now while it is still dark. The team will head out at five o'clock. The sun rises just after seven, so that will give us time to lay the explosives before it gets light. And I want everyone in position before dawn."

Chapter Thirty-One

I t was still dark when Elena woke. Her room was pitch black. All she could hear was Giulia's gentle breathing on the other side of the mattress. She had hardly slept, her anxiety growing about the inspection by Major Heinrich and the lieutenant in a couple of hours. She slowly pulled back the covers on her side of the bed and put her feet on the tiled floor. The terracotta tiles were exceptionally cold and she shivered as she walked over to the single chair where she had thrown some clothes a few hours ago.

Opening the door gingerly, she made her way to the kitchen, where, to her surprise, she found her mother boiling a kettle on the fire.

Elena was startled, but her mother put her finger to her lips. "Don't wake the others. I heard what time you came home last night. Something is going on. These mysterious comings and goings—it's to do with the art, *vero*? Do you want to tell me what is happening?"

Elena sat at the table and took a bite of one of the pastries her mother had laid out on a plate. "I don't suppose it matters now if I tell you. Yes, we are moving the art to Rome today."

Her mother looked troubled. Elena quickly told her what had transpired over the past few weeks since the evening at Luca's house when she had told them all about the plan. She confessed the dinner the evening before had been arranged for the German officer who had arrived with the convoy from Rome—her mother's face fell further at that point. The only part of the story that seemed to cheer her mother up was the official paperwork originating from the papal office. As a devout Catholic, Elisa would never find fault with anything the Pope did, and this revelation gave the foolish scheme some legitimacy in her eyes.

Elisa had been in awe of her headstrong daughter since Elena was a young child who refused to wear dresses to help her father around the farm and instead had insisted on borrowing shirts and pants from Alessandro. It was frightening to hear that Elena had gotten herself so deeply tangled up in this dangerous scheme, but at the same time, she felt a twinge of pride. This girl was something else: smart, passionate, steadfast in her beliefs. Elisa did not really understand why art was considered so important that people would risk being arrested or worse to hide it from the Germans, but she knew it mattered to Elena.

Elisa walked over to the kitchen table and gave her daughter an urgent hug. "You foolish, crazy child. Where on earth did you come from? I can't help but love your strength of mind and the fact that you always stand up for what you believe in. Don't tell me anymore, but please promise me you will stay safe."

Elena felt a sudden lump in her throat at her mother's words. Her mother had not always been the most outwardly affectionate woman—unrelenting hard work tends to produce hardened souls—but Elena had always known that she was deeply loved. She grabbed her mother's hand and squeezed it. "Thank you for your support. It really means everything. To be clear, I'm not actually going to Rome myself, but Luca—"

At that moment, the door opened and her father walked in, stamping his feet to dislodge the snow on his boots. He was surprised to find Elena sitting at the table. "Good lord, girl, this is an early start for you."

Elena and her mother exchanged a quick glance. She knew better than to spell out what was going on—it would be easier to tell her father once the convoy had left.

"Signor Rotondi is coming to collect me soon—we have a lot of archiving to do and we thought we would make an early start given we might be snowed in again before long. I should be home after lunch though."

Francesco grunted. He went over to grab the kettle from the fireplace to make himself a hot drink, which he promptly poured into his aluminum canteen. He had been buoyed earlier, seeing the empty space on the workbench where the goods had been left for Alessandro. He wasn't going to mention it again because any talk of their son always managed to upset his wife.

"Don't let that man overwork you—you are not being paid much."

Francesco turned to his wife. "The cows are a little restless in the barn. The sooner you and Giulia milk them, the better. I am heading up to the top field—when that lazy son of mine deigns to appear, send him up."

Francesco grabbed a pastry and headed to the door again. Elena breathed a sigh of relief. Andrea was in for a tongue lashing, but at least she had escaped unscathed. She just needed Pasquale to arrive as soon as possible.

Half an hour later, Elena, Pasquale, and Zea arrived at the Ducal Palace. It was still dark, but the sky was beginning to lighten in the east. The snow had stopped and a thin layer covered the piazza. Once inside the palace, the group hurried down the ramp from the Courtyard of Honor to the even chillier *sotterranei*. Lavagnino, Vannutelli, and Renon were already there, together with Luca, Giorgio, and the rest of the crew. There was no sign of the Germans.

Luca looked uncharacteristically pale to Elena, his eyes hollowed out from lack of sleep. She fleetingly wondered whether Luca and Giorgio had indulged in a little alcohol as well as the pasta they had talked about. It would hardly be surprising given the stress they had been under the night before, and what might happen in the next hour or two. She smiled at him and then, in a rush of affection, hurried over and threw her arms around him. She suddenly didn't care what anyone thought. Luca was about to embark on a journey from which he might not return. If the convoy was stopped at a Fascist checkpoint, Mussolini's thugs would take the opportunity to remove Luca and any other young Italian and force them to enlist. An Allied plane might decide that the trucks were a legitimate target and strafe them on the road. At any point on the route, the Germans could decide to search the trucks and discover what was inside the crates and then Luca would be in danger of being arrested or, worse, executed as a warning to others.

Luca ignored the sniggers of the young men around him and held her tightly. He too realized what he was about to do. He stroked her cheek and looked again into her brown eyes.

"I love you," he whispered. "I have no intention of not coming home to marry you."

Elena was about to say something in response when she heard footsteps making their way down to the underground cavern where they were standing. She pulled away from Luca as Major Heinrich and Lieutenant Scheibert appeared.

Lavagnino, who had studiously avoided reacting to the interaction between Elena and Luca, stepped forward. "Good morning, good morning. How is everyone feeling today? What a delightful evening we had, *vero*?"

The major said some words of thanks to Zea for her planning.

Lieutenant Scheibert, clearly the worse for wear, sidled up to Elena. "I know you plied me with liquor last night, young lady. I'm not stupid. The big question is what were you hoping to achieve?"

He stared at her intently. Elena was unable to tell if he had somehow worked out their subterfuge or if he thought she had been trying to seduce him. The latter made her cringe. While she was thinking of how to respond, Lavagnino spoke up again.

"Everything looks ready to go. I have been over the list with the team here. All the works have been accounted for. I think the Vatican will be delighted that their treasures will be safely stored with them, at least for the time being."

The major pulled out his own copy of the orders he had been given the day before. "With all due respect, Signor Lavagnino, I'll be the judge of whether everything is complete."

Lieutenant Scheibert glanced at the major with what looked like an equal measure of fear and loathing. "I think I also need to sign off the paperwork as the official representative of the Kunstschutz."

The major ignored him. He turned to Lavagnino. "Come with me." The major turned sharply and made his way back up the ramp. Everyone followed. Once outside, the major marched over to the truck closest to him and signaled to Giorgio. "You, pull back the tarpaulin." Elena felt nauseous.

Lavagnino did not miss a beat. "As you like, Major."

Lavagnino signaled to Giorgio to do what the major had commanded. As the tarpaulin was pulled aside, several large crates with the words '*Basilico di S.Marco*' scrawled on them in large black lettering were revealed. Vannutelli stepped forward and, with Giorgio's help, the two of them unloaded two of the crates. With a couple of wrenches with a crowbar, they opened the tops to reveal the contents. Major Heinrich peered inside one of them.

"Let's take a look at this cargo," said Lavagnino. He seemed to be examining his list. "Here we have several important treasures from the Basilica in Venice. I know the Pope is particularly interested in ensuring that these find a haven." He looked at the major, who showed no response.

"Some rather stunning silver chalices," Lavagnino continued. "I've been fortunate enough to see them in situ in San Marco." He started reading the names and provenance of the pieces from his list.

"I've seen enough," said the major. "Unload another one."

Vannutelli and Giorgio complied, dragging down the next crate and opening it for inspection.

Lavagnino looked at the label on the crate and pretended to match it to his list. "A rather impressive altarpiece decorated with gilded silver. The archbishop in Venice was very keen to send Rotondi as many pieces as possible."

This charade was repeated a couple of times, until the major held up his hand. "I think that will do. How many crates do we have in total?"

"About one hundred and twenty," said Pasquale, who had been silent until now.

The major ignored him and pulled Lieutenant Scheibert into a corner. They spoke for a few minutes in low voices. Elena strained to hear what they were saying. She did not understand German, but she was hoping she could work out which way this might go by the tone of their voices. The two men walked back toward Pasquale and Lavagnino.

"We don't have all day, so that will have to do," said Major Heinrich, clearly irritated. "I will sign off the paperwork so these trucks can start going. Mind you—" He waved the papers in his hand and flashed his cold smile. "If it is discovered later that you have been less than truthful, remember that I know where Signor Rotondi and his wife, and the delightful Signorina Marchetti, live. I would hate to see them suffer the consequences of any deception. Close up the crates."

Elena did not dare look at Luca. She felt clammy despite the bitterly cold temperature. She wasn't sure how much longer she could keep up the pretense. Her mind raced back to the day on the piazza in Sassocorvaro and the terror on Pietro's small face. She felt bile rising into her mouth.

As the major looked around for a flat surface to sign the papers, the spell they had all been under broke. The crates were closed again and reloaded onto the truck. Renon walked to the large wooden doors that led onto the street and started unbolting them. The drivers from Rome climbed up into their trucks.

Luca smiled at Elena but did not move any closer to her. She blinked, trying to stay calm. Reaching inside her coat and sweater, she pulled out the crucifix she always wore and started rubbing it as if it was a good luck charm. Luca shut his eyes for a few seconds, remembering the nights in the hayloft. He had played with that crucifix as it lay between her breasts. Opening his eyes, he focused on her intently, hoping she was reading his mind. *I am coming back to you, Elena. I am coming back.*

Elena looked at Luca and, with her eyes locked on his, started fiddling with the clasp at the back of her neck. She held out the chain and walked toward him. She secured it around his neck and tucked the crucifix inside his woolen sweater. "This will keep you safe," she said quietly. Luca put his hand where the crucifix now lay. He did not want to stop looking at her.

The doors to the outside were now wide open, and through them, they had a good view of the leaden skies and slick street. Luca broke his gaze and turned to Lavagnino and Pasquale. "I know these roads well. I was hoping you would let my truck lead the convoy, at least until we leave the outskirts of the city. We will encounter some rough spots, especially for the first ten miles."

"Local knowledge is worth its weight in gold, my friend," said Lavagnino. "Lead on! My car's at the *albergo*. Why don't you lead the trucks out of here, then wait for us down below at Piazza Mercatale outside the walls? We will join you as soon as we can."

Too quickly for Elena, the group made its preparations to leave. The local men who were staying in Urbino were shaking hands with those who had come with the convoy from Rome and promising to share a bottle of wine somewhere in the future. Lieutenant Scheibert had signed two copies of the authorization form and handed one of them to Pasquale to keep as an official receipt of the transfer of goods. The major looked pensive for a moment.

"I am going to accompany you for the first few miles to ensure that you at least depart the city safely. My car is parked outside the palace. I will lead the convoy for the first few miles and then peel off once we reach the outskirts of Fermignano. After that, you're on your own."

Lavagnino had such a straight face that Elena found it impossible to tell if he was unhappy with this pronouncement or not. The official merely made a short bow as if in assent.

Pasquale gave Lavagnino a bear hug and whispered in his ear. "If it hadn't been you, I would not have given any of these pieces to someone who just turned up with a German officer in tow." His eyes twinkled.

Lavagnino laughed. "Thank you for everything, my dear friend. I'll send you a telegram once we get to Rome. And I will return in January for the next load, never fear."

Five minutes later, as Lavagnino, Vannutelli, and Lieutenant Scheibert walked across the piazza to their cars parked at the *albergo*, the city was beginning to stir. The café was already open and packed with regulars ordering drinks. A couple of housewives were slowly making their way toward the baker's shop. A gaggle of children ran past the three men, hollering and throwing the occasional snowball at one another. With all the activity, nobody paid any attention to the young man standing beside his horse. Carlo tightened the saddle straps before mounting the animal confidently. The man turned the horse's head and trotted away down the street.

Chapter Thirty-Two

Alessandro's heart was beating so fast that he swore he could hear it. He had parked the truck between two oak trees about fifty feet from the main road outside the city walls. A forge was situated on the side of the road nearby, so Alessandro made sure that he was parked far enough from it to avoid any nosy or suspicious workers or customers. From his vantage point, he would notice anything on the road for several hundred feet in either direction. He knew Lorenzo and Bella were hidden behind a hedgerow further down the road from where he was. They had all been in place for a couple of hours now, and Alessandro was grateful that he at least had the advantage of being in the cab of the truck, rather than facing the elements outside. Every time he spotted movement he felt a jolt of adrenaline, only to calm down again once he worked out what it was. His feet were frozen, and he kept bear hugging himself in an attempt to keep the rest of his body from feeling the same way.

Suddenly, Alessandro saw a horse galloping toward him, kicking up the thin layer of snow on the road. He sat up straight and strained his eyes to see if he recognized the rider. As the man got closer, Alessandro made out the familiar cap with ginger hair sticking out of the sides. *My God, this is it*, he thought. *That is Carlo. The convoy must be leaving.*

Alessandro didn't dare signal to his comrade, but instead watched the horse and rider pass the spot where the truck was parked and then gallop further down the road toward Erivo and the ambush team. How long before the first truck would reach this point? Five minutes? Ten minutes? Alessandro knew he had no role to play until after the ambush, but the thought of the approaching convoy filled him with trepidation. He exited the truck to stretch his legs and relieve himself against one of the trees. Mission accomplished, he took out a cigarette with trembling hands and lit it, desperate for a moment of normalcy. He envied the sweaty men inside the forge, hammering away at iron bars and bending them into shapes. As he stood thinking how nice it would feel to be closer to the flames, Alessandro spotted a cart drawn by two oxen being driven at a slow pace by a couple of farmhands. It was moving uphill in the direction of Urbino, and it looked as if the bed of the cart was full of farming implements. The cart was very old, weathered, and misshapen, and the two men were struggling to keep it straight on the slippery surface.

As Alessandro watched the spectacle in front of him, he was filled with an eerie sense of foreboding. He glanced up the road toward the city and, with a jolt, saw two cars appear in his line of vision, followed immediately by a large truck. He dropped his cigarette, crushed it with his heel, and moved to open the door of his truck. At the same moment, the oxen suddenly veered left across the road, heading for the track that led to the forge. The farmhands were wrestling with the rudimentary reins, attempting to turn the cart as well. As the cart moved across the road, one of the farmhands yanked the reins hard. As if in slow motion, the cart tipped to one side, sending the men and everything else tumbling to the ground. The resulting crash turned heads in the forge. A few men rushed outside to find out what had transpired.

Alessandro panicked. The road was now blocked north of where he was parked. One of the farmhands did not appear to be badly injured, judging by the alacrity with which he jumped up, but his companion was lying on the ground, clutching his leg and screaming for help. Bits of metal and wood were strewn everywhere. As the men from the forge reached the scene, it was obvious to Alessandro that they all knew each other. It appeared the farmhands had been about to deliver broken farm implements and wheels to the forge for mending. Would it seem strange if he did not offer help? His mind racing, he watched the convoy get closer to the scene of chaos. Surely the driver of the first vehicle would see what had happened and stop. Where were the German soldiers?

Alessandro reached into his truck and grabbed his rifle. A gun was not an unusual accessory to be carrying, at least not in the countryside, and he wanted to be prepared. Should he stay put and wait for the small crowd of people to remove the injured man and clear the road? He figured it would likely take at least fifteen or twenty minutes before the road was passable again. Alessandro did not like the idea of sitting there in his truck in full view of the convoy. Should he abandon his post and drive further down the road to warn the men at the ambush site?

The convoy had now reached the scene of the accident and stopped. The injured man was being lifted as gently as possible onto what looked like a wooden door. More men from the forge were starting to haul debris from the road. For a minute or two, there was no sign of any movement from the convoy. Suddenly, the passenger side door of the first car opened. Alessandro watched as a German officer in full uniform got out. He surveyed the scene in front of him, then turned to walk back to the other vehicles, no doubt to inform them of what had happened.

Alessandro was paralyzed with indecision. Would it matter if the convoy got to the ambush site late? Surely Erivo would be patient enough to wait for them to appear. Or would they get suspicious when the trucks did not arrive when expected and send one of the men back up the hill to see what was happening? He was frustrated that he had no way of sending them a message.

Now the officer had reappeared, together with several other people from the convoy, including other men in uniform. The officer started shouting orders—Alessandro didn't understand German, but the instructions were clear. The men from the convoy started lifting and carrying the broken wheels and fallen implements to the side of the road.

As one group started to maneuver the damaged cart, Alessandro was drawn to the figure of one tall, slim man with dark curls sticking out from his hat. Something about him looked familiar to Alessandro. He watched as the man put his shoulder to the wooden cart to level it again.

As the man lifted his face, Alessandro stared at him in horror. *Mio Dio, it's Luca,* he realized with a start. *I would know his face anywhere.* What the hell was Luca doing with the convoy? And more to the point, working with Germans? None of it made sense. Alessandro pulled his cap down further to hide his face should Luca look in his direction. *Think, man, think. What is the explanation here?* There was no way his best friend was helping the Germans, especially if Erivo was right and the trucks contained weapons and ammunition. So what was in the trucks?

As he wrestled with this conundrum, Alessandro could see that the addition of so many men had greatly speeded up the clearance of the road. He had very little time left before the road was clear again and the convoy would continue on its way. And Luca was heading to an almost certain death if he was in one of those trucks.

Alessandro took a deep breath. He knew what he had to do. He believed in the partisan cause and he wanted to punish the Germans for what had happened to Pietro. But he had known Luca since they were small boys. He was not going to stand by and watch him being blown into small pieces. He could not let that happen.

Alessandro started walking south down the road as fast as he could without rousing any suspicions. He figured as soon as he turned the corner he would start running. The ambush site was less than a mile down the road. He would find Lorenzo and Bella along the way. Lorenzo was fitter than he was and could run faster. Surely they could make it to Erivo before the convoy would. Something was terribly wrong. Alessandro did not want to lose his best friend if they had made a mistake.

It was hard to walk at a steady pace when his instinct was screaming at him to run as fast as he could. As soon as he reached the bend and had gone another few yards, Alessandro started sprinting. Carrying the rifle and wearing a heavy coat slowed him down, and he almost fell a few times on patches of snow and ice. But within minutes, he had reached the spot where he knew Lorenzo and Bella were hiding. Before he even opened his mouth to call out, he saw the two of them hesitantly pushing through the hedgerow.

"What the hell, Sandro? I almost shot at you. What are you doing?"

Panting, Alessandro bent over to regain his breath. The air was so still that he could hear, albeit faintly, the shouts of the men behind him as they tried to clear the road. Sputtering, in a panic, he quickly told them what he had seen: the trucks, the German officer, Luca.

"This ambush cannot go ahead. There must have been a mistake. I don't know what's going on, but I don't think it is armaments."

He motioned to the others. "Come on, we need to run down to Erivo. If they set off the dynamite, Luca's a dead man."

Lorenzo stood there as if in a reverie. He was frowning and shaking his head.

"Lorenzo, we've got to go. Now."

Lorenzo's face lit up. "I know what is in the trucks. It's the art, remember? It must be Elena's art."

Bella and Alessandro looked at him as if he was insane. *What is he talking about?* thought Alessandro. A tiny spark of memory gnawed at him of his sister talking about the Rocca and the hidden paintings and her request for a truck. Lorenzo was right. It was Rotondi's convoy, not armaments.

"That's it. They're transporting the paintings. So we have to stop Erivo and the others from blowing the convoy to pieces along with your brother. Come on!"

Without waiting for an answer, Alessandro started running down the road again. Bella looked at Lorenzo, her face showing her bewilderment—but seemingly persuaded by Alessandro's passion that something must be amiss, she started running after him.

Lorenzo did not move. He was formulating a plan in his head. There was no need for all three of them to warn the others. He needed to slow the convoy down long enough to allow time for the rest of them to abort the mission and get away to safety.

Lorenzo scrambled back up the bank to the hedgerow he and Bella had been using as cover. His eyes focused on the road. He no longer felt afraid of what he was about to do. He had waited for weeks to see some action and he did not want to be denied his moment now. He thought of the comrades they had lost in that first firefight, the night of the church dance. He remembered all the nights in the barn, listening to the wounded crying out for their mothers until they fell silent. He recalled learning of the brutal execution of young Pietro, a boy he had known since birth. Pietro's proud father had given anyone who came to the café the week he was born a free glass of grappa. Even Luca and Lorenzo, nine and eight years old at the time, had been allowed a small sip each to celebrate the birth of this long-awaited baby. And now that child was dead and buried, yet another victim of this cruel regime. Lorenzo gripped his rifle. He knew exactly what he was going to do.

Chapter Thirty-Three

The minutes passed. Lorenzo waited. At one point, another ox-drawn cart came along the road in the direction of Urbino. Lorenzo watched it make its laborious way up the hill. There was still no movement in the other direction. He gripped his rifle and strained to hear any noise. There it was, the low rumbling of vehicles on the move. Lorenzo went over the information Alessandro had shared about the convoy. There was a car in front, and that car contained the German officer. Then there was a second car. And behind that car would be the first truck, driven by Luca. He needed to be very careful in what he was about to do.

Lorenzo stared at the bend in the road, willing the convoy to appear. All at once, he spotted a car inching its way around the corner. The driver was obviously being very careful, no doubt on account of the snow on the ground. He was probably also trying to avoid the potholes and the patches of ice. Another car drove immediately behind followed by a large truck. Lorenzo took a deep breath to calm himself. The vehicles were too far away to see the occupants clearly, but Lorenzo assumed nothing had changed since the unexpected delay.

He bided his time. One hundred yards. Seventy-five yards. Lorenzo slowly stood up and raised his rifle to his shoulder. *Focus, focus,* he said to himself. He channeled everything his father had ever taught him about hunting wild boar. When the car was about twenty-five yards away, Lorenzo pushed his way through the hedgerow, stepped onto the road, and stood firm. He fired twice at the passenger side of the car, shattering the windscreen. Four shots left. The car screeched to a halt. The driver's side door opened and the driver, a young German soldier, came out firing. Lorenzo felt a bullet pierce his thigh. He fired back at the man, spinning him around as the bullet caught his shoulder.

Lorenzo walked toward the car in a daze. His ears were ringing and he was oblivious to the shouts and movements coming from the rest of the convoy. Suddenly, out of the corner of his eye, he caught sight of his brother, who had jumped down from the first truck. Lorenzo focused all his attention on the car. The passenger door opened. Major Heinrich stumbled out, his face bleeding. Lorenzo raised his rifle at the same moment the major pulled out his handgun. The shots whistled past each other. For a second, Lorenzo felt a burning sensation in his eye, then oblivion.

Luca stood there paralyzed with shock. He found it difficult to comprehend what he had witnessed. The drivers and passengers of the other vehicles were running past him. The three German soldiers from Rome, who had been in the last two trucks, hurried to the car. One of them knelt next to the major, feeling for a pulse. He looked up at his comrades, shaking his head. The soldier who had been driving was injured but still alive. Luca could see Lavagnino bending down to examine the gunman lying on the ground.

Lavagnino looked up, spotted Luca, and signaled him to come and help. Luca started walking toward him, skirting around the body of the major. As he got closer to Lavagnino, he could see that where an eye should be, the gunman had a large hole in his head. That face, that hair coated with blood . . .

Luca fell on the body, throwing his arms around his brother. "Lorenzo, Lorenzo . . . what have you done?"

A wave of grief poured over Luca. His insides felt shredded. He pulled his brother toward him, rocking him like a small child. His fool-hardy brother, who was never content to sit still. His little brother, who had to be rescued constantly from some trouble he had gotten himself into. Luca could hear an unearthly keening coming out of his mouth. He hugged his brother even closer, tears pouring down his face. Why had Lorenzo done it? What had he been thinking? This was the action of a person not in his right mind.

Lavagnino, thrown by Luca's intense grief, stepped back to give him some space. He walked over to Lieutenant Scheibert, who was gesticulating wildly to Vannutelli.

"What the hell was that, eh?" shouted the lieutenant. "Who was the lunatic with the gun? Now we have a dead officer to deal with, goddammit."

Lavagnino thought quickly. The last thing they needed was for the convoy to be derailed. "It looks like a lone wolf, Lieutenant. There's nobody else here. It is possible the man had a grudge against Major Heinrich. From what I could see, he was pretty set on his intended target."

The lieutenant pondered this for a moment. "I am sure you are right, Lavagnino. From my brief encounters with the major, I'm sure many people had it in for him, Germans as well as Italians. Major Heinrich was the kind of man who attracts enemies." He smiled at Lavagnino. "I am sure the gunman was targeting him rather than the convoy."

The lieutenant looked intently at Lavagnino, as if daring him to disagree. He pointed at the soldiers who had accompanied him from Rome. "I will order one of them back to the forge we passed back there. The soldier can take the major's car—he won't be needing it again—and this wounded man. He needs to get to a hospital. They'll have to make the best of it with the broken windscreen. And then someone at the forge can get down here with a cart to take these two bodies back to the city. If anyone questions it later, I'll say that it is a direct order from me."

Lavagnino and Vannutelli exchanged glances. This was the most assertive they had ever seen the lieutenant. He was obviously not going to be shedding any tears over the death of the major.

Lavagnino walked back to where Luca was still kneeling on the road, holding his brother. He knelt next to the shattered young man. "I am guessing you know this person, *vero*? Who is he?"

Luca looked up, distraught. "It is my brother, Signore. My brother Lorenzo. I don't know what to do."

Lavagnino put his hand on Luca's shoulder. He did not know the young man, but from what he had witnessed the past twenty-four hours, he did know that his friend Pasquale trusted him and that young Elena, his assistant, loved him.

He crouched closer. "The lieutenant has sent for help from the forge," he said in a low voice. "You need to decide whether you want to take your brother back with them or continue to Rome with us. I will understand completely if you decide to abandon the journey."

Luca took a deep breath. His mind was in turmoil. He couldn't imagine letting strangers tell his parents what had transpired. What would his father tell him to do if he was here now? What would Elena say? This suddenly seemed like the biggest decision he would ever make.

Lavagnino stood up. "You have a few minutes to decide. Take a few deep breaths—that might calm your thoughts."

A loud shout from the lieutenant made Luca look up. It was directed at two people walking up the road toward them. As they got closer, Luca recognized one of them as Alessandro. He felt like he had woken up in a nightmare where none of the sequence of events made any sense. What was Alessandro doing here, on this road? Had he been with Lorenzo? What was happening right now? Some sense of self-preservation kept him silent—something told him not to acknowledge his friend in any way in front of the lieutenant. The lieutenant raised his hand and told the strangers not to approach any closer.

"We heard shooting," Alessandro called out. "We live further down the road." He signaled vaguely with his arm. "We were on our way to the forge."

The lieutenant looked suspicious, but Lavagnino stepped in. "We could do with some help. We have two dead bodies here." He pointed at the major, now laid out on the tarmac.

Alessandro stood there impassively, not looking in Luca's direction. At that minute, the major's car was heard returning from the forge. The lieutenant turned away to go and brief the new arrivals. Alessandro immediately hurried to where Luca was still kneeling and squatted down next to him. Luca could see tears in his friend's eyes.

"Why are you here?" asked Luca, his face red with anger and grief. "My brother just got himself killed in some kind of suicide mission. Was this a partisan attack on the convoy? We're carrying paintings and music folios—what were you thinking?"

"I cannot explain now," whispered Alessandro urgently, "but Lorenzo did this part on his own. We tried to abort the mission once we realized you were involved. I don't know what possessed him to go rogue."

Alessandro looked around quickly to make sure the lieutenant was still talking. "We heard the shots. Erivo, our leader, sent me and Bella back to see what was happening. I have a truck up there by the forge that I need to retrieve."

The fog that had enveloped Luca since the shooting suddenly lifted. Alessandro was there, the one man he trusted to take his brother home. "You take Lorenzo back. You need to tell my parents what happened. I'm going to Rome and will be back tomorrow. Then I will mourn my brother."

Alessandro looked intently at Luca. He tried to say something but swallowed instead.

"I am a man of my word, Alessandro. I promised Elena that I would take the art to Rome, and I'm going to keep that promise. Lorenzo will still be dead tomorrow."

Without saying anything else, Luca and Alessandro picked up Lorenzo's body between them and carried him toward the lieutenant.

"Lieutenant, this man is my brother," said Luca. Lieutenant Scheibert stared at the young Italian. "All I know is that he had some kind of issue with the major—I have no idea of the details. We weren't close." Luca hated saying this, but he knew it was important to down-play what had just happened.

"This man here," he said, nodding at Alessandro, "knows my family. He has offered to take the body there so our parents can bury him. His truck is at the forge."

There was silence for a minute or so. Luca could see the lieutenant working out what to do next. This was war—people died violent deaths every day. This would be just another incident that would be forgotten in a few days. No need for the lieutenant to make it a bigger deal than it was.

The lieutenant looked at Alessandro. "That is very helpful, thank you. It will save me from having to organize something." He glared at Luca. "Once you have helped carry your brother to this man's truck, I will need some details from you for my report. Then we need to get moving again. That is my priority right now."

Luca nodded. Alessandro and Bella helped him carry Lorenzo's body up the road toward the truck. It felt like a macabre funeral proces-sion—Luca never imagined that this would be how he would say goodbye to his brother. The rest of the convoy removed their hats and silently watched them go.

At the truck, with Lorenzo gently wrapped in a blanket, Alessandro hugged his friend hard. "I'm so terribly sorry, Luca. It wasn't meant to be like this. I'll explain everything when you return."

Luca nodded. "Elena is with Rotondi at the Ducal Palace. Can you make sure she is told? News travels so fast these days—it will be all over Urbino within the hour. I need her to know I'm alive."

Alessandro agreed. "I will drop Bella at the city gate so she can deliver the message before I go to your house. We are then going to lay low for a few days until this blows over. I will come and find you when you return from Rome, I promise."

Luca stood for a minute or two as the truck drove away. He sent a silent prayer with it that his parents would understand why he was not the one bringing their dead son home.

Chapter Thirty-Four

Elena and Pasquale were seated in the café opposite the palace when Renon appeared, looking flustered. He spotted the two of them and hurried over to their table. "I need you back at the office. It is quite urgent, I'm afraid."

The three of them left the warmth of the café and started to walk across the windy piazza.

"Someone's looking for Elena. She said someone called Alessandro sent her. Judging by the state of her clothes and the smell, I would say she's been sleeping rough for a while. I'm guessing—" Renon left the sentence unfinished.

The young woman jumped up when Pasquale opened the door to his office. "I'm sorry for this intrusion, sir. There's been an incident."

The slight woman stood, fidgeting with her cap. Elena did not recognize her. She stepped forward, holding out her hand. "I hear you're looking for me. I'm Alessandro's sister Elena. Has something happened to him?"

"No, not Alessandro. Lorenzo, his friend. Do you know him?"

Elena nodded, staring at her. The young woman had a pained expression. "I don't know how to say this nicely, but I'm sorry to tell you that he's been killed."

The woman started to cry. Pasquale pulled out a chair and motioned to her to sit.

Elena felt numb. She knelt down next to the young woman and took her hand. "Can you tell us what happened? I'm sorry, I don't know your name."

"Bella Mazzi." Bella looked up at Elena, a nervous expression on her face. Elena realized what she was thinking, and signaled to Pasquale and Renon to leave the room.

"It's okay. You're safe here. I know my brother is with the partisans. So you were with Lorenzo and Alessandro—"

Bella slowly told her everything that had happened on the road. She explained that she still didn't understand most of it herself, but she dutifully delivered the message that Luca was safe and that Alessandro was going to take Lorenzo's body home.

Bella stood up, wiping her eyes with her sleeve. "I have to go. I can't risk being caught here." She looked at Elena. "I'm sorry for the death of your friend. Lorenzo was a brave man. And one less Nazi in the world is a good thing, as far as I'm concerned." She gave a stiff bow and left the room.

"Are you feeling alright, Elena?" asked Pasquale, hurrying in. Elena quickly told the two men what Bella had shared. "Lorenzo is Luca's brother," she said quietly.

"Good lord," said Renon. "I'm so sorry, Elena. I had no idea. Why would Luca insist on continuing with the convoy in that case?"

"Luca is a man of his word, Signor Renon. If he said he was driving the truck to Rome, then that is what he was going to do."

Elena was very shaken by the news but determined not to show it. Pasquale put a firm hand on her shoulder. "Luca Rossi is a good man, Elena, as is his father. If Lorenzo was anything like the two of them, then we have lost someone very special. I'm only sorry that I never got a chance to meet him. Do you want me to drive you home? Or to Ca'Boschetto?"

"I should probably let my parents know what has happened. My father and Paolo Rossi are best friends. I know he'll want to visit the family."

"Of course. Give me five minutes to talk to Renon and then we can leave. It has been a hard twenty-four hours for everyone."

Elena excused herself to go to the bathroom.

Pasquale looked at Renon, shaking his head. "These young men—almost children, really—being put in such terrible situations. How many more deaths can we take? What a tragedy! Why do you think Scheibert played this incident down?"

"If you think about it, this is the best thing that could have happened for the lieutenant. He rids himself of the major, who might have made an official complaint about his drunken behavior at your dinner. And he is now in charge of the convoy. In fact, I think he will be determined to ensure that the convoy makes its way safely to Rome without any further disturbances. So there is less chance that he will let anyone search the trucks or hold them up in any way. I hate to say it, but this event probably made us all safer."

Pasquale looked thoughtful, stroking his mustache. "Yes, I think you have a point. If the snow holds off, they should reach Rome later today. Lavagnino has promised to send me a telegram when they arrive. We will have to wait."

Elena returned to the office with her coat in hand. Pasquale grabbed his coat and hat from the coat stand. "I'll see you tomorrow morning, Renon. Let's hope we hear good news by then."

Luca sat at the table, morosely eating a plate of *pasta alla matriciana*. Lavagnino's wife fussed around him, constantly asking if he wanted more bread, or extra cheese, or a glass of wine. Luca kept reminding himself to say "please" and "thank you," but his mind was in turmoil. All day in the truck, he kept having flashbacks to the moment on the road when he saw his brother fall. He was exhausted yet scared to close his eyes, fearful of the nightmares sure to come.

As soon as the major's body had been driven away, Lieutenant

Scheibert had insisted on a swift departure. He had grilled Luca for a few minutes and written some notes, but other than that perfunctory investigation, he had subsequently acted as if nothing untoward had occurred. The journey had been largely uneventful since. After all the weeks of worrying about some kind of calamity occurring, it turned out that Lorenzo's ambush had been the sole cause of any delay. They had been stopped once at an Italian checkpoint, but Lieutenant Scheibert's overbearing manner and the official paperwork from the Vatican had the intended effect and the convoy had been waved through by the bored guards. Luca was nervous as they drew close to the Vatican, wondering whether he would be arrested and interrogated by Germans as soon as they arrived. He was sure that the lieutenant would tell somebody about the ambush and the role his brother had played in it. But they had been greeted with relief by Vatican officials and Lieutenant Scheibert did not mention the major's death to anyone.

Lavagnino sidled up to Luca as the final inventory was being made. "Rossi, my wife will never forgive me if I don't offer you dinner and a bed for the night."

Luca thanked him profusely. He had imagined spending the night in his truck somewhere on Vatican grounds.

Lavagnino brushed the thanks aside. "It is the least I can do. And I don't think there is going to be an official investigation, in case you were concerned. This whole situation has worked out rather well for the lieutenant, if you ask me. Let me organize for a telegram to be sent to Rotondi telling him that the convoy got here safely, and then I'll take you home with me."

An hour later, the two men were devouring pasta, hungry after the stresses of the day. Luca wasn't sure he would be able to eat anything, but he realized that he should, as he was uncertain as to what lay ahead of him on the return journey. Lavagnino suggested that he avoid the main roads and return home via a longer route.

"I can write a letter saying that you are on Vatican business and put an official stamp on it, but it might not be of any use if the Italians stop you. I think you'll be safer going over the mountains from Tuscany. The roads are steep with perilous curves, not easy to navigate in the winter, but I think you have less chance of running into a patrol. Also, your truck is empty now, so if anyone does search it, there is nothing to implicate you."

Luca nodded. He had never left the region of Le Marche before and had no knowledge of the terrain. But he trusted this kind man and felt confident that he would make it home. What he would find there was another matter.

"Let me draw the route on a map for you. I have an old one somewhere. The government has removed some of the road signs to confuse invaders. Just be aware that some of the roads might be impassable—there are bomb craters and checkpoints everywhere, so be prepared to adjust."

Lavagnino's wife cleared the table and the two men pored over the map.

As Lavagnino carefully marked the route, he said casually, "Do you want to talk about it? Your brother, I mean."

Luca did not look at him. He swallowed hard. "I'm not sure what to say. He was my younger brother. We did not always see eye to eye, but I loved him."

Lavagnino put an arm around the young man.

Luca wanted to rest his head on Lavagnino's shoulder. Instead, he kept talking. "We saw things differently, I guess. He wanted to fight the Germans—I thought it was my duty to help my family work the farm. I knew he could be killed, but I never imagined I would watch it happen."

Luca looked at Lavagnino. "The partisans were going to attack the convoy. That's what Alessandro said. They thought it was something else. They only aborted the mission because Alessandro spotted me at the forge when the accident happened. I still don't understand why Lorenzo killed the major. They weren't supposed to be going ahead with the ambush."

Luca's voice started breaking. "Lorenzo would have been safe. He never thinks things through. I had to rescue him from scrapes many times when we were boys. Why couldn't I save him this time?" Luca's breath was ragged. He curled his fists into tight balls and shrugged away Lavagnino's arm.

Lavagnino glanced at his wife, who was watching the young man's distress with a pained expression. She pulled out the chair on the other side of Luca and sat down. Wordlessly, she handed him a handkerchief. "God had other plans, my dear. Each of you had your own path to follow. This war has taken far too many good people. Come on, I have made you up a bed. You must try to get some rest. Your mother will be waiting for you to return, and that is what you need to focus on for now."

Luca blew his nose and smiled gratefully at the woman. He thought of Elena, his sweet Elena. He had promised her that he would help deliver the art, and he had done so. Now he had to fulfill his second promise to her and get home safely.

Chapter Thirty-Five

Christmas Eve dawned bright and sunny. Elena watched Giulia open the bedroom shutters to let in the sunlight before hurrying to get dressed. The air in the room was frigid and Elena could picture the frost lying on the ground outside. She snuggled further under the quilt. There didn't seem much point in getting up. Today was traditionally a day of fasting before the evening celebration of *Vigilia di Natale*, although Elena knew the meal would be meager, and there was little cause for celebration.

Elena closed her eyes and thought about the events of the past few days. She had been shattered by the news of Lorenzo's death and was grieving for the young man she had known her whole life. He had instigated many of the memorable adventures of her youth. His sunny disposition had always lit up every room he was in. Elena smiled sadly when she thought of all the times Sister Caterina had shouted exasperatedly at him as he played the clown at school yet again. It had been devastating to witness how broken Antonella was when they had visited the Rossi house on the night of the shooting. The usually voluble woman had sat in silence, surrounded by her extended family, all with grief-stricken faces. The only sound in the room had been that of young Marco occasionally sobbing in his father's arms.

Elena wanted to join him with her own tears but had held back, not wanting any attention to fall on her. She felt she was to blame for everything. She did not know the facts, but it appeared that the shooting had to do with the convoy. If she had not helped Pasquale, maybe none of this would have happened. Luca would not have been involved at all and he would not have had to witness his own brother being killed. She felt nauseous thinking about it.

The day dragged on. Elena and Giulia helped their mother in the kitchen, preparing food for the next day's Christmas feast. Elisa was making the little *pasta in brodo* for the traditional first course and at the same time directing her daughters to cut up various root vegetables that would be cooked with the main dish. The feast would be small this year compared with the years gone by, but then nobody was in the mood to celebrate. Lorenzo's death hung in the air like a suffocating fog. As in previous years, they had been invited to Ca'Boschetto later in the evening to share in their Christmas Eve meal of *aringhe sotto sale*, or salted herring, but no one knew what the atmosphere would be like when they got there. On the night of the shooting, Paolo had been adamant that the Christmas festivities would continue as planned despite his son's death, and Antonella had not spoken up in disagreement.

Elena was most concerned about Luca. She knew from Pasquale that the convoy had arrived safely at the Vatican and she could only assume that Luca was on his way back. But nobody had heard from him. Pasquale thought he would be taking the back roads to avoid attention and it would take him longer to return. But the absence of a message meant Elena was imagining the worst. She was also worried that Luca would think she was ultimately responsible for his brother's death. Elena already felt guilty, so she could hardly blame him. She sat at the table, half-heartedly peeling carrots, praying Luca would make it back before the dinner that evening.

Across the kitchen, her mother finished making the pasta. Elisa washed her hands at the sink and dried them on a cloth. She came over to where Elena was sitting at the kitchen table and put her arms around her daughter from behind. Elena looked up in surprise.

"My darling, I know this is hard for you. It is hard for everyone. We all loved that boy."

She pulled Elena around to look at her. Elena saw the concern in her mother's eyes. "Lorenzo and Alessandro joined the partisans of their own accord. Nobody made the decision for them. They didn't want to be conscripts in Mussolini's army and they wanted to fight for something they believed in. We should all support them."

Elena felt her tears starting again. Somehow her mother being kind was harder to bear than the heavy silence that had prevailed all day.

Her mother put both hands on Elena's cheeks. "I can see it in your eyes. You think you deserve some of the blame for this tragedy. You think working with Signor Rotondi started this chain of events. It didn't. We don't know the whole story yet, but Lorenzo decided to make his stand on that road, and that was his choice. You too were doing something you believed in. And another thing—"

Elisa paused, as if trying to find the right words. "I probably shouldn't say this, but we're all much safer now that Major Heinrich is dead."

Elena and Giulia stared at their mother. She was a staunch Catholic who believed that all life was sacred. Their mother hated it when their father insisted on drowning kittens that he didn't want around. She even prayed before they slaughtered animals on the farm.

"You told me yourself what the major did to Pietro. Do you think his mother and father are mourning the death of such a man? I doubt it very much. Tonight, they'll be drinking a toast to Lorenzo and singing his praises as an Italian hero. As indeed he is."

Elisa stepped back from the table and looked at her two daughters. "We will go to Ca'Boschetto tonight to support the Rossi family and to celebrate Lorenzo's life. I don't want to talk about the Germans or the convoy or any other distraction. And I don't want you looking like a beaten dog all night, Elena. I want Antonella and Paolo surrounded by our love. That's all."

With her mother's exhortation ringing in her ears, Elena forced herself to have a neutral expression as they arrived at the Rossi home that evening, carrying dishes to add to the meal. It was hard to watch Antonella struggling to contain her grief as she stood at the head of the

Saving Madonna

table, pointing out where everyone should sit. Elena felt even worse than she had earlier in the day.

The meal itself was an ordeal. There was desultory conversation on uncontroversial topics. Giulia tried to engage Giovanna on the subject of ribbons while Andrea attempted to do a couple of his card tricks for Marco and Gianni, who were usually a rapt audience. Nothing lifted the spirits of the assembled group.

Once the main course had been consumed, Aunt Maria carried the large panettone cake to the table. Paolo jumped up and grabbed a bottle of *vin santo*. Slices of cake and small glasses of the *vin santo* made their way around the table. When everyone had been served, Paolo cleared his throat.

"My dear family and closest friends. This is one of the holiest day of the year, and it is only right that we are together tonight to celebrate it."

He looked around the room. "A few days ago, my son Lorenzo was taken from me. From all of us. And the void will never be filled. We will be mourning his loss for a very long time, indeed, forever. That is as it should be."

A few muffled sobs were heard. Elena started breathing heavily.

"But Lorenzo was the very best example of pure joy," continued Paolo. "He delighted in everything: the sun on his face, a newborn lamb in the flock, a swim in the river, climbing a tree."

Around the table, a few people smiled.

"He was just a happy person. He loved life and made sure to get as much out of it as he could. He was troublesome at times, oh yes. He felt my belt on more than one occasion. But he made every day better." Paolo choked up and closed his eyes for a minute.

Seated on the chair next to him, Antonella started crying softly. Paolo put a hand on her shoulder, as if to steady himself as well as to offer comfort.

"Lorenzo made his own decisions these past few months. I didn't always agree with him, but I was proud of him for doing what he thought was right. And when he stood on that road, he was choosing how he would die. I won't say I understand what he did, but I must respect it. As should you all."

Elena felt her face burning. She couldn't look at him.

Paolo turned to his wife, who was still quietly sobbing. "Antonella, nothing I can say will assuage your grief. I know that. But we need to come together as a family and decide how we move on. And being angry with Luca is not going to make things any better."

Elena looked up. This was not what she had been expecting.

Antonella pushed her chair away from the table and stood up. She was silent for a full minute, then gave a tortured sigh. "Why did he not bring his brother home? Did he care so little, for him, for me? Was the art so important that it took precedence over his own kin?"

Her face was a picture of rage and grief and hurt. She turned to Elena. "Elena, I've loved you as a daughter, you know that. I was in the bedroom the day you were born. So it is hard for me to say this, but I think you bear some of the blame. You put big ideas into Luca's head. He was content being a farmer until you came back from Milan. He's changed. I see how he looks at you. You persuaded him to join you in this ridiculous project of yours."

Antonella raised her eyes to look at the beams over her head. She cried out as if summoning the gods. "Where is my eldest son? Why isn't he here, where he is supposed to be?"

Francesco and Paolo both started talking loudly, Francesco defending his daughter and Paolo trying to comfort his wife. Elena stared at the tablecloth. Giulia, sitting next to her, squeezed Elena's hand.

"I love him too." The words came out before Elena could stop them.

The room went quiet. Antonella stared at Elena.

"I love him too. Luca. I love him and he loves me. We're going to be married when the war is over."

Elena stared defiantly at the shocked faces. Her father looked furious. Her mother was agitated, darting her eyes between Antonella and Paolo and back to Elena again. The only calm person in the room seemed to be Paolo, who nodded imperceptibly, encouraging her to go on.

"Zia Antonella, I have been calling you 'aunt' my whole life because you are family to me. I am not going to say I know how you feel because I don't. I've never had a child and I cannot imagine what it is like to lose something so precious. But Lorenzo was doing what he thought was right, fighting for what Italy should be, not what it has become these past few years."

Elena did not dare look at her mother and father. She gripped Giulia's hand tighter. "And Luca is doing what he thinks is right. It wasn't me who changed him. He understands that we need an Italy of enlightenment and beauty, not an Italy of brutality, death, and darkness. That's what the art represents. And helping to save the art is going to help save part of Italy's soul. I'm proud of him for what he is doing. And I hope you can be too."

Antonella looked at Elena, with all the pain of the past few days etched on her face. She still said nothing.

Paolo cleared his throat. "Elena's right. We are all fighting, in our own ways, for the Italy we want to be part of once more. Like I said, I am proud of Lorenzo for living his life on his terms. And for dying for a cause he believed in. Any man would be proud to be able to say that about his son."

He smiled at Elena. "I'm just as proud of Luca. Generations of Italians will be grateful if their cultural heritage survives this ghastly war. Luca is playing his part to ensure it does."

He raised his glass of *vin santo*. "To my sons Lorenzo and Luca!"

Everyone raised their glasses. "To Lorenzo and Luca!"

Antonella put down her glass and walked around the table to where Elena was sitting. Elena shrunk down a little in her seat, fearful of another verbal onslaught. Instead, Antonella held out her arms and Elena stood up gratefully to be enveloped in a tight hug.

"I do love you, my dear child," Antonella whispered. "Please forgive me. I just miss both my boys so much."

Elena closed her eyes. "Luca will come back to us. I know he will."

They stood like that for a long time. Elena felt her breathing slow a little. She felt calm for the first time in days.

Chapter Thirty-Six

Luca could see his breath forming little clouds in front of him. The patched-up windscreen was not doing a good job of keeping out the piercing wind. He was also nervous that the engine was not going to make it all the way to the top of this mountain.

The drive from Rome had been uneventful until he reached the outskirts of Arezzo and turned eastward. The road became a series of switchbacks as it made its way up the foothills of the Apennines. The truck was holding its own on the treacherous curves, but Luca could sense the temperature dropping, which concerned him. There were patches of ice on the road and Luca had struggled in places to keep the truck moving in a straight line. The conditions appeared to be keeping other vehicles off the road, as Luca had seen very few people in the past two hours. Despite being desperate to get home, he knew the safest thing to do was to maintain his slow and steady pace.

Whenever Luca could see somewhere to pull over, he did so, obsessively checking his progress on the map Lavagnino had given him. As Lavagnino had warned him, many road signs had been removed to slow down and confuse enemy troops. Luca found himself having to check landmarks to work out roughly where he might be. It was a small moment of celebration when he realized that he had crossed the border into Le Marche.

Elena, I am coming to you, he said to himself, over and over, like a spell that would keep him safe.

The heavy clouds seemed to surround the truck. Luca peered nervously through the cracked windscreen. First a single flake, then another, and then a white, swirling mass blew at him from all directions. The visibility dropped and he was forced to slow down even more, until Luca felt he was barely making any progress.

Damn, this is the last thing I need, thought Luca. The windscreen wipers were doing a poor job of keeping the snow away. Luca could feel the truck starting to drift on the increasingly slippery surface. He inched forward, praying silently that the snow would ease up. He was not very hopeful.

A mile on, the road widened a little and Luca found himself in a small hamlet. Through the white swirls, he spotted a few pinpoints of light in the buildings on either side of the road. Suddenly, as he approached a bend, he saw in front of him what looked like an *osteria*. There was a large open space on one side of the building. He impulsively pulled off the road and parked the truck. Carrying his small knapsack, he made his way to what looked like an entrance. He pushed open the oak door and found himself in a large room.

A fire was crackling in the hearth. Faces stared at him as he hurried to close the door behind him. An elderly lady was seated in a wooden chair facing the fire, holding out her hands as if to get some warmth. In the middle of the room was a long table with a bench on either side, where a couple of men were sitting, steaming earthenware bowls in front of them. The sight of food made Luca feel very hungry.

"You looking for someone?" asked a suspicious voice. Luca turned in its direction and discovered that it came from a young woman standing behind a bar on the left-hand side of the room. He walked over and sat down on a stool in front of her.

"No, not at all," Luca said, stammering slightly. He gestured vaguely in the direction of the door. "It started snowing and my truck is old, so I thought—"

"—you'd stop for a while," finished the woman. "Where are you heading?"

"Home," replied Luca quickly. "Toward Urbino." Having never ventured too far from the farm, Luca was unsure how well versed other people were with the geography of his province. He figured Urbino was famous enough to be known even in this mountain hamlet.

The woman nodded, although it was hard to tell whether this was because she recognized the name or because she now accepted his presence. "Are you planning on eating? Today's dish is *pasta e fagioli*. Our menu is a little limited at the moment, as you can imagine." She did not wait for Luca to answer but turned and disappeared through the door behind her.

Luca took a deep breath and released it, feeling some of the tension dissipate. He hadn't planned on stopping for a meal, not wanting to draw any attention to himself. But this seemed like the sensible thing to do given the deteriorating weather conditions. He hoped he did not end up snowed in for the next few days.

The woman returned a few minutes later with a bowl of thick soup, pasta, and beans, which she plunked down in front of him unceremoniously. A small boy had followed her from what Luca presumed was the kitchen and was now staring at him from behind the bar.

"What's your name?" asked Luca in what he hoped was a friendly manner.

"He doesn't talk to strangers," said the woman abruptly. "We get all sorts here."

She shooed the boy away and started wiping the glasses draining on the bar, returning them to a narrow shelf.

Luca ate his soup in silence. He had his back to the room, which made him uncomfortable, but it was too late to move to the communal table. He could hear low murmurs behind him and sensed that he was the subject of the muted conversation. He heard a bench scraping on the stone floor and people getting up. A large, older man appeared at the bar next to Luca. His face was ruddy and weather-beaten, his coat threadbare.

"You done, then?" he asked, staring at Luca with hooded eyes. His tone suggested he hoped that the answer was yes.

"Not your concern, Enzo. Let the man eat in peace." The woman accepted coins from the customer, who grunted and turned to leave with his companion, glowering at Luca as he did so. She watched the two men go, the wind blowing some snow inside as they opened the door.

"Don't mind them. They're locals. They come every day. We are not fond of strangers around here. At least not since the war began."

"I understand," said Luca. "I'll be on my way." He paid the bill and reluctantly took his leave. Outside, the snow was falling even more heavily than it had been earlier. Luca hurried to his truck. The cabin was colder than before. He turned the key in the ignition. A strained sound came from the engine. Luca swore to himself. Why had he stopped? He was an idiot. He tried again.

Five minutes later, a tap on the side window startled him. The woman, wearing what looked like an army camouflage jacket, motioned to him to follow her back inside the *osteria*. Luca groaned and did what she was suggesting.

The woman shook the snow off her jacket and hung it on a large metal hook by the door. "That does not sound good. I guess you aren't going anywhere for a while."

"Much as I hate to agree with you, I think you are right."

"I am pretty good with engines, but this is not the weather to be standing outside tinkering under a hood. You are welcome to stay tonight." She gestured to the fireplace. "You can take a seat and try and get some rest later. It is going to be dark very soon, and even if you get that truck moving again, it is a dangerous road to be on in these conditions. I know every curve and I wouldn't even risk it."

An hour later, Luca was sitting at the communal table, playing a board game with the young boy. The woman, who had volunteered that her name was Sofia and that the boy was her son, Marco, had apparently overcome her initial doubts about Luca. The old lady sitting by the fire turned out to be Sofia's mother, who was less keen than Sofia about this stranger staying around, but who had been mollified by her grandson's enthusiasm.

It was pitch black outside. The snow was still falling and whenever he checked out of the window, Luca could see it piling up in drifts against the wall of the building opposite. Even if they could somehow manage to get the truck started in the morning, he was not hopeful about the road ahead of him. Tomorrow was Christmas Day, so he had already failed to get home in time to celebrate with the people he loved. With a start, Luca realized belatedly that today was Christmas Eve. He looked up from the game.

"I am so sorry, Sofia. I had forgotten what day it is. You must be planning on celebrating tonight."

Sofia shook her head. "Not much to celebrate, is there? I don't have any fish and very little meat. I was planning on cooking leftovers. Obviously, you are welcome to join us."

Over a simple but warming dinner, Luca learned that he was in the village of Lamoli. Sofia told Luca that her husband had died a few years ago during the Italian campaign in North Africa. He had been conscripted into the army, leaving Sofia to run the *osteria* by herself.

"He did not want to leave us alone, but then who would? And now the people he was fighting against are no longer the enemy. None of it makes sense to me."

"Has it been difficult? Running this place by yourself?" asked Luca. "It's fairly remote up here, isn't it?"

"It certainly has not been easy. The first few months Leo was gone, the men in the village weren't happy. They thought a woman being in charge would somehow spoil 'their' bar. And suppliers still try to cheat me from time to time. But I'm no walkover." Sofia smiled at Luca. He could see the steel in her eyes. She reminded him a lot of Elena.

"So, what's your story?"

Luca told her a few scant details about where he lived and his family. Marco was excited to learn that Luca's younger brother shared his name. Luca told them very little about his journey, telling them that he was a driver for the art museum at the palace in Urbino and had been delivering some things to Arezzo. He did not mention Lorenzo's death. He hated lying to Sofia when she had been so kind to him. One day, when this war was over, he vowed to himself, he would return with Elena to thank Sofia properly for the part she had played, albeit unwittingly, in their mission.

Sofia stood up. "Young man, it is time for you to go to bed. Say goodnight to Luca and go with your grandmother."

Marco groaned. "It is still early! We haven't finished our game!"

"This must be the tenth game you've played. I'm sure Luca will play another with you tomorrow before he leaves."

Luca promised that he would and Marco finally got up from the table. He walked around and held out his arms for a hug. Luca was taken aback. He enveloped the small boy, holding him tightly against his chest. He tried to push away the thoughts of his own younger brother Marco and of Pietro in the piazza in Sassocorvaro.

"*Buon natale*, Luca! I'll see you tomorrow on Christmas morning!"

"*Buon natale*, Marco. *Sogni d'oro.*" *Sweet dreams, indeed, you precious boy*, thought Luca. He watched as the old lady took her grandson's small hand and kissed her daughter's cheek. She barely looked at Luca.

"I'll come and tuck you in soon," said Sofia. She waited until the two of them had left the room and then turned to Luca with a stern look on her face. She stood there with her hands on her hips. "So, what's the real story, then? Your color suggests you spend a lot of time in the sun and your hands are rough, like someone who works in the fields. You say you live on a farm. I don't think men who work in museums have dark skin or hands like yours."

Sofia looked at him accusingly, but with a slight smile at the corners of her mouth. She removed her apron and took a seat on the bench opposite him. Luca felt a moment of fear and then relief. For some reason, he trusted this woman.

"Well, I *am* doing something for the museum, so I was not lying to you. But you're right. That's not my usual job." Luca told her everything that had happened over the past few months. He told her about Elena and how they had fallen in love. He told her about Pasquale and the mission to save the works of art. He even showed her the crucifix Elena had given him. When Luca got to the events on the road outside

Urbino, he shut his eyes for a few seconds but carried on. Sofia listened in silence.

"That's quite a tale, Luca. I'm so sorry about your brother. I often wonder exactly how my husband died, but I'm glad I wasn't there to witness it." Sofia reached across the table and took Luca's hands. "You may not think this today, but I promise you it does get easier. I mean, it never goes away. The grief comes in waves, so overpowering that you wonder if you will ever be able to go on. But you do. And the next time the wave catches you, it's a little weaker and you're a little stronger. Trust me." She squeezed his hands. "And you'll have Elena by your side to help you heal."

Lights suddenly swept through the small windows facing the road. They pulled apart, startled. They could hear the muted slushing noise of tires on snow and the unnerving sounds of vehicles pulling up at the side of the building. A minute later came heavy pounding on the door.

"*Apra la porta!*" The harsh voice, though speaking Italian, had a German accent.

Sofia and Luca looked at each other.

"I don't think that was a request, do you?" said Sofia grimly. "I will do the talking." She got up from the table, put her apron back on and walked over to the door. As soon as she pushed the bolt back, the door was forced open and six men entered the room. Sofia closed the door behind them.

The men wore gray military coats and fur hats. They glared at Luca, who stayed seated.

"Can I help you, gentlemen?" asked Sofia. "We are closed this evening. It's Christmas Eve."

One of the men removed his hat. "We know what day it is. And we want dinner. What are you going to serve us?"

"We don't have much. Like I said, we're closed tonight and we will be closed tomorrow."

The German moved closer, his face inches from Sofia's. "You are going to serve us some dinner. And some beer. It's Christmas Eve, like you said." He signaled to the other men to sit down at the table.

Luca stood up and started clearing the board game. He knew better than to open his mouth.

As Luca put the game pieces back into their box, the German looked at him with a sneer on his face. "Let the wife do all the talking, eh? That's brave of you. Fetch us some beer."

Luca finished clearing the table and walked toward the bar, where Sofia was already putting glasses out. They exchanged looks. Unspoken between them was the understanding that it was better if Luca was not subjected to questioning. Let the soldiers think they were married.

Sofia disappeared into the kitchen while Luca poured six glasses of beer. He carried them to the table, where the soldiers had already removed their outer layers and were apparently settling in for the evening, talking loudly and teasing each other in German. Luca walked toward the kitchen, hoping to talk to Sofia out of their earshot.

"You! Stay here where I can see you!" came the loud command from the table. Luca hesitated and then headed back behind the bar. No point in aggravating them. He hoped Sofia could find sufficient food.

Luca could make out low voices coming from the rear of the house. He started shuffling bottles behind the bar and making as much noise as he could to mask the sounds. It was better if their visitors did not know that two other people were in the building.

Several agonizing minutes passed before Sofia reappeared, carrying three bowls and spoons on a tray. She placed them on the table and went back into the kitchen, emerging with three more bowls and a loaf of bread. The men grabbed the bowls and the bread and started eating as if they had not had any food for days. They ignored Luca and Sofia, who stood side by side behind the bar.

For five minutes, there was no sound in the room apart from that of cutlery in bowls and glasses clinking on the wooden tabletop. More beer was called for, which Luca delivered. The chatter started up again as beer was drunk and toasts were made. With the soldiers seemingly engrossed in their own conversations, Luca and Sofia risked a few words.

"I have told Mamma to keep Marco in bed."

"Safest place," said Luca in a quiet voice. "Hopefully they will finish their meal and leave."

But they didn't leave. The men kept calling for more drinks. The more they drank, the louder and more raucous the conversation became. Luca and Sofia kept looking at each other, silently hoping that eventu-

209

ally the men would get tired or pass out. The hour hand on the large clock on the wall kept moving: one o'clock, two o'clock.

Suddenly, the kitchen door opened and Marco, wearing pajamas, walked sleepily into the room, followed by his agitated grandmother in her thick cotton nightdress. The soldiers turned toward them, a couple of them scrambling to their feet and picking up their revolvers from the table.

"I tried to stop him!" said Sofia's mother with a wail. "But it was so loud and he woke up, calling for you." She wrapped her arms around her grandson, who had stopped short and was staring in horror at the men.

The German who seemed to be in charge started laughing at the two of them. "Well, well, well. What have we here? Yours, I presume?" he said, looking straight at Luca and Sofia.

"Go back to bed right now," said Sofia sharply, ignoring the German. "I told you—"

"Oh, that won't be necessary," interrupted the officer. "Come over here, boy. I would feel happier if we stay in the same place where I can keep an eye on everyone."

Marco stood still, like a mouse hoping the cat can't see it.

"I said, get over here," repeated the soldier more forcefully. He said something in German to the man sitting next to him, who shuffled awkwardly further down the bench, leaving a gap. The officer patted the bench. "Here's a spot for you."

Marco, terrified, inched toward the table and sat. His grandmother started wailing again.

"Shut up, woman. We're trying to have a nice party here."

Sofia's mother ignored him, her cries only getting louder. She was inconsolable. The German motioned to two of his men, who got up quickly and hurried over to where she was standing, grabbing her on each side. The old woman started shaking violently but kept crying.

"Mother!" said Sofia loudly. "You're scaring Marco."

The small boy was staring at his grandmother, ashen-faced. Luca could see his lower lip trembling and prayed that the boy would not start crying as well.

"I've had enough. I asked nicely," said the German. "I am going to put her outside so we can continue enjoying our evening." He barked an order in German.

The two men started pulling the old woman toward the door.

Sofia ran over and tugged one of the soldier's arms. "Stop it! What are you doing? It's freezing out there!"

Luca, horrified, broke his silence. "Let her go back to bed. She's old and frail and easily startled. She's—"

The German signaled to his men to continue.

They dragged the old woman to the door, Sofia struggling to stop them. One of them pulled back the bolt with his free hand and opened the door. He stepped outside, pulling the woman with him. The other soldier closed the door behind them. He was a young man in his early twenties, Luca guessed. He looked stricken. He started saying something in German to his superior, stammering a little.

The officer looked furious. He started yelling and gesticulating at the young man, who held his ground. The other men laughed at their companion. The young man started speaking again, obviously pleading with the officer.

"*Fünf, vier, drei* . . . !" He pointed his gun at the soldier. The young man looked at Luca, as if seeking redemption, and turned to leave. Through the open door, a quick exchange of words could be heard, followed by the return of the other soldier. He hurried through the door, shivering, and slammed it shut.

Sofia turned and ran toward the table, falling on her knees on the stones. "Please, sir, for the love of God. My mother will die out there. Please don't do this."

There was no further sound from outside. Sofia put her face in her hands and started to sob.

"She's an old lady. Please tell him to bring her back inside," begged Luca. He couldn't believe what was happening. Surely the soldier outside would quickly become unbearably cold himself—he wasn't wearing his coat or hat and the temperature outside was going to be brutal.

The German ignored him. He looked at Sofia, still on her knees next to the table. "Now that's given me an idea."

He got up from the table abruptly and grabbed Sofia's arm. Sofia started pulling away. Marco burst into tears and tried to stand up. The German pushed him back onto the bench with his other hand.

He motioned to the soldier closest to him to hold the boy. Then he turned to Luca. "I'm taking your wife to the back to have some fun. I'll let my companions have their turn when I'm done. They will keep an eye on you in the meantime."

As he yanked the terrified Sofia to her feet, he looked at Luca with contempt. Luca rushed toward him as two of the soldiers jumped up to intercept him. Luca tried to escape their grasp, yelling at the man holding Sofia. The soldiers forced Luca to the floor, one of them pushing his face into the stones and the other twisting his arm behind his back. He could hear both Sofia and Marco screaming but couldn't see either of them. He heard the German laughing.

"I love Italian women—they have so much passion. Remember—your son is staying here with my men. You and I are going to enjoy ourselves. If you keep fighting, your boy is joining his grandmother in the snow."

He pulled Sofia toward the kitchen. "If our young sergeant decides to disobey orders and brings that old cow back inside, my men have my permission to shoot both of them." The officer shouted some orders as he continued pulling Sofia towards the kitchen.

Sofia's cries got weaker as she was being dragged through the kitchen door, which slammed shut behind her.

Chapter Thirty-Seven

Until that moment, Luca had thought that the worst minutes of his life were the ones on the road outside Urbino watching his brother die. He had been wrong. The soldiers found some old cloths behind the bar and fashioned them into ropes, using them to hog-tie him. They stuffed one into his mouth for good measure. For the next few hours, he lay tied up on the stone floor, face down, listening to sounds that came from the depths of hell. The kitchen door did not stop the noises coming from the bedroom beyond as one soldier after another went back to spend their allotted time with Sofia. Each time a man came back into the room, buttoning his pants up, their leader asked him to recount to the group what he had just done. He then repeated the worst depravities to Luca in Italian so he could understand, followed by the occasional kick to his stomach or head. Luca welcomed the intense pain. It gave him something to focus on.

As far as Luca could tell, Marco had sobbed himself into a catatonic state. From where he was lying, he could see the little boy's legs, but there had been no sound from him for a while. The soldier who had been sent outside with the old woman had not returned. Luca did not want to think about what that might mean. The old woman had been in a nightdress. She wouldn't have lasted five minutes in a snowstorm.

The young man had demonstrated some innate goodness and sense of justice. If they were still alive, he hoped they would have the presence of mind to seek refuge in one of the neighboring houses. He knew from his time on the farm how quickly a living creature could die from hypothermia in extreme weather. He did not dare imagine any help was on its way. Even if the soldier had made it to a nearby house, the two local men he had met earlier that afternoon had not looked like they would be a match for a group of young, armed German soldiers.

Luca lost track of time. His feet felt numb and his shoulder sockets were burning with pain from the tight ligatures around his arms.

At one point, he heard the leader stand up and announce something to the assembled group. His men cheered as he made his way across the room, kicking Luca viciously in the head as he passed him. He bent down and whispered in Luca's ear. "I am ready for round two."

The pain was excruciating, but Luca was glad of it. He tried to shut out the noises from the room and concentrate on what he might do when they finally untied him. He heard a muffled scream from the bedroom.

Luca wanted to vomit. He was a coward and a failure. He had done nothing to prevent any of this. The grandmother was probably dead. Sofia had been violated and was possibly badly injured. Marco would be traumatized. And he had not been able to protect them. He thought of his beloved Elena. What would she think of him? She would despise him —he was sure of it. She would see that he was not the heroic figure she believed him to be.

Another half an hour went by, or so it seemed to Luca. He heard the kitchen door open again.

"Fun though this has been, it is going to be light soon. Time to wrap this little party up." The officer spoke to his men. There were groans and catcalls and the sounds of scraping as the soldiers got up from the table. Luca was yanked to his feet. His head was pounding and one of his eyes was swollen and half closed, thanks to one of the many kicks he had received. The German looked at him with a smile on his face.

"I have enjoyed our evening. I have to say the hospitality has been first rate. Particularly from your lovely wife. You're a lucky man."

Luca lunged forward but was held back by two men.

"Sadly, we have to go. For now. We might stop by for some more relaxation on our way back. But unfortunately you won't be here."

He signaled to his men, who started pulling Luca toward the main door. The group, now dressed in their hats and coats, made their way outside.

The snow had stopped and the sky was getting lighter. It would be dawn soon. Luca looked up at the brightening sky. It was Christmas Day. His family would be getting up soon to celebrate. And he would not be there with them. He knew he would never be there again.

Luca could see what looked like two small mounds covered with snow, lying next to the wall. It took him a moment to realize that they were the bodies of the young soldier and the old woman. The strong winds must have blown the snow against the side of the *osteria*, burying them. He said a silent prayer. The young soldier had been drinking earlier in the evening, so it was likely that the extreme cold had disorientated him within minutes. The two of them would have drifted into unconsciousness very quickly. He hoped their deaths had been painless.

The leader of the group stood watching him. "At least we didn't waste any bullets on those two." He signaled to his men to remove the ropes and stand Luca against the wall.

The men did as they were ordered. Luca stood shivering, looking defiantly at the Germans.

The leader walked forward and removed the rag from his mouth. "Any last words?"

"Your time will come," croaked Luca. His voice sounded raw and broken. His mouth and tongue were dry. "You are pure evil. All of you. You'll be driven out of my country and you will suffer. I know it. Evil like this cannot win."

"I'm sure you want to believe that," said the German. "You may be right. But until then, your wife and your son and your beer and your home, they're all mine. The Third Reich is in charge now. I can do whatever I want with them. You Italians are all cowards and traitors, swinging with the wind. I wanted you to hear what happened this evening. I wanted you to know what we were doing to your wife. But now, it is time for you to go."

The German held up his revolver. "Go on. Run, little man. I'm going to count to five."

His men laughed, not understanding the exchange but enjoying the spectacle. Luca continued staring at them, his gaze steady. He slowly raised his sore arm and reached inside the neck of his sweater. His hand closed around the crucifix Elena had given him.

"I'm not running anywhere. Look me in the eyes while you kill me."

"Spoiling my fun, eh? Oh, well, if you insist."

Luca thought of Lorenzo and Elena. At least he would be with one of them on this holiest of days. The German fired.

Chapter Thirty-Eight

Elena tied her long hair back with a ribbon and put on a woolen hat. It was cold in the bedroom, so she knew the barn would be freezing. She took a deep breath and let it out slowly, watching the wispy cloud float away in front of her. *Cows. Just focus on milking the cows.* She slowly breathed in and out once more, this time to steady herself, and left the room.

"Are you two going to manage by yourselves? I need to fold this dough," said her mother, with her hands deep in a large mixing bowl.

Giulia looked up from the table. "We can do it, Mamma. Come on, Elena. Let's just get this over with."

The sisters walked across the yard to the barn, carrying the pails. They didn't speak to each other. Elena had not been in the mood for mindless conversation over the past few weeks, so Giulia found it easier to say nothing. Her sister would talk when she was ready.

The cows were waiting for them, swaying in their stalls. Elena focused on grabbing a stool and walking over to the first animal. She did not want to look up at the hayloft. She found it too distressing to think about Luca and the last time they had lain up there together. She bent her head down and placed her cheek against the warm flank of the cow.

It was strangely comforting. Her fingers instinctively reached for the teats and she started her gentle pumping.

An hour later, Elena and Giulia had finished milking all the cows and had poured most of the milk into the large steel churns. Andrea was going to transport the cans to the creamery later. The sisters started carrying the remaining milk back to the house for the family's use. They were almost at the farmhouse when they heard a car coming down the track. They looked at each other.

"I wonder who that could be?" asked Giulia. She could see the quick flaring of hope in her sister's eyes, followed almost immediately by a blank expression. Giulia knew that there had been too many moments since Christmas when Elena's hopes had been cruelly dashed. The two women put down their pails and watched the car approach.

"It's Pasquale," said Elena in the flat voice she had been using lately. "I don't recognize the others."

The car stopped and Pasquale emerged from the driver's seat. The other passengers stayed inside the car. Pasquale stood looking at the two women. He had a strange look on his face. "I'm glad you're here. Is everyone home?"

Giulia nodded. "Mamma is in the kitchen making bread. Papà and Andrea are in the fields. But you're welcome to come inside."

"Thank you, Giulia. I have two people in the car who want to meet you all. Can we come in?"

Elena nodded, a sense of foreboding coming over her. She did not wait to greet the strangers. Instead she started carrying the brimming pails slowly into the house, followed by Giulia and the three visitors.

They sat awkwardly around the kitchen table. Names were exchanged and warm drinks prepared. The small boy had been fascinated by the frothing milk in the pails, so Giulia had poured him a glass. The room was finally silent.

Pasquale cleared his throat. "There's no easy way to do this. I think I will let Signora Conti tell her story." He turned to the young woman. "Is that alright with you? Or would you rather—"

"No, that's fine," the young woman said in a low voice. "I came all this way. I owe it to Luca."

At the sound of his name, Elena gasped. It hurt to hear that name spoken by a stranger. She had not heard it uttered in her presence for weeks. Everybody had become so fearful of upsetting her that they had started avoiding the topic altogether. Elena leaned forward.

"You know Luca, Signora Conti?" she asked in a whisper. The young woman looked at her with a pained expression.

"Please call me Sofia. And yes, I knew him." Her voice faltered.

"It was Christmas Eve. Around lunchtime. There was a snow-storm." In a slow voice, breaking at times, Sofia started telling the Marchetti women everything that had occurred that day at her *osteria*. At one point, she stopped. She looked at her son and then at Pasquale.

"Signor Rotondi, would you mind taking Marco outside? I am sure there are some things that would interest him on the farm."

Pasquale jumped up immediately and after a brief look at Elena, reached out his hand to the small boy. "You've drank some milk, but I'm sure you would like to meet the cow that produced it!" he said in a jovial tone. Marco looked at his mother for reassurance.

"That sounds like fun, *mio bambino*," said Sofia. "I will be right here with my new friends." The boy stared at his mother, unsure of what to do.

Pasquale held out his hand. "It won't take long, Marco. Your mother isn't leaving without you, I promise." The boy tentatively took the proffered hand and left with Pasquale.

Sofia looked at the three women and then down at the table. She didn't say anything for a minute. "It's been hard. For the longest time, I wished I was dead." She looked up at the three women. "If it wasn't for Marco—"

Elisa, Elena, and Giulia looked at the woman's stricken face.

"I had to come and find you though. I knew that Luca would have wanted me to." Hesitantly at first, but then in a torrent of sentences, words tumbling over each other, Sofia told them everything. The arrival of the Germans. The meal and the drinking. Her mother. The soldier who tried to intervene. She cried when recounting the hours of abuse she had suffered, but she kept talking. The women listened and cried alongside her, feeling the agonies she had endured.

Sofia's voice grew very quiet. The three women leaned in, straining to hear her.

"I was not there when they took him outside. I couldn't move from my bed. But I heard it." She recounted having waited in intense pain until she was sure the Germans had left. How she had dragged herself out of her bedroom. The relief of finding her son sleeping on the bench, followed by the horror of the corpses outside.

"They were all dead," she said, her voice cracking again. "My mother, left to die in the cold like an animal. The soldier, the only one of those bastards with a heart, frozen next to her. And Luca, his blood, red on the snow." Sofia put her hands on her face and started sobbing. She lowered her head to the table, her shoulders heaving. Elisa put her arm around the woman in wordless comfort. Elena felt cold.

"So he's dead?" she asked, knowing the answer.

Sofia raised her head and nodded slowly. "I'm so sorry to be the one to tell you, Elena. I just knew that Luca would want you to know what happened. That he was on his way home to you."

She paused and put her hand into her pocket, pulling out a small package. "I brought you this. He told me it was yours. His hand was clutching it when I found him."

Elena took the package from her and unwrapped it. She held the crucifix up in front of her. "It didn't save him though, did it?" she said in a low voice. "Where was God that night? Why did He let all those terrible things happen?"

Sofia said nothing but held her other hand. The four women sat at the table in silence. There was no point in crying anymore. God had stopped listening.

When Francesco and Andrea returned from the fields for their midday meal a little later, the story was repeated, glossing over some of the more horrific details. Francesco, ever practical, asked Sofia numerous questions. He was concerned that the Germans had seemingly acted with impunity and wanted to know which authorities had been informed of the atrocity. He worried aloud that they might return to harm Sofia again. He was also preoccupied by such matters as the fate of the truck that Luca had been driving and where Luca had been buried.

His wife kept putting her hand on his arm, hoping to stop the inter-rogation. At one point, Sofia started crying again and Elena took her into the bedroom to give her some breathing space. They sat next to each other on the bed.

No words were exchanged for several minutes. Sofia finally stopped crying and the two women sat quietly holding hands and staring at the whitewashed walls. The only sound in the room was of heavy breathing. Elena soon found herself consciously aligning her breathing with that of Sofia. In, out, in, out, in, out. The simple act calmed her down and focused her thoughts. So now she knew. Luca was gone. He was never coming back. There was no more hope, no more imagining scenarios where he could still be alive but unable to reach her. She would never lie in his arms again. Elena felt the tears she had held back for so long pricking her eyes.

"It will never stop hurting."

Elena turned her head and looked at Sofia. The young woman looked shattered, but her eyes were kind. "You'll always feel the pain, but eventually there'll come a time when you have more good hours in the day than bad ones. Trust me, I know. I lost my husband early in the war."

Sofia held both of Elena's hands. "I knew Luca for less than a day, but I know he was a good man. He would want you to live your best life, even if it is without him."

"I no longer know what my life looks like without him," Elena whis-pered. "How do you do it, Sofia? You lost your husband and then this terrible, brutal night happened. They did unspeakable things to you and your family. How does someone recover from that?"

"If I lie down and die, they win. You see that, don't you? You and I have the same enemy. We have to survive, to thrive, to prove to them that we are stronger in the end."

Sofia squeezed Elena's hands hard until they started throbbing. "I'm not going to let you give up, do you hear me?" She pulled Elena in for an embrace and the two women clung together, sobbing for everything lost but grateful in that moment for the comfort of another's arms.

When they returned to the kitchen, Francesco was uncharacteristically quiet. Elena knew that her mother would have had a few sharp words to say to her husband. Pasquale and Marco walked into the room and Sofia busied herself asking her son questions about the cows and the barn.

Francesco pulled Pasquale to one side. "Have you been to see Luca's family yet?" he asked. The farmer had been distinctly cool toward Pasquale since the day of the convoy and the fatal ambush. He had refused to let Elena return to work and was inclined to put some of the blame for Lorenzo's death on the superintendent's shoulders.

"We're heading there now. Sofia wanted to speak to Elena first. Luca apparently made it very clear to her in their short time together that Elena was the most important person in his life."

Francesco did not respond to this and turned back to Sofia. "Signora Conti, can I ask you how you got here? How did you know where to find us?"

"There were clues in Luca's story. He told me that he was working for the art museum in Urbino, the Galleria Nazionale. I went there first and found Signor Rotondi. I am on my way to Pesaro, to stay with my sister for a while, so Urbino was an easy detour. I haven't decided what to do long term."

Sofia did not say anything about the terror she had felt staying in her home. She could not imagine ever living there again.

"Then Signor Rotondi offered to drive me here, to speak to Elena, and then to see the Rossi family. My car is at the palace. I am afraid Luca's truck is still at my home. I'll have to come up with a plan on how to return it to Luca's family."

"The truck belongs to someone else," said Elena. In a few short sentences, she told Sofia how they had acquired it. "At some point, I'm sure Signor Vitali would be grateful to get it back, but it is not a priority."

Pasquale stood up. "I think it is time that we visit the Rossi family. His parents deserve to know what happened to their son. I am so sorry for your loss, Elena. I know this must have been very hard for you to hear."

Sofia and Marco got up from the table and started saying their goodbyes. Elena grabbed Sofia's hands. She did not want to let this young woman leave.

"Sofia, will you come back?" Elena asked. She stumbled over her words. "I mean, I would like to see you again. Is that strange? Or maybe I could come and visit you in Pesaro one day. Would that be alright?" She was suddenly terrified that Sofia would walk out of the house, never to be seen again, and her last link with Luca would be broken.

Sofia smiled. "I would like that. Let me write down my sister's address. Maybe you could write to me. I should be there for a few weeks at least. I can't stay with my sister forever because she has too many children and a very small house."

Elena went in search of a pencil and paper. Sofia wrote down her details and handed the paper back to Elena.

"I need to decide what I am going to do next—Marco and I cannot live on thin air. I know I'll have to return to the *osteria* at some point, if only to pack up our things. I can come and see you on the way back."

Elena admired the strength this young woman was displaying. What Sofia had been through would have destroyed most people.

The family stood in the farmyard and watched as Pasquale's car disappeared down the narrow track. Elena knew that each of them was thinking the same thing: Antonella's hope that her eldest son would return was about to be shattered.

Chapter Thirty-Nine

Sofia's visit landed like a large rock tossed into a pond. Lives that had been suspended in animation for weeks suddenly resumed, albeit changed forever. Paolo and Antonella started planning how they could retrieve Luca's body from the shallow unmarked plot that Sofia's neighbors had dug in the graveyard of the local abbey. Elena spent one day in bed, grieving, and then woke up the next morning, feeling ashamed. Sofia was right—Luca would have hated to see her like this. And thinking about Sofia and everything she had suffered made Elena feel embarrassed to be lying there, wallowing in misery.

Elena tracked down her father and told him that she was returning to work whether he liked it or not. Francesco relented, secretly relieved to see his daughter exhibiting some of her old fire. His fury at the Germans who had murdered his best friend's son, and his desire to see justice done for both Luca and Sofia, superseded any anger he had been harboring toward the superintendent.

The following Monday, Elena cycled to Sassocorvaro. She dismounted in the piazza and started wheeling her bicycle toward the café.

Anna was standing in the doorway talking to a lady with a shopping basket. She spotted Elena and waved. "It is good to see you again. We missed you."

"And I missed your *caffè d'orzo*. How are you?"

Elena immediately regretted the pleasantry. *How is she? Her child is dead—how do you think she is?*

Anna gave a wan smile. "Holding up. Some days are better than others. I heard about Luca. I am so sorry, Elena."

Elena wasn't surprised. News traveled very quickly. The whole town probably knew by now. "Thank you, Anna. At least we know what happened to him now. In fact, I need to speak to your husband about the truck. Is he around?"

Anna pointed toward the stable. "He's sorting stock at the moment. Why don't you go back there and I will bring you your drink?"

Elena found Signor Vitali stacking cases of beer. He offered his condolences. "This war does unspeakable things to people. How many more will have to suffer?"

Elena didn't respond, knowing how much Signor Vitali and his wife had already endured. She sat down on one of the crates. "I need to tell you about your truck."

Signor Vitali listened patiently as Elena explained where it was. "I'll have to come up with a plan to get it back to you. Signora Conti is in Pesaro now, but she will be coming back. Maybe I can bring her to town when she does and we can decide what to do next."

"As I told you all previously, that truck will just be a gift for me. There's no rush to return it. If the lady needs it, she's welcome to use it."

"I think she is keen to get it back to you. She strikes me as someone who does not like to leave loose ends."

"Well, then, it's a date. I'll be happy to meet her."

"Who's the date? Are you replacing me?!" asked Anna, as she walked in with a large cup in her hand.

Elena smiled, repeating the story in brief. It was good to see Anna teasing her husband again.

"Please bring her and her little boy for lunch. I would enjoy that," said Anna in a wistful tone.

Elena thought of Pietro's cheeky face and swallowed hard. "I'd enjoy that too. I'll let you know when she is coming back." Elena returned the cup. "Back to work, I guess. Is it okay if I leave my bike here?"

"Anytime, Elena. We'll keep it safe." They all knew it was easier to keep bicycles safe than people.

Over the next two months, Elena and Sofia kept up a steady stream of correspondence. They quickly became close friends, writing long letters to each other, sharing their innermost thoughts as well as snippets about their daily lives. Something about the written word allowed Elena to act as if she was in the confessional. She told Sofia intimate details about her relationship with Luca, things she had not even told her sister. In return, Sofia shared her concerns about the future and her worries about the lasting effects of the trauma she and her son had been through. She wrote about the nights when she lay beside her son, praying fervently that the two of them would go to sleep and never wake up again. She also wrote of the mornings when she cried for a few minutes upon waking up to the harsh reality, but then looked at her son and knew that she had to stay strong.

It was Sofia who found out first that Elena had stopped seeing blood appear each month and who sent her a stern note in early March.

> *You must talk to your mother. You'll start showing any week now and it's better to get ahead of it. It won't be as bad as you think, I am sure. Your mother seemed like a kind woman to me and it is clear she loves you very much.*

Elena read the letter three times, then did as Sofia had advised. Her mother cried, and raged, and finally hugged her daughter.

"We'll get through this, my dear. This isn't how I wanted you to have your first child, but if God has blessed you, who am I to challenge His plan? We'll have to go and talk to Antonella."

Unlike Elisa, Antonella was overjoyed immediately when she heard the news. "This is the best gift I could have asked for. Nothing will bring back my sons, but to have a piece of Luca in the world? Indeed, that's a blessing."

Elena defied her parents and kept working for Pasquale. But she was wracked with guilt. She had told everyone, especially Luca, that they were saving the art for Italy. The art had indeed been saved, and she was proud of what they had achieved. But Elena had to admit to herself that the main reason she had put so much effort into making the convoy a success was so that she could prove to Pasquale that she had what it took to be an art curator like him. She spent many nights awake, tortured by the thought that her ambition was ultimately what had killed Luca. What if she had never gone to Milan but remained on the farm, following her parents' directives, until she was ready to become a wife and mother? She finally shared her guilt with Sofia, who was swift to disabuse her of the notion.

None of this can be blamed on you. To me, there is nothing wrong with you wanting more than a life on the farm. Luca would be the first to agree with me. Do you think I gave a damn about those old men in my village who said I couldn't run the osteria when my husband was killed, simply because I am a woman! If anything, you owe it to yourself and to this child to make a living. If that means doing something you love, even better.

Elena was thankful for the vote of confidence. She became even more driven than her boss, working late into the night, helping with Pasquale's voluminous correspondence to the various museums and churches that had entrusted him with their treasures. Pasquale wanted to ensure that all the records were up to date so it would be easier to return everything to their rightful homes once the war was over.

Lavagnino had returned to Urbino as promised and completed the transfer of all objects to the Vatican. He had been distraught on learning about Luca's fate.

"He was a good man, Elena. He did not deserve to die like that. Rest assured that once we kick those bastards out of our country and help the Allies win this thing, there'll be punishments. I have to believe that they will be made to pay for what they have all done."

At the beginning of April, Sofia wrote that she was going to leave Pesaro and return home to Lamoli via Urbino.

> I need to pack up my home and find somewhere else to live. I'll try to sell the place after the war. But for now, I must find a haven for Marco. Somewhere he will feel safe. I know how to cook and clean and run a bar. I'll have to look for work and try to earn enough to keep us alive.

Elena was excited that she was going to see her new friend again. She persuaded her parents to let Sofia and Marco stay with them and visited Anna at the café to let her know. They agreed on a date and time for lunch.

A week later, Elena, Sofia and Marco were sitting at the dining table in the Vitali family apartment above their café in Sassocorvaro. It was a cold April day, and there had been persistent rain all morning. Despite the gloom outside, the room rang with laughter as Sofia regaled the table with little anecdotes from her time running the *osteria*. She focused on recipes going wrong, beer barrels exploding, and the peculiarities of some of her regular customers. But Elena could see the effort it took on Sofia's part to keep the conversation light. From time to time, a shadow crossed her face and her smile froze.

Whenever the table fell silent, Anna picked up the conversation, telling her own tales of life running a café. Occasionally, Anna would reach out and gently rest a hand on top of Sofia's. The women would exchange sad smiles. Elena wondered how many times this tableau was being repeated in bereaved homes across Italy.

After they had finished the meal and Signor Vitali had poured some small glasses of *amaro*, Anna looked at Sofia with a gleam in her eye. "I have an idea. I think it could be the answer to all our prayers."

Elena looked at her in surprise. Despite the evident sorrow hanging over the table, the meal seemed to have lifted something from Anna's shoulders.

"My husband can go with you to Lamoli. He can help you pack up and lock the place securely. Then you can all return here, with my husband driving the truck. I am sure you have more belongings than what will fit in your small car anyway, so you could use an additional vehicle. We will scrounge fuel from somewhere"

Anna looked around the table excitedly. "But that's not the best part. You can move in with us. I always need help in the café, and Marco can go to school. It would be lovely to have a child living here again. We have the room."

She looked at her husband with tears in her eyes. "We'll never get over Pietro's death, but I have a lot of love to give."

Her husband looked at Anna fondly, not trying to hide his own tears. "So do I," he said softly.

Anna turned back to Sofia expectantly. "Think about it, Sofia. Please. You'd be doing us a favor."

Elena could see that Sofia was shocked at the suggestion. Sofia opened her mouth and then closed it again. Finally, she spoke. "You would do this? For me, someone you've just met?" She looked at Anna and then Elena, as if needing an explanation.

Signor Vitali cleared his throat. "This war has made me realize that you need to hold on to the good wherever you find it. Life is too short to just wait and see. You seem like a good woman to me. And I trust Elena's judgment. Pietro always said that she was his favorite customer. If you're Elena's friend, then you're our friend too. It would be an honor to have you here."

Sofia looked around the table.

Marco was fidgeting in his seat. "Mamma! Can we stay? This pasta is so good. And if we live here, I can visit Elena's farm and see the cows whenever I want." They all laughed at the little boy's enthusiasm.

Sofia ruffled his hair. "Well, if you'd like to stay, then I think that's a yes. Yes, thank you. I will accept your incredible offer."

Later that evening, when everyone was asleep, Elena slipped out of the house. She made her way to the barn and opened the large wooden doors. The cows started mooing gently. Elena climbed up the ladder to the hayloft and lay down in the straw. She clutched her crucifix in one hand.

"Luca, this was a good day." She had started coming to the hayloft at night several weeks ago. Every few days, she got an overwhelming urge to talk to Luca and the hayloft was where she felt closest to him. Maybe when Paolo worked out how to transport Luca's body to the nearby cemetery so he could be buried next to his brother, that might change. But for now, the hayloft would have to do.

"My friend is going to be nearby, so I can see her whenever I want. Anna gets to spoil a little boy again. And our child is growing inside me and, before the year is out, I will get to meet him or her and see your beautiful eyes again. Your parents will have a grandchild, which may alleviate some of their terrible pain. Life is good."

Elena rubbed her crucifix like a lucky charm. "Remember that night in this barn? When I told you about Pasquale's plan and we had our first argument? And then you changed your mind and told me you would help? I remember it so clearly. You were laughing because I was so riled up, and you told me that you would help me save the Madonnas. Do you remember that?"

She paused, as if waiting for a reply. "Luca, I think without meaning to, you might have saved more Madonnas than you could possibly know."

Epilogue

October 25, 1986

Elena was getting exasperated. Her granddaughter had been in the bathroom for at least half an hour. For some inexplicable reason, she always waited until shortly before they were due to leave the house to decide to get ready.

"Cristina! What is taking so long? We're going to miss the start if we don't leave soon."

"Nonna, calm down!" said Cristina, emerging at last, waving the car keys at her. "I'm driving and you know I go much faster than you do."

"And don't I always tell you to slow down on these roads? I'm hoping to die in my bed!" Elena sounded annoyed, but her face said otherwise. She loved all her grandchildren, but she had a soft spot for this one. She admired Cristina's fearlessness and her huge ambition. Nothing fazed this young woman.

Elena couldn't help smiling at her. She straightened Cristina's hat and gave her a peck on the cheek. "Can we leave now? Anyone would think it was you being honored today."

Twenty minutes later, Cristina had parked her car in the Piazza Mercatale, just outside the city walls, and the two of them were walking slowly up the helicoidal ramp which led to Corso Giuseppe Garibaldi. Elena brushed her fingers on the smooth wall as they made their way up to the street—she wondered how many townspeople had walked on these flagstones over the centuries. Emerging into the daylight again, the sight of the *torricini* of the palace stirred Elena's soul as it always did. She never got tired of seeing these fairytale towers that seemed straight out of a children's fable.

The courtyard inside the Ducal Palace was lined with chairs. Several people were already seated. Elena could see the rest of her family sitting near the front. Alessandro spotted her and waved. His wife turned and gave Elena a huge smile. Sofia was in the row behind, next to her son and his wife. The Vitalis sat next to them, Anna with one of Marco's children on her knees. Sofia motioned to Elena to join them.

Elena noticed Renon and his family sitting on the other side, close to the small stage, and went over to say hello to the curator. She hadn't seen him since he retired. Renon shared with her the news that he and his wife were thinking of moving to Pesaro to live by the sea.

"I like the idea of starting the day with a walk on the beach," he said. "I think I have spent far too many years in dusty archives and underground vaults."

Elena laughed. "That sounds like a wonderful idea. I just wish my mother had decided to do the same. She might not have left us so soon. But my father is going to draw his last breath plowing a field."

"Well, at least you still come to the university every day to teach those lucky students. I am glad the art world did not lose you to the cows."

"Lucky me, more like it. Those kids can drive me crazy at times, but there is nothing better than being in a classroom talking about paintings all day. I owe Pasquale a huge debt of thanks."

"And speak of the devil. Pasquale! You made it. I really wasn't sure if you would."

Elena turned and watched her old boss and his wife as they made their way toward them. It had been so long since they had seen each other. She felt a surge of affection toward the man who had changed the course of her life.

"Pasquale, I am so happy to see you. Today is truly a momentous occasion and nobody deserves it more than you." She kissed him on both cheeks, then stood back to take a good look at him.

His wife laughed. "You should have heard what a fuss he made about dressing up. I swear he was looking for excuses to duck out. He hates being the center of attention."

There was a sudden flurry of activity from inside the Ducal Palace as a group of dignitaries made their way to the platform. Elena spotted her son among them and gave him a wave. People started sitting down in anticipation of the start of the proceedings.

Pasquale and Zea were ushered to the front row by a young woman with a clipboard. Elena walked over to where her family and friends were sitting. Cristina patted the empty seat next to hers.

"Nonna, I saved this one for you. You need to have a good view of the stage." Elena sat down gratefully and wrapped her scarf tightly around her neck. She was glad that she had decided to wear a hat—the air was cold, and her winter coat was not keeping her as warm as she would have liked.

The mayor stood up and made one of his customary interminable speeches about the many attributes of Urbino and its people. Elena felt her eyelids closing until Cristina nudged her.

"Nonna, you'll miss it if you fall asleep."

Elena stirred herself and tuned in again to what the mayor was saying.

"But sometimes an outsider comes along who falls in love with this glorious city we call home and uses his considerable talents to make us better. I dare say not since Duke Federico has one man done so much for the cultural heritage of this place. Signor Rotondi, you made those momentous decisions during the war to protect our treasures, at great personal risk. We owe you tremendous thanks, and I can only apologize that it has taken so long for us to offer them to you. So today, it is my great honor to bestow upon you an honorary citizenship of the city of Urbino, with our eternal gratitude."

The mayor beamed as Pasquale stood up and made his way slowly to the small stage. Pasquale hesitated in front of the platform but managed to step up with the help of his cane. The two men shook hands and then posed for photographs as the mayor made a big deal of handing over a framed certificate. The crowd rose to its feet and gave him a standing ovation. Elena felt her eyes filling with tears. Finally, some small acknowledgment of what Pasquale had managed to achieve against overwhelming odds. For decades, it had seemed as if nobody cared about what they had done together.

Cristina nudged her grandmother again. "Look, Papa is going to say something."

Elena's son, a tall, slim man who looked exactly like his father, stood up and made his way to the microphone. He shook hands with Pasquale and spoke softly to him. Pasquale sat down in a chair at the side of the stage.

"Good morning, everyone. My name is Luca Rossi, and for those who don't know me, I am the director of the Galleria. It is truly an honor to be here today with Signor Rotondi and to remember with awe the actions he took during the darkest hours of our country's history to help save our cultural heritage. We owe him so much."

Luca paused and then looked straight into the crowd at Elena. "My mother read me numerous stories when I was a small boy and taught me many valuable lessons. But it was her love of art that influenced me the most and led me to where I am today. She taught me that art is a universal language, a way of expressing our deepest thoughts and beliefs. Art connects us across geographies and demographics. It is a window to the past and a portal to the future. Above all, it gives us beauty in a world that can be very ugly. Signor Rotondi recognized that power and risked everything to ensure that this generation and those to come would not be robbed of it. In a world where money and political power seem to reign supreme, we need constant reminders of what matters."

Luca looked over at Pasquale, who was noticeably squirming on the small stage.

"Today, the city of Urbino recognizes Pasquale Rotondi, a man who moved mountains for what he believed in. Many people doubted him and the importance of his cause. I am very proud that my mother and father were among those who supported him in this mission. But I think today generations of Italians are grateful to this man who was willing to risk everything to save what should matter to us all. I can only hope to live up to the example of men like Pasquale Rotondi, who recognized that we must always fight for the light."

The audience rose to its feet once more, applauding the sentiment. Pasquale did not move for a few minutes. He finally stood up and turned to face the crowd, acknowledging their applause with a wave. Elena clapped louder, happy that the reticent man had finally been given his due from the city, indeed the country, that owed him so much.

Her son turned to the crowd. "We have planned a small reception upstairs in the Ducal Palace. Please join us to congratulate Signor Rotondi in person."

Luca helped Pasquale down from the platform and led the way across the courtyard to the stone steps that led to the upper floors.

Cristina looked at her grandmother, grinning. "Doesn't Papa look so handsome today? Like a movie star!"

"Well, I agree with you, obviously, but don't let him hear you saying that. You know how modest your father is."

Elena got to her feet to follow the crowd into the palace. Cristina was right—her son looked particularly handsome in his expensive suit. She wondered whether her Luca would have looked the same at this age. It was disconcerting to remember that her son was already twice as old as his father had been when he died. Her Luca would always be eighteen years old to her.

A glass of prosecco in hand, Elena looked for Zea at the reception. Zea and Pasquale were living in Rome, as Pasquale was now working for the Vatican as a technical consultant for the restoration works there. Elena rarely saw them and was happy for an opportunity to catch up. Zea and Elena were engrossed in their conversation when Pasquale and Luca hurried over to join them.

"Mamma, I need to show you something," said Luca, taking her elbow. "Pasquale and I have been planning a surprise."

Elena looked at her son, bewildered, and then at Pasquale and Zea. It was clear from Zea's expression that she was in on the secret.

"Come and see," Luca insisted. He gallantly took her arm and led her back down the wide stone steps to the courtyard. Pasquale and Zea followed more slowly, with Pasquale leaning on his cane. The four of them went through the small doorway into the walled garden of the palace.

Luca steered his mother to one side of the garden. Elena could see a newly planted olive tree. Her son stopped and waited for Pasquale and Zea to catch up.

Luca smiled at his mother. "Mamma, ever since we found out that the city was going to honor Pasquale today, the two of us have been in frequent communication. He wanted the museum to do something to mark your contribution, not only in helping the convoy all those years ago but also to acknowledge the generations of students you have inspired, both here in the museum and at the university."

Elena felt herself blushing. She looked down at the ground.

"You deserve this, Nonna," whispered a voice behind her. Cristina had followed them into the garden. She put her arms around her grandmother's waist and squeezed her.

"Yesterday we planted this tree in your honor. And can you see the plaque on the ground next to it?" Luca pointed at the small metal plate.

"Let me tell her!" said Cristina excitedly. "Nonna, it has your name and my grandfather's name. It recognizes your contributions to the preservation of art in this country. Papa really wanted to do something specifically for you."

Elena was stunned. She looked at her son and at Pasquale and Zea. "This is . . . this is too much," she said in a quiet voice.

Pasquale smiled at her. "It really isn't, my dear Elena. Luca was instrumental in getting the art to a safe place and died as a result. You have been teaching students for decades about the importance of preserving art in war zones. Both of you deserve to be recognized as much as I do."

"I couldn't wait to show you, Mamma," whispered Luca. "You do deserve this."

Elena's eyes filled with tears. She felt an overwhelming sense of pride tinged with sadness. *You should be here, my darling*, she thought to herself. *I wish you were here to see this. What we did mattered.*

But my Luca is here, she chided herself. *He's always been here.* Elena looked at her beautiful, soulful son she and the man she loved had made together all those years ago, in a freezing cattle barn in the middle of the darkest winter of her life.

THE END

Afterword

I first came across the story of Pasquale Rotondi in 2000, when my late husband, Huw, and I bought our dream home in the countryside outside Sassocorvaro in central Italy. It took longer than we thought to renovate the five-hundred-year-old farmhouse, so between our frequent visits with architects and builders, we spent time in Sassocorvaro, drinking coffee outside a café or eating incredible pasta at one of the small restaurants. One day, we decided to check out the imposing Rocca in the center of town. Facsimiles of famous paintings were mounted on the walls with explanations for each in Italian. At the time, my Italian was virtually nonexistent, so it was a mystery to us as to what these displays meant.

Some research gave us the story of Pasquale Rotondi and the race to first keep the art safe from the ravages of war, and subsequently, after the German invasion of Italy in 1943, to save it from Hitler's henchmen. We were surprised that we had never heard this story before. Several years later, our surprise turned to something more akin to frustration when Robert Edsel's well-researched nonfiction book *The Monuments Men* was turned into a Hollywood movie starring George Clooney. The movie highlighted the role played by American and British art historians in saving the art after the war but said little about the dangerous work done in 1943 and 1944 by Italians under the watchful eye of the German invaders. The movie scarcely mentioned the people who had put their lives on the line during the war years.

We talked about this many times with our neighbors and friends, Luca and Germana. I said I was determined to write this story one day. Luca joked that he could play the lead in the subsequent movie of my novel. Years went by, and I did nothing.

In 2019, my dear husband, Huw, died prematurely from the ravages of cancer, and six months later we were hit by a global pandemic. I was forced to close our business. I was left bereft and a little lost as to how I was going to fill my time. I started a new venture with close friends, but I still had more free time than I was used to. Luca had also suffered the loss of his dear Germana a few years earlier. Life suddenly seemed cruelly short. My daughters, Tara and Savannah, encouraged me to do something with my extra time.

"Why not finally write that book?"

So I did. This book is a work of fiction inspired by real events and real people. Many of the incidents in this book are written about in the diary of Pasquale Rotondi, which offers a detailed chronology of his daily life between 1943 and 1944. My Pasquale Rotondi, however, although based on an historical figure, is a fictional character, as are other historical figures depicted in this story: his wife, Zea, who was a renowned art historian in her own right; Signor Renon, the curator; Signor Montagna the builder in Sassocorvaro; Signor Pretelli, Rotondi's driver; Lieutenant Scheibert from the Kunstschutz; Erivo Ferri, an anti-Fascist who founded the first partisan brigade in this region; Emilio Lavagnino and Italo Vannutelli from the ministry in Rome. (Emilio Lavagnino also kept a diary, so it was interesting to read about his perspective on his colleague Pasquale Rotondi. The two men clearly liked and respected each other very much.) All other characters and events are entirely fictional.

Where the action dictated it, I have changed the chronology and locations of certain real-life episodes. For example, the cases of art were never consolidated at the Ducal Palace—the convoy eventually left from Sassocorvaro rather than Urbino. There was indeed a partisan attack planned on the convoy but the plan was halted well before the convoy departed thanks to information passed to the partisan unit in good time.

I was also inspired by actual events at our Italian farmhouse, which is represented by Ca'Boschetto in the book. One day many years ago, we were visited by an elderly couple and their granddaughters, the latter telling us that their grandfather, who spoke no English, had been brought up as a child in our house together with his cousins' family. We welcomed them in and learned some fascinating details about life in the house during the war. The moment when Marco hides the wine in the pigsty, for example, is based on an actual event shared with us on that summer day.

I hope I have done justice to this story. What frightens me the most is that this is not just a tale of something that happened many decades ago. Art, historic buildings, literature, and culture are being systemically destroyed right now in places like Syria, Afghanistan, and Ukraine. The easiest way to erase a people and a sense of self is for the enemy to destroy what makes those people special.

Acknowledgments

Writing a novel is often depicted in the movies as a fairly lonely experience. I have been lucky enough to have a whole village along for the ride. So many people have encouraged, cajoled and pushed me to finally put pen to paper and this story would not have been told without them.

I am lucky enough to be a member of two book clubs and the experience of dissecting and debating the merits of other people's work in public has been a learning experience in and of itself. Thank you to the members of the frequently raucous book club formed at my old company which managed to thrive even after the demise of the business and offered an online place of refuge during the pandemic. Huge thanks also to the ladies of my Amici book club who can make me laugh until I cry.

A special shout-out to my dear friends and beta readers who gave me valuable feedback and suggestions for improvements. Cindy Gallop, who has had my back for thirty-six years and is always ready with a martini. Tat Small, who never says no to a cup of tea and will happily talk nonsense with me for hours. Rebecca McGough and Maria Salvador Smith, my brilliant friends who make my actual day job such a joy, and whose notes on the book and other elements have been so useful. Moira Fielding, my book soul mate. The biggest thanks go to my writer friends. Diane Hatz and Angie Annetts have been my spirited guides to the independent publishing world. Angela Petch, the best-selling writer of several books set in Italy, was generous with both her time and her experience, and her thoughtful edits, suggestions and corrections have made this novel so much better.

My Italian community welcomed me with open arms. I am never happier than when we are eating and drinking together in our beautiful valley. Apologies for borrowing some of your names for my characters. Luca, I told you I would write this book one day. Special thanks to my beloved patient friend Cristina for taking care of my Italian home when I am not there and for helping me deal with numerous house emergencies.

There are a number of books, articles and papers that I have referred to while writing this novel. I have highlighted some of the most influential below but there have been numerous trips down rabbit holes on the internet as well.

Robert Edsel has written superbly researched books on the efforts to save art in Europe during the war. *The Monuments Men: Allied Heroes, Nazi Thieves, and the Greatest Treasure Hunt in History* by Robert Edsel and Bret Witter and *Saving Italy: The Race to Rescue a Nation's Treasures from the Nazis* were invaluable. I was fortunate enough to attend a lecture Mr Edsel gave at the Getty Museum in Los Angeles, and we were able to have a quick conversation about Sassocorvaro and La Rocca afterwards.

My financial advisor Aaron Werner of Raymond James kindly sent me a copy of his grandfather's book, '*Fighting Back: A Memoir of Jewish Resistance in World War 2*' by Harold Werner. Although focused on his experiences as a resistance fighter in Ukraine, rather than Italy, during WW2, this memoir gave me some important universal insights into the partisan experience. Aaron's grandfather was a remarkable man, as were all partisans—ordinary people in most cases who took up the fight to save their homelands. The character of Erivo Ferri, my partisan leader, is based on a historical figure. In the summer of 2023, I tracked down the real Erivo Ferri's grave in the village of Schieti, Le Marche, to pay my respects.

'*War in Val D'Orcia: An Italian War Diary, 1943-44*' by Iris Cutting is an evocative description of day-to-day life in war-torn Italy.

'*Italy's Sorrow: A Year of War, 1944-45*' by James Holland.

'*The German Side of the Hill: Nazi Conquest and Exploitation of Italy, 1943-1945*' by Timothy D. Saxon, University of Virginia 1999.

Nehrt, Jennifer L., '*The model of masculinity: Youth, gender, and education in Fascist Italy, 1922-1939*' (2015). Senior Honors Projects, 2010-current. 66.

Anna Melograni: '*Per non ricordare invano: il diario di Pasquale Rotondi e la corrispondenza con i colleghi delle soprintendenze e la direzione generale delle arti (1940-1946)*' ('Do not remember in vain: the diary of Pasquale Rotondi and the correspondence with fellow superintendents and the general directorate of the arts'.)

'*L'Arca dell'Arte*' (The Ark of Art) by Umberto Palestini

'*La lista di Pasquale Rotondi*' (Pasquale Rotondi's list) a documentary produced by RAI Cultura.

If you happen to find yourself in Le Marche, be sure to visit the Ducal Palace in Urbino, and the Rocca in Sassocorvaro. I spent an inspiring morning at the Rocca talking to Silvano Tiberi about the events of 1943 and 1944, and his input was invaluable. You can purchase '*Diario di Pasquale Rotondi: 1939-1946 : Opere D'Arte Nella Tempesta Della Guerra*' (The Diary of Pasquale Rotondi, 1939-1946, Artworks in the Storm of War), a beautifully designed book curated by Silvano, at the ticket office there.

I wish Huw was here to share this with me. Can you believe it, darling? I actually went and did it.

And finally to my girls Tara and Savannah. Your father and I were so proud that we'd managed to create such wonderful human beings. Thank you for being the lights of my life.

About the Author

Kate Bristow was born in London. She fell in love with reading when she got her library card at the age of four. Her first attempt at writing and publishing for a wide audience was a local newspaper typed laboriously at home on her mother's typewriter while at primary (elementary) school in north London. It is surely a loss to cutting-edge journalism that only one issue was ever produced. Kate divides her time between her small-but-perfectly-formed modern home in Los Angeles and her five-hundred-year-old farmhouse just outside Sassocorvaro in Italy.

For news and updates: www.katebristow.com